THE JUSTICE WE SERVE

MEG JOLLY

Published in 2022 by
Eldarkin Publishing Limited
United Kingdom
© 2022 Meg Jolly
www.megjolly.com

Cover design © Meg Jolly 2022

ISBN 9798403872393

CHAPTER ONE

SUNDAY EVENING

I t is the deadly things we cannot see that we ought to fear. The things that make us too uncomfortable with our human mortality to acknowledge. The things that surround us in the very air, slip insidiously into our bodies, and take hold before we have even realised.

And when we do?

It's already too late.

We are well versed to avoid fire, hypnotic and dangerous. We know to look before we cross the road, lest our lives end in an inelegant crunch of blood and bone. We fear the lulling cold of innocent looking dark water. And yet, these obvious sources of death still take the most foolish or unlucky of us.

The comfort of our modern lives offers us a traitorously deceptive falsehood of safety. An ignorance—willful and naïve—of all else that could harm us. One that we ignore to our folly. Life is fragile. Never let down your guard. Especially when you deserve death.

Paul Moore realised it too—that he had childishly trusted life to keep him in its fickle grasp—as the stabs of pain twisted through him. They were the metaphorical Sword of Damocles swinging overhead that felt all too real. Falling. Plunging in. Over and over.

He groaned, curling over on his stomach as it racked him, contracting every muscle in his body into a painful spasm as it tried desperately to expel. Expel he did then. He shoved his chair back from the table as he felt the convulsions bubbling—the tide surging up his throat. Acrid vomit sprayed all over the vinyl floor, painting a violent abstract of the dinner he had recently consumed.

Every mouthful had been bliss, from the tender chicken falling apart on his tongue to the sweet berry and red wine *jus* that had been drizzled on it and the crunch of golden, crispy roasted potatoes. Now it burned on the way out, bile-filled as it dragged past his tongue. He groaned as shudders racked him once more. Beads of sweat popped on his forehead and his skin prickled.

Something was very wrong.

Paul reached into his back pocket for his phone, but his fingers were too clumsy, like sausages trying to thread a needle and the pocket seemed clenched shut to his best efforts. Before him, the darkening kitchen diner swam in and out of focus as though it were filled with water that shifted around him. It only made him dizzier.

He bent his head low to rest it on the table, the cool wood a momentary relief, before another round of lightning-fire surged through him, that stabbing pain incandescent upon his every jarred nerve. His entire body felt like it was on fire—and yet, he was drowning. He gasped, adrenaline and panic firing up another notch as his breath seemed to stutter and stall, though he could not pinpoint why. Each breath was a fight and suffocation blackened his vision.

He wanted to scream with the pain of it, but it merely served to deplete him of more breath when he tried. Gasping desperately, he clawed at his throat, only to vomit again and gag upon the bile that caught in the back of his throat, inhaling some in a burning gulp that seared itself down his windpipe.

The world turned sideways as he tried to stand. Instead, he fell and the chair crashed with him, tangled around his legs when he convulsed. Every muscle was a screaming cacophony of pain. A symphony of death played upon the strings of his remaining heartbeats, few and frenzied that they were.

It was a tune that he railed against, but one he could not silence. He was a marionette, but his new master was inside him and it was a cruel one that would not relinquish control. Not until his lungs had been strangled of breath, every organ crushed into failing, and every shard of his consciousness starved of its life.

Against his cheek, the floor was cold and wet, his already cooled stomach contents now plastered to the side of his face. Through fading, star-laced vision, he gazed at the darkness in the corner. It seemed to grow, detaching from the shadows until it swamped him. Watching. Waiting. It claimed him into the void of death one excruciating spasm at a time, one ineffective breath after another, one desperate heartbeat and then the next. Each shallower than the last. Until the symphony of his living-self ended.

He was the first.

He would not be the last.

The time had come.

CHAPTER TWO

SUNDAY EVENING

Detective Inspector Daniel Ward hunched in one of the half-broken desk chairs in the stiflingly hot Incident Room, muttering curses under his breath as he deciphered the scrawled, handwritten, evidential notes. The room became an overflowing cesspit of burglary cases every winter, and this winter, it had claimed him too, unwillingly though he had come.

The irony was, usually the heating was broken and it was freezing—this November, by some twist, it was stuck on some setting north of 'hotter than the fires of hell'. His formal work attire clung to a thin sheen of sweat that would have suited a beach in Barbados better than a desk in Bradford South Police Station and he'd abandoned the tie in favour of the top two buttons undone and rolled up his sleeves to create the illusion of relief. It didn't really work. He yanked at the collar again, pulling it away from his clammy neck.

Beside him, DC Kasim Shahzad worked quietly. The

young man was plugged into his earphones and working through a mountain of paperwork about as happily as anyone could. Which was not very. Shahzad wasn't best pleased about being stuck in burglary either, but it was the luck of the unluckiest draw. Some poor bugger had to do it and they rotated the caseload through winter to make it fair on everyone in the team. It was his week.

For Ward, luck had less to do with it. He'd been there three weeks already and it felt like an eternity. For him, it was a punishment.

Ward had been sternly disciplined following the weapons discharge incident during the Varga warehouse raid and that hellish night down in Manningham, which had ended with a lot of death and destruction and very few answers. Ward ought to have been grateful that he'd kept his job—it had been a close call, with the DCI standing up to the Super on his behalf, to Ward's surprise —but he didn't relish the punishment, even when he knew he damn well deserved it.

Instead of being dismissed, Ward had received a right bollocking from the Super and marching orders to 'get his arse out of sight' with 'not a peep of a bad word' against him, or he'd be finished. The DCI had docked him off field duty for the foreseeable. Ward had taken over the burglary caseload from DS Chakrabarti so she could get out and stretch her legs—indefinitely. It was serious, alright. Only long-standing good service had seen him avoid a suspension or dismissal.

Either way, he was in the doghouse.

It was a miracle they'd managed to keep the worst of

it out of the press too, but even so, the journalists had had a field day with stories of gun battles between police and major criminals and the fire that had devastated a whole street's worth of warehousing property before being brought under control... not to mention the fatalities.

In the end, seven bodies had been found inside the gutted warehouse, the building itself dangerously damaged by the fire. It had rampaged through the structure by the time the fire service brought it under control. Then the grisly discovery had been made that they had not died as a result of the fire, but from the bullets riddling their charred corpses.

Ward shuddered. That was never a nice sight. Or smell. He didn't envy the pathology lab or the mortuary that. They were still trying to identify five of them, several weeks later.

The force had found no hint of Varga there, nor any drugs supply from the Khans who owned the premises. Just traces in one corner that had miraculously escaped damage from the fire, suggesting what supply had been there, had been moved. By whom, Ward couldn't even guess yet—not until they had some key pieces of evidence analysed by forensics. He reckoned it had been taken in the Range Rover that Ward had fired upon, bearing one of Varga's known registration plates, before being transferred to another vehicle.

Inside the vehicle, which had later turned up abandoned, had been a forensic goldmine. They had uncovered traces of Class A drugs—that DI Ward hoped might match the samples from the warehouse—and perhaps more crucially, *blood.* Precious flecks dotted the back seats and was smeared on the steering wheel from two different sources.

The reports were due any day now on all of that. If they had any matches to the blood on file. If they could link the traces of drugs found at either location—the car or the warehouse—to each other or any other known sources. It felt as though they were possibly on the cusp of a breakthrough.

However, it was difficult for Ward to feel glad he'd kept his job when he could see the rest of his team, including his usual partner DS Emma Nowak, through the tall internal windows tackling their cases—leaving DI Ward stuck in exile in the room where investigations went to die. The room of mostly unsolved and unsolvable burglaries smelled permanently of coffee and curry flavoured Pot Noodle thanks to the seemingly indestructible stain on the carpet under one of the desks.

Now, the sole reason Ward had to get out of the Incident Room was to keep up with the one other case he'd been permitted to remain involved with—and only because he was so deeply immersed in it as Senior Investigating Officer that they couldn't do without him. The ongoing, sprawling expanse of the Bogdan Varga caseload, which had, as usual, poor DC David Norris buried in his corner of the open-plan office and tangled up in a web that seemed to keep growing.

There had been a *lot* of paperwork to add to that pile after the farce at the warehouse in Manningham. DC

Norris hadn't complained one bit, even though a stack of it was Ward's fault.

Ward sat back in his chair, stomach growling. He glanced outside. Pitch black, save for the usual orange glow of the city at night. It was dinner time, but he was on until eight. It'd be a late, small bite for him after he picked up Oliver from his doggy daycare. At least the pup was having the time of his life with a doting dogsitter who was graciously accepting of Ward's odd hours of work.

Just one hour left.

The phone rang and with Shahzad still deep in his tunes, bopping his head as he typed, Ward hooked a finger around the phone to pick up the call from the switchboard. It could only be one thing for them— another fresh burglary to visit. Another case to add to the pile.

'Aye, fire away,' he said, pen in hand, ready to take the details. A commercial burglary, forced entry through the front door, cash taken from the till, some other items of value missing. 'What's the address?'

He stilled, cold flooding through him. 'Eh?' He cleared his throat. 'Sorry, could you repeat that?'

As the voice on the other end of the line did so, Ward's eyes slipped closed. Ten seconds ago, he'd been dragging his heels at the thought of heading out to another crime scene that would no doubt leave him working late *again* with unpaid overtime whilst he processed it, on a dark, cold, and wet November evening. Now...

Ward hung up the call, with his heart hammering, he stood and threw on his coat. He didn't need to take the address with him, or the scant details he'd been fed. He knew precisely where *Griffiths' Fine Art & Framing* was.

DC Shahzad didn't bother looking up as Ward fled the office, car key in hand and mind tumbling with worries about one Eve Griffiths.

CHAPTER THREE

The roads were too damned slow. Thirty miles per hour speed limits. Every damn traffic light on red. Every bloody slow driver in front of him. DI Ward cursed under his breath with frustration as he got stuck behind a tractor trundling along at ten miles an hour on the outskirts of the city. From the opposite direction, a steady torrent of headlights dazzled and blinded with no room to overtake.

The inside of the VW Golf R seemed too hot, then too cold, then too hot again as Ward raced to Wilsden, his nerves racing with worry. He shouldn't have personally overseen it. He should have left it to CSI, or Shahzad at best. It was a low-priority commercial burglary, after all.

The worst of it was, he already knew what he would probably find—naff all evidence to go about solving it or bringing anyone to justice, let alone retrieving any stolen items or cash. It was always the way. It was why they all hated burglary duty in the HMET department—which as the Homicide and Murder Enquiry Team was hardly in their remit, but thanks to budget cuts, left everyone available across the force contributing. It was a hopeless cesspit that reminded them all how fragile the semblance of civility was. How easily and wantonly it could all be ruined by a few choice scrotes, who operated seemingly with impunity.

But picturing Eve, he just couldn't leave it to someone else to pick through the shards of her life, comfort her with hollow eyes and empty words, knowing they were as good as useless. He had to make sure she was ok, check she hadn't been personally there, *involved...* the thought of someone harming her made him feel sick. That added to the churning mess in his stomach.

After what seemed like an age, he pulled up outside on the dimly lit street before the small, quaint gallery. A squad car was already there and CSI would follow if Ward thought there was anything useful to glean.

As he cut the engine, he glanced up at the front door. He could see what had happened. The door was half-solid with a large pane of glass at the top that, when last he had visited, had held a cheerful open/closed sign in embellished writing decorated with flowers. Now the sign was gone. So was the glass. Shattered, jagged shards lined that opening. They caught the warm, bright light from inside that spilled out onto the dark, freezing street.

Ward climbed out from that pocket of warm air in the

car into the frigid November night. The sweat against his skin clammed up at once, cold and unpleasant as it clung to him.

His lips thinned into a grim line as he saw the once-proud display inside the window. It had been an easel with a glorious piece of artwork propped up on it. The window display now lay on its side; the easel tipped over and the painting face down on the floor beside it.

Anger warred with worry as Ward hurriedly pulled on some gloves and shoe covers, before striding in—carefully, holding himself back, knowing he ought to disturb things as little as possible, no matter how concerned he was for Eve Griffiths' safety.

He gingerly opened the door, the metal handle ice-cold through the thin rubbery glove. The tiny bell tinkled overhead, as welcoming as ever, but his heart sank.

It was carnage inside.

Eve stood behind the counter, her arms folded around herself, her face red, blotchy, and tear-stained. At his entrance, she jumped, her face paling under the red on her cheeks—then recognition sparked.

'Detective Ward?' she greeted him with a frown—she had not expected to see him again then, it was plain. Perhaps she didn't care as much as he had for their scant interactions. He shoved that thought away.

He sidestepped the shattered glass littering the floor inside the door—the intruder's point of entry, it looked like. The 'open' sign, cracked, in the midst of the mess. He'd seen that method plenty of times before. Smash the glass, undo the bolts, attack the key lock, get in. Child's play, really, for anyone who went equipped, knew vaguely what to do, and had enough brute force to go the rest of the distance.

Ward looked up and murmured, 'Ms. Griffith,' in return.

She glanced between him and the female uniformed police officer standing with her—he hadn't noticed the petite officer at first, shadowed by a huge display cabinet.

'DI Ward, SIO,' he said to the PC, ignoring the frown of confusion that also swept across the PC's face—for a very different reason to Eve's confusion. What would a DI be doing on a low-rank burglary case, after all? 'I was passing,' he said blandly.

The woman nodded. 'Aye, sir. PC Small. First officer on the scene.' She flicked back a couple of pages in her pocketbook and tucked a stray strand of short, blonde hair behind her ear. When she spoke again, Ward noticed the Welsh lilt in her voice. 'Standard commercial burglary, sir. Entry through the front door, as you can see. Till emptied, amount taken being approximately one hundred and thirty-five pounds. A couple of other items missing—soldering iron and supplies, some small trinkets, and general damage consistent with breaking and entering.' She gestured to the mess at the door.

'Aye. Thanks. I'll take it from here, if you'll let CSI know they'll be needed, please. Might be something here.'

Ward had seen enough burglaries in the area over recent weeks with the same calling cards to suspect it was the same gang combing through vulnerable businesses. They might not get the twats that time, but over time, with enough evidence, they might just get lucky—though Ward hated that he had to rely on any kind of chance. Even with the massive advances in forensic evidencing and technology, they still couldn't catch the criminals who did this sort of thing very often.

Ward liked to think of them like lions stalking their prey, though. Serial criminals needed to get lucky every time. Ward and his team only needed to get lucky once.

Eve murmured her thanks as PC Small departed.

'It's no trouble, love,' PC Small replied. 'I hope you'll be alright.'

A big gust of chilly air flooded in as she opened the door. It didn't warm up as she shut it, however, that shattered mess of a pane letting in an insipid frigid cold that seeped through Ward's jacket.

'Ms. Griffiths,' Ward started.

'Eve,' she cut in insistently, grimacing. Her arms tightened around her again, the dark cardigan she wore pulling thin against her. He noticed she was shaking slightly. Cold or fear, he couldn't tell. *Probably both.*

'Eve,' he amended. 'Are *you* alright?' He wasn't asking for the polite answer—*fine*—he wanted the honest one. *Was she here when it happened?*

'No,' she admitted, though that was blindly bloody obvious.

'Were you here?' *Did they hurt you?* Ward's chest tightened.

Eve swallowed and shook her head.

Something in Ward loosened again with relief.

'I'd just closed up and left. The app—I have an app for my alarm—notified me that there was an issue. I thought I hadn't set it right, to be honest. But when I returned, it was like this.' Her voice was so hushed, Ward had to lean closer to hear her.

'I was terrified they'd still be here, inside, I mean. I didn't know what to do. I could see from my car that the door was smashed in, the display overturned, the till moved... I called the police right away.'

Her shaking had intensified. Probably shock setting in and the upset of it all starting to kindle. She pressed a trembling knuckle to her lips, her shoulders hunched. It wasn't his place to comfort her, much as he wanted to. The best he could do was offer platitudes that felt too hollow, that they'd do their utmost to find who was responsible—but he couldn't bring himself to voice such rubbish.

'Was anyone here?'

'No, I think they'd gone. I waited until the police came though. I just... I didn't dare come in. Just in case they were still here.'

'Did you touch anything?'

'No. I mean, yes. Sorry. I touched the till, before the officer said not to disturb anything.'

'That's alright.' It wasn't the end of the world. They'd eliminate her prints from any that they found. They would have had to do that anyway. 'Is there anything else you've noticed missing other than what you told my colleague?'

'Not that I've noticed, but I need to have a proper look.' As Eve gazed around, wide-eyed, he knew the real thing of value that had been taken from her, and it had nothing to do with money or possessions—it was her perception of safety. Her sacred space had been violated and he saw how vulnerable she now felt, standing amidst the chaos of what was left of her livelihood.

'If you could, that would be helpful. Just let me know anything else that's gone. Our Crime Scene Investigation team will dust for prints and any other forensic evidence they can find to see if we can link this to anyone.'

'Will you catch them?' she asked, pinning him with a piercing stare—one that was filled with hope and edged with righteous indignation.

Ward stalled. 'We'll do our best,' was the only lame answer he could give.

Something darker flickered across her face. 'I understand. Thank you.'

Did she? he wondered, as she turned away to survey the empty, busted open till beside her.

'This place is my baby, you know. I've only owned it for a few years, but I put my heart and soul into it.' Her smile was sad, her eyes hollow. 'It was always my dream to paint and sell my artwork. I worked hard for this. Against my better judgement and whatever everyone else told me wasn't possible. Now...'

She fell silent, gazing around, her glance landing on one small focal point after another, until it fixed on that kaleidoscope of glass fragments littering the floor. She shook her head.

Ward sighed. She didn't have to say it, really. He knew. It didn't feel like hers anymore. Didn't feel like she'd made it. Her dream was as shattered as the glass strewn on the floor. Another gust blasted in, rattling the door in its frame as it swept through the broken window and snatched any shred of warmth left inside.

Ward stirred. 'Do you have anyone who can help you secure the property, so you can go home and get some rest once CSI is done?' *Before dealing with the inevitable pile of shite to sort tomorrow*, he did not add.

'Dad's on his way,' Eve answered with a sigh and checked the small watch hidden under the sleeve of her cardigan. 'He'll help with it.'

'How long will he be?'

'Um...' She glanced at her watch again and grimaced. 'Maybe another ten minutes. They live a while away.'

'I think I have everything I need, but I'm in no rush.' He was off duty now, after all. 'Do you want me to wait until he's here?'

Eve's attention rose from the glass to him. 'Really? Are you sure?'

Ward nodded. 'No trouble, honestly. If it'll help you feel safer. I'm on my way home from here anyway.'

She broke into a smile—a tired, drained smile, but a smile nonetheless. 'Thank you. I'd appreciate that.' She reached out to him, her hand almost spanning the arm's length between them, before she seemed to realise the impropriety and her hand dropped away. 'Thanks,' she said again. 'It's nice to have a familiar face to help me feel slightly better about all this for a few minutes.'

'I'm sure it's safe,' he said, reading between the lines of what she said. 'I doubt they'll come back now. They have what they came for.' He gestured to the till. He was confident in that; they wouldn't come back and she was safe, but to her, a threat would still lurk in every shadow for a long time after this.

Whilst he waited, she moved into the back to start a detailed look for anything that had been disturbed or taken, careful not to disturb anything herself. Silence yawned between them. There was little else to say, after all, and he was not daft enough to start trying to exchange pointless pleasantries.

Eve wasn't far wrong though. Fifteen minutes later, her father arrived. Eve was the spit of him, though he was shorter than her by a few inches. Ward towered over the balding man, who did a double-take when he saw DI Ward lurking inside. He relaxed once DI Ward held out his warrant card.

'Dad!' Eve burst from the back and her father enveloped her in a giant hug.

'Are you alright, love?' he said as she pulled away.

Together, Ward took in the resemblance. Eve had her father's kind eyes and his mousy brown hair—though his had threads of grey running through what was left on his scalp.

Tears shone in her eyes now. 'No.' She turned to DI Ward. 'Thank you for waiting with me, Detective.'

Her father held out a hand, standing straighter. 'William Griffiths. Thank you, sir.'

'Detective Inspector Ward.' Ward shook his hand.

His attention flicked back to Eve. 'I have everything I need for now, Eve, so I'll head off.' He smiled—a professional, distant smile that betrayed nothing of the unease he felt at leaving her in the mess, father present or not.

'CSI will be along in the next hour or two,' he continued. 'I'm sorry for the wait.'

William Griffiths nodded and clamped an arm around Eve's shoulders, holding her close. 'We understand.'

'Aye. Not enough funding and luckily or unluckily, this isn't a serious case, so I'm afraid it's not been given top priority. They will be out tonight though and once they've finished, you're free to secure the property and get yourselves home for some much-needed rest.'

'Thank you for coming personally,' Eve said, pulling away from her father. 'I appreciate it—I really do. Especially if you've stayed late on my account.'

Ward's answering smile was genuine for a moment before it faded. 'It's no trouble. I'm glad you're alright and I'm sorry you're in this mess.' At least now she had her dad with her.

He hoped CSI would find something. Much as there was naff all hope, he hoped all the same. DI Ward fished a card out of his inside pocket and held it out for her. 'My details. I live just over the hill in Thornton, so I'm not too far away at all.'

She took it. 'Oh, I couldn't, you've been far too kind already.'

'Not at all. It's my job. I'm happy to help. Please, if

you need *anything* at all, if you have any new information, or if you're in need of help, call.'

'Thank you.' She held it tightly, clutching it in both hands as though it might vanish. He bade them both goodnight and stepped past the broken glass once more and outside into the darkness.

CHAPTER FOUR

D I Ward slammed the car door behind him harder than he intended, pissed off about the state of the world even more than usual. He'd be glad to get home to Oliver, his faithful and fun-loving Beagle, once he'd picked up the pup from his doting doggy daycare. Oliver, at least, made him forget it all for a short time and feel like maybe the world wasn't entirely damned to hopelessness.

As he slid the car into gear—the rough rumble of the throttle a soothing sound to drown out the discontent inside him—his phone rang, coming up over the Bluetooth.

DCI Kipling.

Ward spat out a choice swearword.

If the DCI wanted him, it meant he was absolutely not going home and Olly would be getting *another* impromptu sleepover with his second family. Not that the fickle hound would mind. *The little bugger can be bought for a good bone, as I well know…*

Ward glared at the centre console. He was off duty. Technically. He debated the merits of not answering for a mere split second before he connected the call.

'What kept you so long?' DCI Kipling barked at him.

'Sorry sir,' he muttered with as much contrition as he could muster. If the DCI was snappy, Ward wasn't about to add his own neck to the pile for wringing. 'I was attending a burglary.' His hands tightened on the steering wheel as he blasted up the hill, the heating on as high as it would go, as he attempted to thaw the chill out of his bones.

'Well,' DCI Kipling snapped. 'You're off burglary for now. A suspicious death's come in. I have no more hands, so I have no choice but to call on you.' And he didn't sound happy about it in the bloody slightest.

But at the sniff of freedom, Ward's spirits lifted.

'Suspicious, you say, sir?'

'It's your lucky day,' said DCI Kipling, disgruntlement oozing from every word. 'If it was up to me, you'd be buried in burglary to the end of the year—and according to the Super, the end of next.'

Lovely, thought Ward, but he didn't dare mutter it aloud. Ward pulled over at the side of the road, wedging into a small ditch so he wasn't causing an obstruction, his indicator lighting up the dark hedgerow beside him on the unlit road.

'Thanks to that winter vomiting bug taking out my staff like we all don't have anything better to do, we're so short that even *you* become an option. A death's been reported in East Morton and I need you to head it up.'

At the word 'suspicious', Ward's curiosity had piqued. He kept his mouth shut, not wanting to blow his chances.

'Do you think you can manage this without causing a major incident?'

Annoyance stabbed in Ward. He had a pretty damn good track record and years of experience, thank you very much. The one incident in Manningham seemed to be overshadowing a run of good years, like salt in a fresh wound. It was unfair, to say the least, but he wasn't about to complain and get his arse sent back to the burglary caseload, when it seemed there was a sniff at something more promising.

'Aye, sir,' DI Ward grudgingly acknowledged, with as much contrition as he could muster.

He'd take it, after all. He was sick of burglaries; poking about in the shreds of people's lives and not being able to get the bastards who'd done it. Even more so now he'd just seen Eve again, knowing her pride and joy had suffered such a fate.

A suspicious death sounded intriguing, if nothing else. If it was a stabbing, shooting, or straightforward homicide, DCI Kipling would have said. Suspicious meant something altogether more unique.

'What do we already know, sir?'

DCI Kipling's annoyance came through in his answer. 'What do you take me for, Ward, your bloody

PA? I'm the DCI for goodness sake. Take DS Nowak and find out the details yourself.'

Christ, someone's got their knickers in a twist. Wonder what's pissing him off today?

The line disconnected before Ward could answer. Or figure out what to say to that.

Ward stared at the control panel of the car for a second. Taking in his senior officer's order. Then, he put the car back in first gear, executed a swift three-point-turn and sped off in the opposite direction to East Morton.

As he did so, he flicked through his recent contacts on the car's interface.

Susanna Wright – Doggy Daycare.

It looked like Olly would be due an extra big bone tonight with his second family (again) whilst Ward would be going hungry (again). It was a good thing they loved the pup to pieces and were forgiving of Ward's entirely antisocial working pattern and last-minute schedule changes.

No rest for the wicked. Or paid overtime.

But at least now, DI Ward had something more interesting than doomed burglary investigations to sink his teeth into and he'd be back with his long-time investigative partner, the brilliant DS Emma Nowak.

It's about time we reunited the dream team.

CHAPTER FIVE

D
S Emma Nowak's voice crackled a little as it came over the car's speakers. Ward could tell from the grainy quality that she was driving too. His fingers flexed on the cold leather of the steering wheel, wishing he'd gone for the heated option. Yorkshireman that he was, he'd not plumped for it at the eye-watering price it'd been on 'offer' for. Regrettable now, seeing as he couldn't feel some of his fingers, though an unpleasant burning tingling sensation worked its way through his extremities as the heating kicked in.

Emma would probably not be there too much after Ward, she reckoned. She had set off directly from the police station, but he was closer with faster and less busy routes through the West Yorkshire countryside just outside the suburbs of Bradford Metropolitan District. They would converge on East Morton village, a small, pretty place on the sides of the Aire Valley. As they drove, DS Nowak filled him in.

It was good to hear her voice, Ward reflected. He'd missed their rapport. He enjoyed working with the young, capable, and hungry detective. She was sharp-minded and observant with a good sense of humour and a knack for relating to people, the latter of which he felt rather useless at. He'd fallen lucky with her. The DS was everything he liked in a partner, and by heck, he'd missed her whilst he'd been locked up in the burglary caseload.

'So, from what I've been passed,' she said, 'the circumstances sound a little unusual. We could be looking at a possible medical episode, but it could be something else entirely. I think we've been called as a precaution as the death is unexplained for now.'

'Hmm.' Ward didn't know what to make of that. 'Unexplained' was a difficult one to deal with. Usually, they had *some* kind of hint at the cause of death. A dirty great knife wound. A blow to the head. A tumble from somewhere high. Something obvious to work with.

'It's not pretty though.'

'Eh?'

'I've been warned.' He could practically see her wrinkling her nose from the distaste in her voice.

'When *is* death pretty?' he said and huffed a laugh out that clouded his breath in front of him.

She chuckled too. 'Well yes, fair enough. I suppose I can't recall seeing too many lookers of the dead kind.'

When Ward arrived, it was to a tree-lined narrow lane nestled on the hillside. The road continued up the hill to East Morton village. He turned onto a heavily shrub-shrouded driveway that went further back than he realised. He followed the unlit tarmac onto a shared entrance for another few houses that blazed light down the track.

The address he needed was the first one on the corner of the main road and as the garden hedges ended, a multiple-car driveway in front of a row of three garages opened up, deeply shaded and lit by a single lamp from a neighbouring house that cast an insignificant glow against the pooling shadows. He tucked in next to the deserted ambulance that was parked there.

At the side of the driveway, a small gate nestled in the high hedges, hung open. It led into the corner plot where a secluded and private bungalow huddled, almost invis-ible from the road. The garden was mostly decked, his footsteps echoing hollowly as he stepped onto it and glanced down, having expected paving.

Emma wasn't there yet, her Mini nowhere in sight, but he headed in anyway, curious to see what had happened. He strode across the large deck to the front door, rapping on the glass, the sound echoing sharply in the still air.

Every light inside was on and it spilled out through un-curtained windows and the glass panes of the door to illuminate the garden, the silver wood of the aged deck beneath him, the empty garden furniture covered over for winter, and a closed up greenhouse in the corner of the plot.

As Ward raised his hand to knock again, the door opened to him and two paramedics filed out. After a cursory look, they murmured a greeting. One headed out, the other waited. 'Police, I presume?'

'Aye.' Ward introduced himself. 'What have we got?'

She pursed her lips and led him back inside as she stripped off her protective gloves. Ward edged past a couple of vast pots inside the hallway boasting a large cheese plant and something else he didn't recognise. The massive leaves seemed to clutch at him as he passed.

'We have an IC1 male, aged early fifties, deceased. We weren't able to resuscitate. Seems he was violently ill before he passed, but without an autopsy, we don't have a cause of death. His wife says he had no underlying health issues. From all we can see, he simply died. However...'

Ward glanced aside as she led him past the open door of a living room, where a sobbing woman sat on a couch, curled over her knees, her words unintelligible as she spoke into a mobile phone.

'There were some... *odd* things that I noticed, shall we say? That's why we called it in.' The paramedic frowned and stopped, turning to Ward. 'Dilated pupils, some very odd skin discolouration, and the painful and sudden nature of his death seem very inconsistent with anything we'd expect from a callout like this. See for yourself.' She waved him into the kitchen.

'Sorry. I know your crime scene'll be a mess if you need to evidence this,' she said. Their duty was to preserve life where possible, not worry about the fine details of forensics.

'Hmm.' Ward didn't comment. It would be the head of the CSI team, Victoria Foster, or one of her lackeys, who would tear a new one over it. At least this time, it wasn't his fault. He stepped carefully into the modest kitchen, the wood-effect vinyl lino slightly sticky beneath his covered shoes. As soon as he passed the threshold, the acrid tang of vomit intensified.

Ward breathed shallowly through his mouth as it curdled his stomach. He stared down at the husk of a man on the floor. Paul Moore, the log said. A man about ten years Ward's senior, in his early fifties, with a thick crop of light hair. Average height, average build, though he had the start of a pot belly. A ruddy rash covered his cheek with blotchy patches and his hands too, Ward noticed, as he cast his attention down the body. He saw nothing else, for the man wore a long-sleeved jumper and jeans that were stained with the puddle of vomit he had fallen into.

Paul lay at an awkward angle, half spreadeagled upon the floor, and like a ragdoll abandoned, contorted so he was almost bent back on himself. Worst of all was his face. A soundless howl of agony was frozen there, a testament to whatever suffering he'd endured.

His dinner, plastered across everything from the floor to his clothes, also smeared across one side of his face like watery paint, with chunks of undigested, chewed food in it. His wallet was half out of his arse pocket, his phone laying discarded under the nearby table, as though it had been dropped just out of reach.

'Right. So. We received the call to say he was unresponsive, made by his wife, approximately an hour and a half ago. We responded and found him on his back there on the floor, but the wife says she turned him over and he'd originally been on his belly here.' She pointed.

Ward could see exactly where he'd been from the smeared trail of vomit across the floor. *Nice.*

'Now, she'd not been with him; she returned home and found him in this unresponsive state, so we believe he was already deceased at that point. She reports having seen him this morning before he went to work at approximately eight and he seemed absolutely fine then.

'You can see from his expression, those strange symptoms I mentioned, and this,' —she gestured at the chaos— 'that he didn't go gently. I'm concerned this isn't natural, but I can't give you any more than that.' She glanced down at the victim, silent, her brows furrowed and then gave her head a small shake. 'I'm sorry. Can I be of any more help?'

Ward shifted his weight from one foot to the other. Taking another small breath through his mouth to try and minimise that awful stench worming into him anymore. 'I don't think so, but thank you.'

She left with a murmured goodbye and Ward followed her out, turning into the living room where a couple of sofas were overshadowed by more greenery. Someone here was green-fingered, he reckoned. He'd have managed to kill all of these plants in a week. He never remembered to water them.

As the woman glanced up at him, he fished out his warrant card and murmured an introduction. Her phone idled in her slack hand, the screen going black as he looked.

Her gaze darted past him to the hallway and the kitchen beyond. Back and forth, as though she wasn't sure which to be more disturbed by in that moment, the hulking stranger in her front room, or the dead body in her kitchen. She was pale, waxy, and glassy-eyed.

He gently pried her name from her, Janice Moore, and that the man in her kitchen was her husband, Paul Moore, as expected.

At a rap on the front door, Mrs Moore rose automatically to answer it and drifted past DI Ward almost in a daze. Seconds later, DS Emma Nowak filed in behind her. Mrs Moore sunk onto the plump couch again, as Emma mouthed a greeting to Ward and flashed him a quick smile.

She raised an eyebrow at him.

Ward inclined his head.

One look and they instinctively knew what to do. Divide and conquer. Emma, more personable, softer in approach than Ward, would speak to the wife who was clearly in shock, to pry out what details she could, whilst Ward took a more detailed look at the scene and made sure that CSI had marked it as a priority and that the body would be collected for further examination by the pathology laboratory at Bradford Royal Infirmary.

CHAPTER SIX

The acidic scent of vomit permeated the whole house, the smell strengthening as Ward returned to the kitchen, crinkling in his forensic boot covers. He paused on the threshold, eying the food on the floor with a frown, and then the body.

Had Paul Moore eaten something that disagreed with him? Food poisoning didn't do *that* to people. He made a mental note to ask the wife if she knew what he'd eaten that day, all the same. It wasn't a medical condition according to his wife, but that didn't rule anything out. It could have been undiagnosed, perhaps an allergic reaction, Ward mused, as his mind chewed over the dead man-shaped problem before him.

He peered around the kitchen diner. There was a dirty plate with a sauce that resembled the vomit—the same dish, probably—on the counter, a knife and fork slung across it. An empty cup stood next to it and some dishes were stacked in the sink. The kitchen was otherwise ordinary and nothing caught his eye. A brown paper takeaway bag wedged the bin lid open. The open bin coloured the top notes of vomit and death with delightful middle notes of rotting food waste and rubbish.

There was nothing out of the ordinary and nothing suspicious at all, except for the fact there was a dead man on the floor who appeared to have suffered a horrifically painful and yet inexplicable death without obvious injury. Ward would be relying heavily on CSI and pathology to get to the bottom of it without any more obvious clues to follow.

He slipped back to the living room, glad for the relief of the worst of the stench, which was starting to make him lightheaded. DS Nowak chatted away to Paul Moore's wife in a low voice.

Ward silently perched on the sofa beside Nowak. Sat opposite, Janice Moore ignored them both. She stared at the floor, phone still limply in hand. Ward took the opportunity to examine her too. At first glance, she appeared to be a similar age to her husband, though she had already aged in the minutes he had been present in her home, with the weight of shock and grief already crushing more years onto her than were kind. A worn gold band on her ring finger hinted at the long length of their marriage. What a way for it to end.

Ward glanced over Nowak's shoulder to read her notes.

Mr Paul Moore, it read, listing the man's date of birth, age, and occupation—a van driver for a local freight company up the valley in Keighley. His wife, according to Emma's notes, had found him when she had come home from work at a local supermarket, where she'd been on a mid-shift until eight that evening. She had returned home straightaway as normal and noticed the smell as soon as she opened the door.

The TV had been on, but other than that it had been silent and she just... knew. Something was wrong. Like the house felt still, different. Janice had found Paul collapsed on the kitchen floor in a pool of his own vomit and called an ambulance straightaway, but she hadn't been able to wake him and she'd feared the worst then and freaked out.

'And can you tell me a little about your family, Janice?' Emma continued, still scribbling away in her notepad as she spoke. 'Does anyone else live here with you both?'

'No,' sniffed Janice. 'Our daughter left years ago, she's thirty and our son went to university this September, in Sheffield. Neither have keys. It's empty without them here.' She dragged a desperate glance around the photos hanging on the walls of the four of them over the years and crumpled into herself anew, as the realisation punched into her again, that now it would be even emptier.

'No one else has access?'

'No.'

'No signs of forced entry?' They had to discount that someone else had done it, even if that possibility already seemed slim.

'I...I didn't notice.'

'I'll go and check,' Emma said. Her voice was kind but her glance at Ward brimmed with cool focus as she stood and left to pad quietly through the house and see if any locks had been jimmied, or windows left open, anything that might have hinted at someone else entering the property.

...Entering the property and what? Scaring Paul Moore to death? Ward couldn't finish the thought with any plausible answer.

'Do you know what Paul did today?' Ward asked, slipping out his own pocketbook and pen. He did not add on the end, 'before his death.'

'No. I, um, yes. He went to work this morning—they needed overtime doing. He usually goes golfing on Sunday so they went after work tonight instead, or at least, that's what he told me they were doing. At East Morton Golf Club—they have a driving range. He wouldn't have had time for the main course after work,' she added at Ward's prompt.

'He said he'd be home around seven, I think, and have dinner. I eat later when I get in from work. I work 'til eight every Sunday. We always have takeout on a Sunday, because it makes life easier.' She rubbed a hand across her nose and sniffed wetly. 'He won't cook and I don't have the energy when I get home, so one of us picks something up. Tonight was his turn. It couldn't have made him sick, could it?' Her eyes widened with that realisation.

'It's unlikely,' Ward said. 'But of course, we'll be investigating.'

'There'll probably be a portion in the fridge for me to reheat as normal.' She looked positively queasy, gripping the sofa arm with whitened knuckles—whether from the thought of her husband's food being the cause of his demise or her own, Ward couldn't say. 'I think I'll throw it out,' she muttered faintly.

'We'll hold onto it for now, please. In case it's relevant. I'm sorry to deprive you of your supper.' Ward smiled in what he hoped was an easygoing, reassuring manner. Likely the food had nothing to do with it, but they couldn't have her dispose of potential evidence—by eating it or binning it.

'Trust him to leave me hungry,' she huffed a sudden bitter sigh and then sniffed again, her lip wobbling.

'What do you mean?' Ward asked, his pen stilling.

'Oh, just that Paul always makes life harder for me and I don't know what's worse, that he doesn't care or doesn't realise.' She stopped and shook her head. Fresh tears slipped from the corner of her puffy eyes. 'He's an arsehole and it's been so hard since the kids left. I'm glad to work late sometimes and stay out of his hair. He's such a mardy arse. Look at me moaning I don't get tea... like I could eat now anyway.' She muffled a sob into her palm. 'I should have been here. What if I could have helped him?'

She turned those tear-filled eyes upon Ward, but he could do or say nothing to ease her guilt or suffering. Her attention passed to the wedding photo of them standing proudly on the TV cabinet. Two young and happy looking souls a lifetime ago, he in a suit that was too big on the shoulders, her in a puffy white dress, drowning in layers.

'He's hard work, but I've always loved him. Always. And he died *alone*.' That was it. She crumbled into sobs.

DS Nowak slipped back into the living room. She shook her head at Ward. No sign of forced entry or anything overtly suspicious then. That would be in line with Paul Moore not seeming to have suffered anything consistent with injuries of assault they'd expect from a breaking and entering of some kind.

Ward leaned closer and Emma edged towards him. He muttered into her ear, below the sound of Janice's crying, 'Check in the fridge if you can get past the scene without disturbing anything. See if there's a takeaway container with any branding on. If so, it needs to be mentioned to CSI, in case there's something wrong with the food.'

Toxicology reports would be able to confirm if there was anything untoward, as slim as the chances were. Food poisoning wouldn't act so quickly.

Janice jumped at the thundering on the door and Ward stood to get it. 'It's alright. Leave it to me, Mrs Moore.'

She sank back down into the cushions, looking slightly relieved not to have to deal with any more people for a moment.

'Now then,' Ward said as he opened the door to one of his least-favourite colleagues, exceptional though she was at her job. He and Victoria Foster had a rapport alright. One that rubbed them both up entirely the wrong way.

'Haven't seen you in a while,' she beamed up at him from behind a typically bright pair of spectacles—that evening's were canary yellow with pink spots—before her smile turned vicious. 'It's been absolutely *lovely*.'

She tugged up the white hood of her paper forensics suit and brushed past him, two members of her team following.

'I've missed you too,' he muttered darkly. 'He's in the kitchen.' But Foster had already gone and Ward wanted nothing more than to stay out of her way.

For some reason, she'd never let him forget the one time he'd traipsed through a crime scene and destroyed some evidence as a much younger and more inexperienced detective. It hadn't even been *material* evidence, damn it, but still, he'd carried that reputation for being a clod-footed imbecile in her mind ever since. Never mind that he'd had an excellent track record since.

He glanced outside. Another vehicle had pulled up too. One to take the body away to the mortuary to be examined by Mark Baker and his pathology team. Much as Ward didn't enjoy Victoria Foster's company, he was glad she was there, and Baker's transport too. He was keen to know what had happened because as far as he could see, Paul Moore was inexplicably and suspiciously dead and he was stumped.

CHAPTER SEVEN

MONDAY MORNING

'I'm not happy about this, no, I'm not happy at all,' said Mark Baker. From his voice, Ward could tell the usually jovial pathologist was frowning into his phone.

Ward had made it back home and to bed too late for his liking from the Moore household—and with no dog to greet him. No doubt Oliver the Beagle would be living it up at his second home, being thoroughly spoiled by his pup-sitter. A stab of guilt bit Ward at the thought of his dog. He knew he didn't need to feel guilty—the dog was happy as anything—but Ward did all the same. Ward had taken Olly on knowingly and yet his schedule was so all over the place sometimes, the pup had to play second fiddle to his career.

It was the next morning and Ward had hauled himself out of bed reluctantly, the dark November mornings not helping his inclination to get up, especially after the late night. But drag himself in Ward had, with a double dose of coffee to try and wake up.

He and Nowak had combed through the scant details they had so far, gathering the first of the information they'd need to make a running start at the case if it turned out foul play had been involved in Paul Moore's death.

'I'd estimate the time of death to be around eight last night and I'd probably say between seven and nine to be more confident,' Mark said.

Just before Paul Moore's wife had returned home, and covering her arrival time. Ward grimaced. He swirled the teaspoon in his mug and took the coffee to a quiet corner of the canteen.

'Now, I don't know that he could have been saved by a medical intervention at that point,' Mark said, a rush of static bristling Ward's ear as the pathologist sighed down the phone. 'He would have been in a very bad way, you see. I can't determine an exact cause of death yet. As the paramedics noted, he has some symptoms inconsistent with what I would expect to see for a wide variety of normal causes. He had a rash covering a significant portion of his body, which possibly alludes to some kind of anaphylaxis, perhaps.

'There are plenty of diseases that cause rashes, of course, some fatal, but none like *this* one. All that to say, m'boy, that I'm afraid there's nothing obvious at first glance that I can tell you to go on. You'll have to wait until I've conducted the full postmortem. Has dear Victoria found anything more useful?'

Ward cringed at the fondness in the pathologist's voice for Victoria Foster. He couldn't imagine thinking of her with anything other than irritation and distaste. 'Er, afraid not. They've bagged up plenty of evidence, and the contents of our deceased's stomach, but nothing else yet.'

Ward stirred with a sudden thought. 'Could it be untreated appendicitis? It can be fatal with the complications that arise, can't it?'

'Yes, absolutely! That's very astute of you to bring up. Unfortunately, the chap's medical record suggests he's already had his appendix out as a child and it simply doesn't match some of his other symptoms. It's that rash which concerns me most, alongside the sudden and inexplicable rapidity of his decline.'

'Do you think there's been foul play?' Ward asked frankly.

Baker was careful in his answer. 'I can't *definitively* say. Not yet. However, I'm not happy this is natural causes and that's what concerns me greatly, Daniel.' He fell into silence.

'Right,' said Ward, chewing his lip. 'I'll wait for the full report then. Thanks, Mark.'

He hung up, though the phone remained to his ear for an extra second or two as he processed. Baker's full report would be with them soon, he hoped, and with it, answers. What had the DCI sent him? Had Kipling put him on a duff case to teach him a lesson? He wasn't sure he'd put it past the DCI to make him earn his way back onto HMET.

However, if Baker wasn't happy it was natural causes... Perhaps Kipling hadn't sent him a humdinger. Perhaps he'd sent Ward a case with enough meat to chew on.

CHAPTER EIGHT

D I Ward punched another name into his phone and braced himself.

'Foster speaking.'

'Morning, Victoria. Daniel Ward.' Knowing she never stopped to exchange pleasantries—neither did he, in fairness—he got straight to it. 'Do you have anything for us?'

'Not much, I'm afraid,' she said around a half-stifled yawn. 'There's nothing to suggest anyone else broke into the property or was present, no signs of any weapons, damage, assault. I mean really, just a dead guy laying in a pool of his own puke.'

Ward grimaced.

Her tone turned sourer. 'Which was gross, thanks for that. We examined the food containers in the bin and fridge and we've taken samples of the vomit to test, in case there's anything relevant there. Honestly, there's nothing to go on. Are you sure this is murder?'

'No, and that's the problem,' Ward said. 'It's not clean-cut enough yet to be natural causes, but not exactly obvious enough to be suspicious. DCI said to investigate so, here we are.'

'Yes, well, understandable. There was that case a couple of years ago, right?'

Ward lowered the volume of his voice as a group of bodies sauntered in for a coffee run. 'Exactly. I think he's making sure everyone's arses are covered.' An accidental death had, in fact, been later revealed to be a murder. It had been an utter mess to sort out. The DCI had taken a lot of flak for that—it had happened on his watch, after all.

Ward hoped this was an accident, but he couldn't help but think, all too viscerally, of that anguished snarl of pure pain and fear frozen upon Paul Moore's face. Ward ended the call and headed back to the office. Forensics and pathology so far had turned up nothing, which pointed towards no foul play.

No answers yet, he mused. Usually, by now, something had stuck out. Usually, they'd have had some idea of what had happened, even if they had to wait for a postmortem or some forensic results to back up their theory with hard proof. But this time, there was nothing, not really, only that Mr Moore had died suddenly and in agony.

Well, sometimes that just happened, didn't it? Even young, healthy, fit people dropped dead, never mind middle-aged men with a lifetime of bad habits stacked against them. And, let's face it, death did not always take mildly or meekly. It was messy, it was painful, it was *scary*.

Ward sighed and pushed his way into the office, brew in hand, holding the door open for Patterson as he dodged out with an armful of files.

'Alright, Sarge,' he greeted Nowak, who was head down and shoulders hunched, furiously making notes at her desk.

Nowak looked up and hurt flashed across her face. 'Oi, sir, you didn't even offer!'

'What?' Ward glanced down at his brew. 'Ah, sorry. Autopilot today.'

Emma narrowed her eyes. 'I'm not sure you're awake enough that there's even a pilot in there, sir.'

Behind Ward, DS Scott Metcalfe's dark chuckle rumbled.

'You know, just because you stick a 'sir' on the end doesn't make it respectful,' Ward warned. He turned to Metcalfe. 'And don't *you* start.'

Nowak grinned wickedly. Metcalfe winked.

Ward rolled his eyes. 'Right. Come on then. On with it. Can you request his medical records today please, Emma? Baker says he can't see anything obvious, but he's not completed his full examination yet, so who knows. Same for CSI, Foster hasn't got anything. I reckon we might be dealing with natural causes here, but we have to run the full gamut if the DCI wants us to do it by the book, alright?'

Especially if he wanted let out of burglary any time

soon. Oh yes, Ward had to do this one by the book, get a good result, and absolutely not stuff it up.

'Yes, sir.'

Ward was banking on a medical condition unknown to Moore's wife—it was about the only straw left to clutch on the information they had. They needed more.

'What else have you got?' he asked.

Nowak had leaned a whiteboard against the vacant desk next to hers. She'd started putting together a Big Board of sorts, as she usually liked to, to try and visually put together key aspects of any case they worked on.

She wheeled her chair over to it and he walked around the desks to stand beside her to look.

'Well, sir, so far, we have our victim as Paul Anthony Moore. Aged fifty. Married to Janice Theresa Moore. Father of Lesley Jean Moore and Thomas Paul Moore. He worked at T. Brown Haulage in Keighley as a van driver and according to their website, they ship everything from house moves to hazardous waste everywhere from Bradford to Bulgaria. I'll speak to the company for more background information on Paul's direct duties, if that's relevant?' She looked up at Ward.

He nodded.

'Alright. So, I spoke to Janice last night at the house and she mentioned that Paul had been to golf before he returned home. One potential theory is an accident—could he have received, say, a very severe concussion? Untreated, severe head injuries can cause vomiting and death.' She sounded unsure.

'Aye, keep spitballing. It might feel like we're grasping at straws but it's all worth pursuing.'

'Right. Well, I took down the details of Paul's golf buddies from Janice. He didn't go alone, you see. He usually goes with three friends. We have...' She leaned over to her desk to scan for a note. 'Tony Brown, who owns the firm Moore works for, Lee Brown, who is Tony's brother, and Andrew Collins.'

'They'd be the perfect starting point then. If he did suffer an injury at golf, they'd know. Do we have any other obvious lines of enquiry? The wife, perhaps?'

'What makes you say that, sir?'

'Well, she didn't seem too happy.'

Nowak scoffed. 'I think that's more to do with the fact they had an old fashioned marriage, don't you?'

'Old fashioned?' Ward raised an eyebrow.

'Yes, you know. People nowadays, if it's not working out, you get divorced, move on, right?'

Ward would know, after all. He was waiting for the final papers to come through for his own divorce to end an ill-fated marriage.

Nowak took his silence for acquiescence. 'Well, I don't know too many older people who do it. Back then, you got married for life, right? And women relied on men more—they couldn't go out and work and raise the kids and all of it, like I guess we do now. They didn't have independence and the freedom. So you put up and shut up and stayed with your husband even if he's a bit of an arsehole, because it's comfort and safety and you have no better options.'

'Savage,' murmured Ward. 'Sounds like you're speaking from experience.' At twenty-six or so and not yet married to her fiancé Adam, that couldn't be the case. He wandered back around to his desk and sat, logging in with a few quick taps.

'Yeah, well, my grandparents were like that. My granny hated my pops. He was a, "Women and children should be seen and not heard" type of guy and my feisty granny wasn't too on board. When my mum and her brothers grew up and left, she had no one to be a buffer between the two of them. My mum thinks granny irritated him to death and he passed just to escape her pecking. She was much happier after. I wouldn't be surprised if she danced on his grave.'

Ward snorted with laughter. 'Charming!'

The corner of Nowak's lip turned up in a half-smile. 'I never met him, so I don't know, but my mum talks about them all the time. But that's what I think, anyway. I think Janice Moore loved her husband in that kind of way —the old way. Love, loyalty, and sticking to her vows, even if they didn't exactly get on too well anymore.

'All those plants were hers, by the way, and the green-house outside—that's how Janice kept herself busy. He golfed. She gardened. They were happier that way by the sounds of it, but she was genuinely upset and you can't fake that. Not easily, anyway. Besides, she has an alibi for the day. She was at work long before and until after Paul Moore passed.'

'That only applies if his death was caused by something in that time frame, though.'

'True,' Nowak conceded, flashing him a grin.

Ward's answering smirk faded. 'Nowak, come look at this.'

Her brows furrowed but she slipped from her chair and came to stand behind him, leaning on the back of his chair and peering over his shoulder. 'Moore's criminal record? What am I looking f... Oh.'

'Oh, indeed,' Ward said quietly. It was routine to examine someone's criminal record, driving records, whatever details the Police National Computer held on them, to build a picture of a potential victim's life and to pursue any lines of enquiry. Or create them.

Ward had to admit, this, he hadn't expected.

On Paul Moore's criminal record was a particular stain. He had no criminal record per se, but on there had been marked, three decades prior, a 'not guilty' verdict of rape following a trial.

An unsettling feeling in the pit of his stomach curdled the fresh mouthfuls of coffee in there. Nasty business. Ward hated looking into cases like that. The bias at the time, the systemic failure to properly investigate serious crimes of that nature and the lack of forensic technology back then did not make for many successful cases and subsequent convictions. 'Not guilty' did not mean 'innocent'.

He pulled up an internet browser to search for more details—newspaper articles from the time, any other information he could find. 'Let's see,' he murmured. 'Here we go. Okay. It was a case of alleged gang rape of a young woman named Elizabeth Munroe, who was...

Christ.' Ward gritted his teeth. 'She was seventeen at the time of the alleged offence.'

Over his shoulder, he could practically feel Nowak's seething. 'Did he do it?'

'Who knows but the two of them.' Ward shook his head. 'If it went to court though, that means something. Oh...' He'd flicked to another tab. A photo in black and white of a young teenager smiling, joy beaming from her eyes, sat under the header 'Obituary'. 'She passed away. Took her own life, shortly after the trial.'

'What does that tell you, then,' Nowak murmured, leaning closer to stare at the girl, but her words held no question.

It couldn't be a coincidence, and Ward agreed. He felt a tinge of sadness for the lass. Like Ward's own mother, who had died after a violent attack at the hands of his father when Ward had been a teenager—which had also remained unproven and his father unconvicted—Ward sensed there was more to this than met the eye. This young woman had ended up dead too, most likely as an indirect consequence of male violence. But with her death ended any notion that this could be some kind of far-fetched and long-planned revenge crime. Ward didn't believe in ghosts, that was for sure.

'He was found not guilty in a court of law and that's all we have to go on, I'm afraid, Sarge. Moore has no other criminal history. The only thing I can see is three points on his driving licence, which is hardly far-fetched if he drives for a job, so it seems that this is a blip on an otherwise normal life.'

He stared at the photo on Moore's driving licence. The man looked entirely different to the anguished corpse Ward had encountered the previous evening. Serious faced and grey-eyed, Paul Moore stared into the camera. *A possible rapist?* Ward wondered.

Not guilty in a court of law... Innocent? Guilty? The young woman had taken her own life as a result of that trial, it appeared. What did that mean? And now, Ward was investigating Paul Moore's death... her possible attacker.

Life was so rarely black and white, more like a tangle of greys. Should that colour this? Whatever had happened then, did not change what had happened now; Paul Moore had died and DI Ward and his team were duty-bound to investigate his death. Fairly.

Innocent until proven guilty, right? Everyone deserves justice and peace in death, right?

CHAPTER NINE

MONDAY AFTERNOON

The radio buzzed on low volume, the jingling beat of early Christmas songs dropping like punctuation between the rain battering the car. In November, the weather was as unforgiving as ever in the Yorkshire hills.

Ward drove his Golf with Nowak in the passenger seat, the windscreen wipers on furious overtime to try and clear the unrelenting downpour. Steaming travel cups of pumpkin spice lattes sat in the cupholders between them from a drive-through Starbucks on their route. Ward had never tried one, but Nowak had insisted. 'Divine,' she'd called them. Ward thought they smelled a little bit sickly if he was honest.

That afternoon, they had arranged to meet with Paul Moore's golfing buddies. Two, the Brown brothers, worked with Paul and another was close by down the valley at a mechanics. That hit two birds with one stone at least, so they could scope out Paul's workplace for any potential evidence that could link to his death, in the seemingly complete lack of any other useful leads so far.

In the passenger seat, DS Nowak scrolled through Paul Moore's medical record which had been sent over by his GP surgery. His wife had reported he had no problems and indeed, no health conditions were showing on the report. Not that related to his death, in any case.

Nowak said, 'Standard stuff, sir. He was prediabetic, had a blood pressure to make your eyes water and a few historical surgeries. Knee surgery, a hernia, and he had his appendix out as a kid, like Baker said.'

'Hmm. Unlucky for us, then.' Ward had been hoping for an easy solution, especially after the criminal record he'd unearthed. It soiled the case with an unclean taste he couldn't seem to shake. Much as he didn't want to bias the investigation, Ward was human and he hated the thought that a terrible injustice resulting in a young woman's death might have taken place.

'Nothing that could have caused the strange rash that Baker noted? Did he have any allergies?'

'No, sir. No allergies noted at all.'

Ward sighed. *Then what on earth could kill a man in such a manner?*

———

DI Ward slowed in the centre of a small industrial estate backing onto the dual carriageway on the south end of Keighley to find the right address. The older part of the sprawl was a tangle of Victorian brick buildings, but the newer was prefabricated warehouses of modern stone and corrugated metal.

This one was a typical freight yard, with signage fixed on the high, spiked, metal fencing in red and gold reading *T. Brown Haulage*, which Ward could clearly read now as the deluge had lessened to a miserable, but more manageable, steady rain. Trucks and vans clogged the yard up to a large warehouse with huge open roller doors where vans and a lorry were parked up to be loaded or unloaded.

There was a small amount of visitor parking located next to the gate, but Ward parked on the road outside, well away from the hustle and bustle. He wasn't going to risk getting his prized car pranged in the chaos, thank you very much.

Ward and Nowak walked through the open gates, Ward holding a brolly over their heads. A distinct brew of unappealing scents permeated through the rain—chemicals from some of the factories nearby and the quite literal smell of crap which had somehow managed to drift up the valley from Marley sewage works between Crossflatts and Keighley.

Ward glanced down the valley. High hills soared behind the buildings around them, and nearby, the giant, cylindrical, metal structures of the gas storage towers rose to punctuate the horizon. Not the most alluring part of Yorkshire, he had to admit, though Keighley town itself, to the North, was a pretty little hub with a central, flower-filled square and Victorian stone facades lining the high street.

They made for the small building next to the ware-house, housing the reception and offices, by the look of it —a paper sign labelled 'reception' with an arrow directed them to the right entrance. Ward held the door for Nowak.

'Thanks, sir,' she said, slipping inside gratefully and smoothing a hand over her hair to try and tame some of the wild, rain-frazzled strands.

Ward collapsed the umbrella and followed her inside to the woman waiting there behind a desk. 'Detectives Ward and Nowak. We have an appointment with Tony Brown.'

She frowned, her gaze lingering over the two of them. Nowak, auburn hair in a ponytail, a long, sleek, dark coat. Ward, hulking over the both of them, collar and tie poking out under his own woollen winter jacket. She made a quick call to Tony and though she spoke in a quiet voice, Ward and Nowak could hear every word. She hung up.

'Follow me.' She led them past the reception desk, through a door, and up a narrow set of stairs in a dim hall-way. The rain seemed amplified inside and it was cold too. Ward glanced up and noticed the uninsulated metal roof.

Upstairs, she showed them into a modest boardroom at the end of a hallway lined with offices and storerooms. Ward noted as they passed one with a plaque on the door stating 'Tony Brown, The Boss Man'. Sense of humour, then, Ward reckoned.

'Wait here, he'll be along in a minute.' She didn't

offer them any drinks. Ward could have done with a proper coffee after the sweet and sickly abomination that had been the pumpkin spiced latte.

Whilst they waited, Ward drifted around the board-room with Nowak, glancing at the small number of award plaques and certificates on the walls, alongside press clip-pings and professional photographs, including one of a beaming man in a suit that Ward presumed would be Tony Brown himself.

A couple of minutes later, the man from the photos walked in, devoid of a suit and instead in a black polo bearing the company logo and dark jeans scuffed with dust. Balding and chunkily built, with a budding belly, but shoulders, arms, and thighs brimming with muscles, he exuded strength and confidence. He extended a tattooed arm to shake Ward's hand and then Nowak's, in a crushing grip.

'Tony Brown. What can I do for you, Detectives?' he introduced himself in a deep, rich, Yorkshire accent, before stepping back to regard them with thinned lips and a troubled frown. 'I heard what happened.' He shook his head. 'Can't believe it. I only saw him yesterday and he seemed fine.'

'Thanks for agreeing to chat,' Ward said after introducing them both, having to raise his voice as the battering on the roof intensified as the rain picked up once more. No one made a move to sit at the board-room table. Tony hovered near the door still and Ward and Nowak stood shoulder to shoulder in front of him.

'We have a few questions if that's alright, to try and understand what happened to Paul Moore.'

'Is he..?' Tony's mouth sagged and he looked up at Ward, horrified. 'Do you think someone killed him? I thought... I mean, I thought maybe he'd had a heart attack or something, from how sudden it was,' he blurted out.

Ward shared a glance with Nowak. 'I'm afraid we can't comment on an ongoing investigation, but we are investigating his death at this point.'

Tony clamped his lips together and nodded, arms folding across his burly chest. 'Aye. Jan told me what happened, how she found Paul. Nasty way to go.' He shook his head again. 'I can't believe that anyone might...' He trailed off.

'How long did you know Paul?' Ward asked.

'A lifetime,' Tony said and a nostalgia-laced chuckle slipped out. 'We all knocked about at school together— him, me, my brother, and Andrew. A few others, like, but us four have stayed tight over the years. I don't see much of anyone else these days.'

'This must be hard, then, if you knew him well.'

'Aye.'

A man of few words, perhaps. Ward got the feeling that Tony wouldn't be breaking down and blubbering all over them, but that didn't mean he wasn't feeling deeply hurt by the loss of his friend.

'We appreciate your help,' Nowak said having come to the same conclusion. Ward let her lead. She excelled at lowering guards and drawing out information in a way that he couldn't. It was another reason they worked so well together; their different strengths combining to make an investigative team that could handle anything.

Nowak added, 'We're trying to build a picture of Paul's life and what may have happened to him. Anything you can tell us will be helpful.'

Tony nodded. The only hint of the tamped down feelings inside him was the bob of his throat as he swallowed.

'Paul worked with you yesterday, is that right?'

'Aye.'

'On a Sunday?'

Tony winced and shook his head. 'We're really busy running up to Christmas.'

Ward nodded. 'Between what times?'

Tony stirred and his arms unfolded. He leaned heavily on the back of one of the chairs tucked under the table. 'He started at... would have been eight, but I can guarantee he was ten minutes late. Always is. I don't mind. He grafts hard enough to make up for it.'

'Until?' Nowak jotted notes in her pocketbook.

'Five normally. We finished an hour early yesterday with it being Sunday.'

'And he seemed alright, you said? Nothing different about his appearance, or his behaviour?'

'Aye, nothing that I noticed. He was out driving all day and when he came back at half four, he was alright.'

'Any injuries or illnesses that you know about?'

'Uh, no.' Tony shook his head emphatically.

'You saw him at golf too,' Nowak prompted. 'East

Morton, right?' She continued at Tony's nod. 'Can you tell us what time that was?'

'Eh, yeah. We all went straight from work—Paul, my brother, me, and we met our mate Andrew there. So, half four or thereabouts.'

'And Paul was fine there too?'

'No, he was the same cocky bastard as always,' Tony said with a dark chuckle, but one that quickly stuttered out with the sobering realisation once more that his friend was dead.

'Can you tell us what you did there?'

'Same as always. Spent half an hour smashing out a bucket of balls each at the driving range and then went to the pub. And he was fine,' Tony said abruptly, anticipating her next question. 'We didn't speak much. I was in a separate lane down the end. Andrew and Paul were next to each other.'

She glanced up. 'That's Andrew Collins, right?'

'Aye.'

'Sorry for the interruptions, please continue.'

'Er...' Tony looked like he didn't have much more to say. 'Well, I suppose, we're not as good as we like to think, but it takes the edge off the stress. Things are tough here right now and all. Winter makes things harder. We have a few drivers off as well and everyone's having to pick up the slack. Hence the Sunday overtime.'

He looked tired with dark shadows under his eyes. As Ward watched Tony, the man dragged a hand over his face.

'We've all been picking up more hours. I've been up

since three already, pulling doubles this week.' He looked up and straightened. 'Legally, I mean. It's all legal. We have our logs. Everyone's getting the appropriate breaks and all that. No one's going over their maximum hours.'

Ward wasn't convinced, but that wasn't the can of worms he was there to open. 'What happened next at or after golf?'

Tony glanced at him, then back to Nowak, as though confused that they had changed direction and Ward had taken charge once more.

'Well, we went to the pub. The Busfeild Arms in East Morton. No,' he added, raising a hand as Nowak scrawled. 'It won't be spelled how you think. It's Busfeild with the 'e' before the 'i'—I couldn't tell you why, just is.'

'What did you all drink?' asked Ward, an idea sparking. Could Paul Moore have ingested something that caused a fatal reaction? Could his pint at the pub have been contaminated with something toxic or poisonous? It was about as good a theory as he had at that moment, in any case.

'Er...' Tony mumbled as he thought. 'Well, I had a Guinness, I always do. Paul and Andrew tried a new pale ale they have on tap.'

Interesting. So if Paul drank the same as Andrew... We need to check if Andrew Collins is well for that theory to hold up.

'What about your brother? You said he came too?'

'Oh, normally he does, aye, but last night he was working late, so it was the three of us. Lee had a night run to Heathrow to do for one of our customers, so he went home for some tea before he set off.'

'I see.'

'And, do you know if Andrew Collins is alright?'

'Aye. I spoke to him this morning, let him know what's happened. He's fine. Well, obviously aside from all this.' Tony waved a hand in their direction and his gaze fell to the table. For a moment he seemed lost in deep thought.

'What time did you finish at the pub?'

'I'm not sure, around six maybe?'

'And what happened then?'

Tony shrugged. 'We all went home, as far as I know.'

'Is there anything else you can tell us that might be able to shed light on what happened to Paul?'

Tony looked up quickly and cleared his throat. 'No. I mean... no. I'm sorry. I'm just in shock, to be honest, but no, he was right as rain yesterday. I never would have seen this coming.'

Ward took a deep breath and waited until Nowak had finished writing. 'Right then, well thank you for your time, Mr Brown. Is your brother here for a chat?'

'Aye, but I don't think he'll be able to help. Like I say, he was working a lot of hours yesterday, I doubt he even saw Paul.'

'Still.' Ward smiled, though no warmth reached his eyes.

'Aye, well I'll take you to him now.' He turned and they followed him back downstairs to the warehouse, where he led them to a slightly younger man who was the spit of him.

'Thanks for your help, Mr Brown. We'll be in touch if we need anything else.'

Tony nodded and his gaze was troubled as he left, glancing back at them a couple of times.

CHAPTER TEN

Ward and Nowak briefly spoke to Tony Brown's brother Lee. About five years Tony's junior and his spit, aside from a gnarly beard, Lee was about as forthcoming as a stone. He looked dog-tired like his brother, which Ward could understand. He too was a man of few words when he was knackered.

Lee Brown could tell them nothing more than he hadn't seen Paul at work since the previous week as their schedules hadn't crossed and he'd not been to golf as Tony had said, due to work commitments.

Nowak and Ward excused themselves and with Andrew Collin's contact details in hand, headed off to speak to him next. Ward had the distinct feeling that they were beating their heads against a wall, being busy fools who weren't actually getting anywhere.

Frankly, he was still half-convinced the case was a waste of time that the DCI had sent him on to further punish him. His temper already fraying, his fingers beat a pattern on the leather-wrapped steering wheel as he drove to the mechanics where Andrew Collins worked, down the valley beside the delightful odour of the waste plant.

———

Ward's mood brightened en route—unlike the pissing down weather—when Mark Baker's name flashed up on the screen and the radio cut off mid-Christmas tune as the Bluetooth rang.

'What've you got, Mark?' Ward asked, flying past a glacially slow car on the bypass.

'Well, Daniel, something very interesting indeed. I think your man's been poisoned.'

'What?' Ward tucked back into the slow lane, easing off the accelerator as he focused on Mark's voice.

'Based on my examinations, I suspect severe poisoning. There's absolutely nothing medical I can find that would have caused Paul Moore to die in the manner he did. Based on the symptoms I can see—pupil dilation, the rash and the violent and abrupt nature of his ah, *demise*—it's the only conclusion I can draw at this point.'

'What does that mean?' Ward's mind was already firing with possibilities, all of which felt ludicrous.

'Well, first, I have to note that poisoning might not mean what you think—you know, some dramatic slipping of poison into a chalice of wine.' Baker's hearty warm laughter rumbled through the car. 'I mean poisoned in that Mr Moore seems to have come into contact with or ingested some severely potent toxic substance.'

'Do you know what?' They needed that information —without it, they couldn't even begin to narrow things down.

'I'm afraid not.'

Ward's heart sank.

'I've sent off for a full toxicology report, of course, but honestly, it could take weeks.'

Weeks?

Ward indicated to pull off the bypass at the Cross-flatts roundabout by the shitworks. 'I see. Is there anything else?'

'That's all, Daniel. I recognise that might be disappointing, but that's as definitive as I can be. At least now you know how he died.'

'Just not from what.'

'I'll keep hounding toxicology to process it as quickly as they can, rest assured, m'boy.'

Ward injected warmth into his tone, though he felt more akin to crushing disappointment. 'As always, I appreciate it, Mark.'

'Poisoned...' murmured Nowak beside him as Ward hung up.

'Aye,' Ward replied grimly.

Nowak smoothed back her hair. 'What does that even mean?'

Ward sighed. 'I'm not sure. But for starters, perhaps that beer's back on the table. We need to check if there could have been any contaminants present and see if

Collins is alright, seeing as they drank the same beer, probably from the same cask or pump.'

'What about Moore's work?' Nowak asked, turning to Ward with a frown.

'What do you mean?'

'Well, I checked out their website and they transport hazardous waste, it says. I mean, if Baker's telling us that he's either come into contact with or ingested something highly toxic or poisonous, well isn't that the obvious place to start looking?'

'Definitely. Well spotted. That opens up a whole can of worms we need to look into.'

'Can you imagine if he was exposed to something at work?' Nowak shuddered. 'Poor guy.'

'Hmm.' Ward wasn't as naturally compassionate as Nowak, he reckoned. That *not guilty* verdict on Moore's criminal record still lurked in the back of his mind.

They arrived at the mechanics where Andrew Collins worked and Ward pulled up, switched off, and opened the door. 'Eurgh.'

'The rain isn't doing much to dampen the stink,' groaned Nowak. They were still close to the waste centre in the bottom of the valley. Lucky for them.

'At least you don't have to work here all the time,' Ward said. It was a silver lining at least.

Together, they approached the man inside, busy underneath a car raised on a platform.

'Andrew Collins?' Ward said, raising his voice above the rumble and whir of tools and the radio blasting eighties rock out at full volume.

The man emerged, smeared in grime. He was burlier than Ward and just as tall, blue overalls braced tightly on his bulky chest. He looked darkly at them, his frown laced with suspicion and he did not put down the giant wrench clenched in his right hand. 'Yeah?'

He doesn't like the police. Wonder why? It was usually easy to tell, though the reasons were harder to discern. They usually amounted to some form of prior offence or run in personally, an issue with friends or family, or a current outstanding crime of some sort. Ward introduced them, giving nothing of his internal thoughts away.

'I take it you've heard the news about Paul Moore?' Ward said.

'Aye.' Andrew Collins looked none too happy about it —or life in general—and his scowl deepened.

Ward gave him a polite smile, trying to make it as pleasant and un-grimace-like as he could. Emma was far better at charming people than he was—he didn't have the damned patience for it, half the time. She stood to his side and slightly behind, notebook out and pen moving.

Ward said, 'We're sorry to bother you at a time like this. We have a few questions about Paul, to try and understand what happened to him, as his death is currently treated as being unexplained.' *And suspicious as hell.*

Andrew didn't respond, so Ward continued.

'Can you tell us when you last saw Paul?'

'Yesterday. At golf.'

'Did you see him in the week before that?'

'No. Golf. Same again. Last week.'

'Alright. Could you tell us what happened at golf?'

'What do you mean?' Andrew said sharply. He narrowed his eyes at Ward, glancing between him and Nowak as she too watched him, waiting for an answer.

'Just that. Can you tell us what happened? Did you speak to Paul at the driving range? Did he seem alright? Was he acting differently? That sort of thing.'

'Right.' Andrew folded his arms, that wrench gripped tightly in his fist. 'He was fine at golf, if that's what you're asking. We didn't talk much.'

'Did you play close together?'

Andrew paused, his stare not leaving Ward's. Eventually, he answered, 'Yes and no. We played in separate lanes, though they were near each other. There's not a chance to talk there.'

'Right. And how did Paul seem?'

'Fine.'

This is like drawing blood out of a stone. 'Did he sustain any injuries whilst you were there?'

'Eh?' That seemed to throw him and he frowned, his confusion clear. And then, 'No.'

'Alright. What happened after golf?'

'We went home.'

'Did you?' Ward cocked his head.

Andrew shuffled. 'After the pub, I mean. We got a pint. Then went home.'

'Did you mean to forget that?'

'No,' retorted Andrew, his glare hardening again.

'Alright. You must have chatted at the pub then, if

you didn't at golf. What came up in conversation, anything of note?'

'Not much, same old shit, different day, moaning about work, women, you know.' His glance flicked to Nowak at that, provoking, challenging, but she didn't react.

Ward ignored it tactfully too. 'You drank the same at the pub as Paul, right?'

'Yes, why?' He seemed to close even more. 'Was there something wrong with the beer?' His eyes widened and his mouth slackened. 'Was it poisoned or something?'

'Why do you assume that?'

'Well, from what his wife told Tony, he dropped dead and I had the same IPA.' His face paled. Ward could practically see the 'what if?!' thoughts whirring to life in his mind.

'If you're fine now and you haven't been ill, I wouldn't worry about that,' Ward said, with Baker's theory in mind. 'Are you feeling alright in yourself too? No signs of illness?'

'No.' His arms flexed, loosening slightly and he chewed his lip, his attention on nothing as he fell into a world of his own for a second.

'Would there be any other reason to be worried about poison? That's a pretty specific word.' Had he stumbled onto something meaningful in this otherwise probably banal investigation?

'No.' He closed up again, his attention snapping back to them. 'You mentioned the beer and I thought...What happened to Paul? Should we be worried? Was it the pub? The beer?'

Ward and Nowak shared a look and Ward held up his hands. 'I'm afraid we can't comment on an ongoing investigation, but we're looking at several lines of enquiry.' He smiled, but this time it was threatening. 'We want to make sure we have the full facts. One is making sure that yourself and Tony are fit and well so we can rule out anything that might have occurred at golf... or after.'

Andrew drew himself tall and nodded. His lips thinned into an impenetrable line, clamped shut.

'Is there anything else at all you can tell us that might help?' Nowak prompted, but Ward didn't think even she would be able to open up this clam. *What isn't he telling us?*

Nowak added. 'We know from Tony that you've been friends for an awfully long time and we can appreciate how difficult this is for you. We just have to understand what happened to Paul. Janice most of all needs closure.'

Andrew gritted his teeth, but he nodded. 'I get that. I can't tell you anything else. We went to golf, got a drink, went home. Paul was fine. I don't know what happened.'

'Right. Thanks for your help. We'll be in touch.' Ward's tone was more ominous than he intended. As though it were a warning.

With inscrutable eyes, Andrew nodded and watched them leave, before the hammering started up again as they rounded the corner.

'I don't like him,' Nowak muttered as they sat in the car. 'Something about him sets me on edge.'

'Mmm,' replied Ward noncommittally. 'I get the feeling he doesn't like us either. Maybe he has priors. You know how people are. We're all the same to them and it brings back bad memories. Hard to shake that suspicion and distrust, I suppose. Let's go to the pub whilst we're over this way, anyway.' Ward yawned and eased the car into gear, to turn around.

'Eh, sir? Drinking on the job? That's not like you.'

Ward laughed gruffly. 'Fat chance. You know me, I rarely partake these days. DCI works us too hard for the chance and like we get paid well enough.'

'You can't say that, you're a DI.'

'Aye, and I get knack all for it, let me tell you. You're in the wrong career for a pretty penny, you know that, right?'

'Hmm.'

'I want to speak to the bar staff, see if we can get a sample of the pale ale Moore drank. Long shot, probably a dead end, but we need to check it out anyway now we suspect he could've been poisoned.'

Nowak shivered.

'What's up?'

'Just... scary, isn't it, sir? You can't even see it and it could kill you.'

'Aye. I suppose so. Plenty we can see that can kill us too, mind.'

'Well, isn't that a cheerful thought for a Monday afternoon.'

'Font of sunshine, me, Sergeant. Happy to please.'

She smirked at that. 'To the pub then, sir. Drinks on you.'

'You can have a tap water or a tap water, lass.'

'You know how to treat a girl, sir.'

Ward chuckled darkly. His impending divorce would suggest otherwise.

CHAPTER ELEVEN

MONDAY LATE AFTERNOON

The Busfeild Arms was closed. They'd have to call another time. Back in the sweltering office, Ward shed his outer layers, his tie, and loosened his collar again, the drive-through coffee he had consumed seeming to boil him from the inside as well as the outside.

Whilst they'd been gone, Paul Moore's phone records had landed. Ward tasked DC Jake Patterson with cross-referencing them against possible contacts of interest.

Mark Baker had emailed his provisional postmortem report through, without the toxicology report, of course. Without that, there was nothing much to go on, really, only to say that Paul Moore did not appear to have died of natural causes and that as Baker had already told them, he suspected some kind of poisoning from exposure to a fast-acting toxic substance.

That brought a small thrill to Ward—one that he used to feel guilty for—because it meant that he wasn't looking at a tedious dud case after all. They had *something*, even if it felt like they had no answers so far.

All they could do now was wait. It could take up to four weeks for the toxicology reports to return, though Baker had marked them as URGENT and followed up with a strongly suggestive phone call that the laboratory in Leeds do their utmost to get the results back *pronto*.

Already, the office had started to clear, with DC Shahzad absent from the incident room and the stacks of burglary paperwork, and DC Patterson racing through the phone records so he could be out the door too.

David Norris, buried in his usual corner amidst the Varga caseload, was the only one with his head down and not clock-watching like the rest of them. He took a deep breath and looked up, blinking a few times as he spotted Ward, as though he had not realised Ward had returned. 'Ah, sir. A word, please?'

'Aye, David, what's up?'

Leaving a note to chase the pub on his desk, lest he forget, Ward ambled over. David leaned back in his chair and stretched out his neck with a relieved groan. 'An update on the Varga case, sir. I didn't catch you yesterday, sorry.' Despite the late hour of the day, some energy lit up his face and coloured his tone with fresh vigour.

'Go on?' Ward was intrigued. He perched on the corner of Norris' desk.

'We've received back the blood work from the Range Rover, sir. Oho, it's good. Better than good. *Excellent*. We have two matches.'

Ward waited, his breath stalling.

'One of them is Havel Marko.'

What? Ward's eyebrow rose. Marko was a known high-level associate of Bogdan Varga. One of his right-hand men, if their investigative work was right.

'And the other?' Havel Marko was a high-level prize enough, but any other subordinates they could take off the streets would be gold. His chest seemed to contract, waiting, the seconds dragging out inexorably.

David smiled, the dark satisfaction of that grin out of place on his usually placid visage, such was the satisfaction he drew from the moment. 'Bogdan Varga himself.'

'*No.*' It couldn't be. It simply *couldn't*. That would be too good to be true, surely.

'Oh yes, sir.'

Ward lets out a low whistle. *This is it.* If Varga's blood was in that car, they could directly tie him to the vehicle and a string of other crimes that it was connected to. Most importantly, they could link him to the events of that night, the warehouse fire, the deaths there... It was a crucial piece of evidence in the case they were so painstakingly building against him.

Ward said, 'This is huge. This is the breakthrough we needed.'

'I hope so, sir.'

'Have you told Milanova?' Their contact in the Organised Crime Bureau of the Slovak Police Force, *Praporcik*, or Sergeant, Marika Milanova.

'I was just about to fill her in.'

'Excellent. Now that we have the blood linking them

forensically to that car, do we have enough to move on Marko?'

'I believe so, sir. Certainly, we can arrest him.'

'Excellent.' The fallout from the Varga raid on the Khan warehouse had been pandemonium, with pockets of violence directly related to the incident breaking out through the area and across the wider city, as the gangs fought a turf war.

Already, they'd hauled in some lower-level criminals on drugs and violence charges in relation to it and found traces of the drugs stolen from the warehouse moving through the system and onto the streets.

'Where's he dealing right now?' Ward asked.

Norris brought up a map and indicated some streets in East Manningham. 'There's a den here, according to our surveillance and the word on the streets. There's been an increased number of visitors coming and going from the property, signs of drug use in and around it—discarded needles and the like—and the place is a hub for antisocial behaviour. A lot of calls from around there, but you know how hard it is to pin down that sort of thing on any one individual to make it stop.'

'Aye,' Ward nodded. 'And Marko runs it?'

'We're pretty certain, yes. I've managed to tie him to another vehicle.' Norris plucked out a Post-it note. 'This one here. An Audi R8 running on false plates registered to, of all vehicles, a Nissan Micra down south.'

Ward snorted. That couldn't have been further from an Audi R8.

'I've made sure no one pulls it yet, though, because

it's our only lead as to where Marko is, but it's markered up to the sky on the system, believe me. Any ANPR or traffic units will know it's a problem, so we're going to have to move quickly now that we can tie it all together.'

'Good thinking.' Much as it pained Ward to know a car most likely uninsured, untaxed, and running on someone else's plates was running around their city, it was worth it, for now, as long as they moved swiftly. 'Have you found anything helpful from it? ANPR data? Registered keeper?'

'Yes, sir. No registered owner, since we don't know the original plate number or VIN. It makes weekly cross-Pennine trips, presumably for a drop. I'm presuming it's him, because I don't know that he would trust anyone else with such a high-value job in that car.'

Ward shook his head. 'County lines. I suppose we shouldn't be surprised.' Varga's operation imported at least some drugs through Liverpool Harbour that Ward knew of, though the police hadn't managed to seize any yet that they could tie to Varga and they hadn't managed to join the dots to Varga's enterprises in Bradford and the surrounding area directly. 'If we have enough to move and that car is the key, I want a sting operation setting up on it post-haste.'

Norris nodded, his expression serious. 'If it goes the same time and day every week, well... that's on Thursday.'

'Whenever we have a clear shot to move on that vehicle, I want it taken. Can we notify traffic and interceptors?' It would be the high-speed police cars patrolling the county's network of roads that would be responsible for that operation. The desk jockeys like Ward and Norris would have no part in it.

'Yes, sir. I'll do that right away. I'll make sure our lot are briefed and those in neighbouring counties. There have been occasional trips to Nottingham, Sheffield, and Leicester in recent weeks too, though they're rarer. I think the cross-Pennine route will be our best bet. It's a regular, same night every week.'

'If we can get him on the M62 across the hills where there's no way off, reduced risk to those around... Aye, I think that'd be best.'

'As I say, sir, I'll pass it on with the urgent markers for drugs, violence, and weapons. They'll love a crack at that.'

'I'll bet.' Ward wouldn't have minded being a police interceptor if he were able to chase down the bad guys at high speed, but those few seconds of glory were few and far between on that job. More like drunk drivers, traffic accidents, and untaxed knobheads to round up all day long.

'We might have enough to get Marko,' Ward said, 'but do we have enough to get Varga?'

Norris stalled and grimaced. 'Do we ever?'

'Too much circumstantial evidence, I know. We need to find his hand wrapped around a gun, pulling a trigger, with a big old bag of drugs in his other hand, don't we?' said Ward, sighing.

'That would be very helpful,' chuckled Norris.

'Well, we keep building the case. However long it

takes. We'll keep digging the sand out from under him, take out all his people, all his cronies and eventually, we'll take him out too.'

Ward didn't add that he knew someone else would simply fill Varga's shoes. That went without saying. It would be someone just as bad—possibly worse. That was inevitable in their job. They kept fighting against the tide. Sometimes they won, but always, it kept coming, inexorable as the North Sea beating down the Filey Cliffs.

'Let me know if you have any updates. And if Milanova has anything to add to our information, perhaps we can tie something back to one of her ongoing Varga cases too.' The data pooling between the two international police forces had already helped *Prap*. Milanova put away two of Varga's associates in Slovakia and she was closing in on the weak link of his brother-in-law, too, by the sounds of it.

'Excellent work though, David, I mean that. Keep it up. I don't know what I'd do without you.' And he didn't. The diligent DC was a credit to Ward's team, his aptitude for meticulous record keeping and data acquisition was critical to pulling the whole bulging, tenuous web of the Varga crime empire one millimetre closer together at a time.

Ward straightened. Patterson was still buried in Paul Moore's telephone records. 'Give it up for today, Jake,' Ward called across.

Patterson groaned in relief. It was charging towards six and none of them would get any paid overtime that quarter. 'Thanks, sir. See you tomorrow.'

Ward had barely made it back to his desk before the lad had shut down his computer, grabbed his coat, and fled into the night.

Ward would take a reasonable home time too. 'You as well, David. Don't be staying here all night, alright?'

'Yes, sir.' But David didn't look up as he waved his acknowledgement. He had the same dedication as Ward, in the end; he had to get things to a neat edge before he could call it a day.

Ward sat back down at his desk. There was one more thing he had to do too before he'd be happy to call an end to the day too.

———

'Busfeild Arms,' a man answered the phone on the other end.

Ward held the phone closer to his ear, the call irritatingly grainy. 'Good evening. Detective Inspector Ward, West Yorkshire Police. Would I be able to speak to whoever worked behind the bar on Sunday night, please?'

'Uh, sure, that'd be me. What's it regarding?' The man's words were formal, but his voice wobbled slightly. A call from the police did tend to have that effect on people.

'Perfect. Do you recall three or four men who stopped for a pint around half six that night? They possibly come in most Sundays around that time.'

'Oh, aye. Normally there's four, just three this week,

they're some of our regulars. Can I ask what's up? I don't understand.'

'Sorry. I can't comment on an ongoing investigation. Did you notice anything unusual about any of them?'

Static reared down the phone as the man blew out a breath, contemplating his answer. 'Well, I suppose I normally wouldn't remember the specifics, but this week they had a right barney, actually. I thought it'd come to blows, to be honest. I had to tell them to shut up or piss off. I would have chucked them out if they weren't regulars. Never seen 'em have a to-do like that before.'

Ward's attention piqued. Neither Tony nor Andrew had mentioned an argument. He needed to dig into that with the two of them.

'An argument, you say. About what?'

'Well, I didn't hear much. One wasn't happy with another, the third stayed out of it, watching, then he stepped between them to try break it up and calm them down before it came to blows. Nothing physical, but the pair of 'em were raging.'

His breath rattled down the phone again. 'I think one was asking the other for money—it was as though he owed him it.'

'I see. Is there anything else you noticed whilst they were there, or after they left?'

'No, I mean after that they settled down, but they drunk up and left quickly. I kept an eye on them and well, those two weren't talking, put it that way.'

'Thanks for your help, you've been very useful.'

'Are they in some kind of trouble?'

Ward debated how much to tell the man. The beer was still a potential concern, even if Andrew Collins had consumed the same as Paul Moore and turned out fine. 'We're currently investigating the death of one of those men.'

'Bloody hell, what happened?'

'I can't comment on that. Would you be able to describe the three men involved in the argument?'

'Aye, I see them every week. The two who were arguing... Well, the one asking for money was built like a brick shithouse, is the best way to put it. He's a strapping chap. Towers over me. T'other was shorter, light hair, normal build. The one who tried to separate them was probably somewhere inbetween, balding. Does that help?'

'Very much, thanks.' Ward banked on those rudimentary descriptions meaning that Paul had owed Andrew some money, Andrew was calling in his debt, and Tony had stepped between the two to try and keep the peace.

Brilliant. 'There's just one more thing. We are looking into a potential contamination contributing to the man's death and he had your new IPA. Has anyone else reported illness after trying it?'

'Oh no. I drunk a pint of that the same night too— would have been the same cask—and nothing's wrong with me. Well, I hope.' He let out a quickly stifled nervous laugh.

'Right, thanks.' If Andrew Collins and even the barman, not to mention who knows how many others, had sampled the same beer without ill effects, it looked even more unlikely that the beer was the source of the toxin that had killed Paul Moore.

However...Why had neither Andrew Collins nor Tony Brown mentioned an argument when they'd spoken to them? Had that argument been connected to Paul Moore's death?

Tony Brown and Andrew Collins have some answering to do.

CHAPTER TWELVE

MONDAY EVENING

Thud thud thud!

Janice Moore's heart thundered in her chest, but that hammering drowned it out. It sounded as though the front door would come crashing through in the next moment. She glanced at the window again, glad she'd drawn all the curtains and blinds against the dark of night. The lights were on. Her car was outside. He knew she was home. She knew he knew it too.

Thud thud thud!

It was constant along with the muffled shouts coming through the front door. She didn't need to hear the words to know they were threats she'd rather not hear.

Janice sobbed as she cowered behind the sofa. She'd tugged the plant pot and side table back into place to hide her—no one would see her, not unless they were looking.

But the man at the door *was* looking.

He would turn the whole house upside down and

tear it to pieces to get what he was coming for... but she didn't have it.

Had he done Paul in? She didn't know, and she was so scared. Was she next? That made her want to vomit or faint—or both. She leaned heavily on the wall, propped up on all fours.

What had Paul become mixed up in? He'd told her not to worry about the money he'd borrowed, that it would all be fine—and yet there she was, fearing for her life, hiding behind her own sofa whilst the door got smashed in by thugs. She couldn't pay any of it back. Paul had long since spent it down to the last penny.

At first, it had been responsible things—fixing the car, getting the leaking roof done, that sort of thing. She'd been so grateful then. It had seemed like a God-send. But then, he'd had a taste for it. The all-inclusive holiday to Spain had wooed her. She should never have been fooled. Everything came at a cost.

Thud thud thud.

Janice Moore cowered and cried silent tears, her hand covering her mouth to stop any sound escaping, whilst she waited, wishing more than anything that Paul was there to protect her.

Eventually, the hammering and shouting ceased, but she didn't move.

Not until the early hours of the morning, when her bladder hurt so much that her only options were to chance a dash to the loo or piss herself.

She didn't dare switch another light on. Or go near

the bathroom window. Just in case, somehow, someone still lurked outside and were waiting for her.

As soon as it was daylight, she was packing a bag and leaving. She couldn't stay here another night.

CHAPTER THIRTEEN

TUESDAY MORNING

'What've you got, Patterson?' Ward asked, ambling over to the young DC's desk with a coffee in hand.

'You didn't make me one?' Jake asked indignantly as he spied the brew.

'Nope.'

'You didn't even ask!'

'Didn't want to. I can go make you one if you like?' His voice was light and inviting, but Ward smiled. *Evilly.* Patterson had pranked him on two occasions now by adding salt to his cups. Ward was waiting for precisely the opportune moment to return the favour.

Patterson's eyes narrowed and he swallowed. 'Uh...no thanks, sir.'

'Thought so. Go on. Cough up. What've you found?'

Patterson cleared his throat. 'I've been through all his phone records. Most of the text numbers are automatic texts from banks, service providers, and the like. I think he used WhatsApp or something for his personal messages, but I can't access those unless we have his phone.'

'It's in evidence. Take what you need from it.'

'Right. Thanks, sir. Erm, oh yes and the phone calls, not much there either. Occasional calls to the wife, his mates, and local takeaways, roughly one a week. A couple hours before his death that night, he did make a phone call to a restaurant and takeaway called Forage—some fancy new thing that uses local, natural ingredients.'

Ward felt a little queasy. *How much can we ever really trust food?* There were constant supermarket recalls of food for contaminants as innocuous and dangerous as bits of plastic, or frankly as terrifying as E.coli. It at least felt better to consume something a local producer had made from good quality local ingredients, compared to a supermarket factory combining goodness knew what from goodness knew where, anyway. Except, now, he wasn't so sure.

'Right. Well, I don't think it's anything to do with them, anyway,' Patterson said. He chewed the end of his biro. The thing was half-shattered and yet the lad still gnawed on it like Olly did with his bones. Ward refrained from mentioning it, even though it grossed him out.

'How so?' he said instead.

'I rang them up. Spoke to the lady that owns it, as it happens.' Patterson leaned across his desk to check a sticky note on the partition between his desk and the next. 'Becky Callahan. She says no one with that name— Paul's, I mean—placed any order for delivery that night.

She did receive an enquiry about delivery to East Morton, but the address was outside her radius, so the chap didn't order as he didn't want to collect it. She didn't get his name, since he didn't place an order, but that sounds like our guy.'

'Hmm. Alright. Wonder why he picked there, but he must have gone somewhere closer.'

'They've been in the press recently and their ads are all over my Facebook account. I reckon they're doing a big marketing push. He probably saw something like that and rang up.'

'Aye, probably.'

'That was the last call on his phone.'

'He went for takeout *somewhere,* though. The cartons weren't marked, were they?'

'No, sir.'

'Any clue as to what's in them?' Perhaps they could narrow it down based on cuisine.

'Uh...Food.'

Ward's glare narrowed.

Patterson covered by hastily clearing his throat. 'I mean, it wasn't curry, or Chinese. Maybe British or Italian. Could be from a number of local restaurants or takeaways.'

Ward chewed on his lip. That meant Paul had turned up somewhere in person to collect food. They couldn't know where Paul Moore had purchased from—not without knowing precisely where he'd travelled that night. Which was impossible, even with technology, short of being psychic.

There were still enough takeaways in the radius of his home, the pub, and the golf club to be possibilities too vast to explore. They didn't have the time to call each and every one to follow what was quite probably a complete dead-end.

'Alright then. New tack. Please, will you get access to his bank? Call his wife and see if she can check the account he would have used. Or confirm if it's cash—in which case, it's a dead end. But if he used his bank, we could narrow down a payment to any local takeaway from there, in case that's the source of the toxin or contaminant that killed him.'

'Aye, sir. On it.'

Ward strode back to his desk, muttering a choice curse to himself. They were getting nowhere with this damn case. It wasn't exactly the best start to his newfound and very tenuous at best parole from the burglary room.

It was time to poke the bears that were Tony Brown and Andrew Collins and hope he could shake loose something more promising.

CHAPTER FOURTEEN

D I Ward made the trip to Keighley again, alone, since DS Nowak was buried in another case and out of the office. It would have been easier to phone him, but you could never see the look on someone's face when you spoke over the phone. You couldn't read their body language, from the open expression that implied a good liar or honesty, to a closed posture that indicated secrets.

Ward had called ahead to check Tony was around. The man strode out to meet him as he pulled into the car park. Ward saw clenched fists and a concerned expression.

'Follow me?' Tony said as Ward stepped out of his car. It was spoken like a question, but Tony had already turned away. 'Got a massive shipment to get out, need all hands on deck. I can't spare any time, sorry. I'll have to graft and talk. What can I do for you?'

'I just have a few follow-up questions to clarify a couple things,' Ward said noncommittally, falling into stride beside Tony. He tried not to appear too interested —the man appeared jumpy, but Ward didn't know why.

Tony glanced up at him, raising an eyebrow, before looking away quickly.

Ward continued, 'I spoke to the chap on the bar on Sunday at the pub and funnily enough, none of you mentioned there'd been an argument.'

'Eh?' said Tony, but he darted down the side of a lorry so that Ward was forced to follow him single file, and grabbed a box.

'Just that, Tony. Why didn't you mention it?'

'I forgot,' came back the instant answer.

'Sure, I can understand that. What did you argue about?'

That stopped him. He turned, the box straining his bulging arms and shoulders. 'What? I didn't argue with anyone.'

Ward waited.

Tony huffed with annoyance and turned away, disappearing around the back of the lorry and returning a moment later without the box. 'Paul and Andrew had a set-to, alright?'

'What about?'

Tony sighed and folded his arms, looking disgruntled as his brows knitted together thunderously. 'Same old shit, to be quite honest with you. Right ruined a good pint, did that. Tossers.' He shuffled uncomfortably. 'Well, I mean I don't want to speak ill of the dead and all.'

Ward didn't respond.

'Andrew was stewing at the pub again over it all.

Ages back, Paul borrowed money off him to fix his car. Only, turns out, Paul never paid him back. He had enough money to go to Spain for a week with the missus, but not pay Andrew back. You know?' Tony raised an expectant eyebrow at Ward.

He continued, 'I've had the same trouble from him in the past. I don't lend anythin' to him anymore. Andrew was pissed off, to say the least. He ain't rich. He needed it back and Paul wouldn't pay. Well, Paul said he *couldn't* pay, but I know Paul. He's as tight-fisted as they come and I reckon he's got summat squirrelled away for a rainy day. He was being a right stubborn sod.'

'What happened?'

Tony shrugged. 'It got heated. Slanging match, you know? Name calling. I stepped between the two of them and got them to pack it in before we all got chucked out, but it didn't get far.'

'Did it get physical?'

'What? Oh, no, nothing like that. They're not that daft. Paul stormed out shortly after and honestly, I left too, because a rock would be better company than Andrew in a mood.'

'I see.' Ward scrawled loose notes in his notepad. 'As far as you know, what happened next? You went...?'

'Home.'

'And Andrew and Paul?'

'Home too, I'd have assumed.'

Ward grimaced.

Tony caught the inference. 'Look, Andrew wouldn't have hurt him. Honest. He's got a mean temper and he can be a bit of a dick, but he's a good lad. I've known him for years. He wouldn't hurt anyone—not over that. He's not in bother, is he?'

Ward didn't answer. He couldn't. Only talking to Andrew Collins might determine that.

CHAPTER FIFTEEN

TUESDAY LATE MORNING

Clang.

C'What are you doing here?' Andrew Collins bent to retrieve his tool from the floor, glaring at Ward, who hovered in the open doorway of his mechanic's garage.

'I've come to ask you a few more questions about Paul Moore's death, if you don't mind.'

'And what if I do?' said Andrew defensively. 'I'm busy. I don't have time to chat.'

'Aye, well, I shan't be long. Or I can wait til you're free?' Ward raised an eyebrow, pausing pointedly.

Andrew ground his teeth together.

'Perfect. What happened on Sunday night, Andrew?'

Andrew didn't answer.

Ward waited, shoving his hands deep in the pockets of his coat as the cold air licked the back of his neck unpleasantly and the scent of diesel clogged his nose.

'We went to golf, then to the pub and home,' Andrew said eventually.

'And what happened at the pub?'

Andrew scowled at Ward. He knew he'd been rumbled. He folded his arms tightly. 'I had an argument with Paul, but I suppose you already know that, since you're here. Doesn't mean nothing.'

'I think you'll understand that we have to treat it as though it does until proven otherwise. What were you fighting about?'

'Paul owed me money.'

Ward waited.

Collins was not forthcoming.

'Come on. You'll have to do better than that. If you want me to stop pestering you, give me a good enough reason, Andrew. I've got better things to do too, if this doesn't matter.'

'Fine,' the man ground out. 'Paul owed me five hundred quid. Lent him it a year ago now, to fix his car, it broke down last winter. I did the labour for free but the parts were five hundred. He didn't have any money. I said I'd lend it to him. He didn't pay it back and I was sick of asking. I got angry. Can you blame me?'

'So you...?'

Andrew scoffed. 'I didn't do nothing. We argued, I shouted, called him a few things, and Tony stepped in the way to cool us both off. Prolly for the best, Paul wasn't going to cough it up, the tight bastard. I'm not the only one he owes.' He scowled.

Ward filed away that information. *Paul Moore borrowed money...from whom?* He asked the question.

'I don't know. I just know what he's like.'

'What happened next?'

'I went home and mouthed off to the girlfriend. She wasn't best pleased either. We wanted that money to go on holiday with. Been a shite year. Paul and Janice got away on an all-inclusive, but could he pay me back? No.' His scowl widened.

'You were angry though. You didn't follow him?'

Andrew laughed darkly. 'I didn't kill him, no, if that's what you're getting at. Why would I want him dead? I aren't gonna get my money back now, am I?' He muttered a curse under his breath that sounded an awful lot like the C-word.

'Do you know how Paul died?'

Andrew's face closed up again. 'Aye. Janice told Tony and Tony told me. Said he'd been poisoned or something?'

'Perhaps. We're still investigating.'

'Well there you go. Nothing to do with me.'

'How so?'

Andrew stared flatly at him. 'Do I look like I know anything about...*that*? If you want something toxic, go talk to Tony. He's got lots of *dirty* little secrets about that sorta thing.'

'What's that supposed to mean?'

Andrew looked triumphantly malevolent as he grinned darkly for a second. 'I aren't dobbing him in it. There's plenty nasty things go through that business and the hazardous waste training and cleaning ain't what it should be, if you catch my drift. Go ask him, that's all I'll say.'

'You're saying there are leaks of toxic waste there? That Paul could have been exposed?'

'Maybe. Maybe not. Wouldn't be the first time.'

Ward pressed his lips together as Andrew failed to elaborate.

'Go talk to Tony about it. And if you speak to Janice, tell her I want my money back.'

'Her husband just died.'

'Aye, and she still owes me.'

What a charming man. But it seemed he'd get little else of value from the clammed up witness. 'I'll be back if I think you're keeping anything else from me,' Ward warned.

Andrew glared at him, arms folded, and refused to say another word.

'For the love of God,' Ward grumbled to himself as he trudged back to the car, stepping in a puddle-filled pothole up to his ankle and earning an entirely drenched foot in the process. 'Can today get any bloody worse?'

He needn't have worried.

It was about to.

CHAPTER SIXTEEN

TUESDAY AFTERNOON

I f Tony Brown was surprised to see DI Daniel Ward again, he didn't show it. Wait. No. He didn't *hide* it.

The boxes in his arms tumbled to the warehouse floor with a crunch and a clatter, goodness knows what inside probably breaking as they smashed onto the concrete.

A cursory Google by DI Ward and a quick call to the office on the way back over had turned up a worrying amount on Tony Brown's firm. There were several articles in a few of the local papers that described several chemical *incidents* at the firm. One had resulted in life-changing injuries for a colleague who had retired with permanent disabilities, on a massive pile of cash he'd sued for and won. On another occasion, the firm had been fined for a hazardous waste spillage that had polluted the street for a week afterwards.

That was just the incidents the press had found. Looking into the records that HMET could access back at the office, it seemed that Tony Brown had a track record for treating toxic substances carelessly. Only last month there had been a leak of arsenic, which hadn't been properly cleaned up and two staff had ended up in hospital poorly from exposure.

'It's not true, you know,' Tony stammered. 'I swear.'

Close by, drivers and warehouse staff paused or slowed, glancing at them with open curiosity.

'What's not true, Tony?' said Ward affably, but his tone hardened. 'Because it's certainly true that you've been wasting my damn time.' Ward didn't mind Tony making a scene. Not at all. That was the man's own business.

'I swear he wasn't poisoned. Not here. Not with anything we have here.'

'Did Paul Moore transport hazardous material in the days and weeks leading up to his death?'

'Well…yes,' said Tony, cringing as he gathered the boxes, dented corners and all. As he turned towards the warehouse, the yard became a flurry of movement as his staff hurried to look busy and pretend they hadn't been staring and trying to eavesdrop.

'And were all of those transportations *safe*? Bearing in mind, I know your firm's track record on hazardous materials.' Ward's addendum was a warning for Tony not to mess him around.

Tony didn't answer and bit his lip.

'Tell me exactly what he transported, how much, and what the risk was,' Ward said, his voice deadly quiet, but Tony heard every word.

Tony nodded. Lots. Like a nodding dog on a dashboard, to the point Ward wanted to tap him on the head to make him stop.

'Now.'

'Right. Yes. Er, come with me.' Tony led Ward into the offices, abandoning the damaged boxes at the side of the warehouse.

Trip hazard, Ward noted, but he wasn't about to pull Tony in on it then. Not when he potentially had a death to explain.

Could that have been the answer DI Ward sought? Had Paul Moore been exposed to toxic waste at work? This was a tragic accident after all—not murder, but gross negligence by his employer, who he should have been able to trust with his safety?

―――――

'Arsenic,' came the answer, as Tony returned to the boardroom that he'd left Ward in whilst he pulled the files needed to identify shipments Paul Moore had come into contact with.

'How much? When?'

'Last week, about seven days ago, give or take. Seven crates. It was safely sealed, so it shouldn't have been an issue.' The confidence in Tony's tone wavered and he dropped his gaze to the table, leaning heavily on the back of the chair.

'And yet, here we are.' Ward would feed the information back to Mark Baker as soon as he could. Mark would know if Paul Moore's death could have been consistent with arsenic poisoning. Ward thought back to the strange rash Baker had noted.

'Look, he had all the right permits, the training... It's dangerous stuff that we move here and we do our best, but accidents happen, you know?'

'That's not good enough,' Ward said softly. 'A man is *dead*, Tony, and it could be your fault. He's not the first either, is he? How about the ones who've been injured, some so severely they can't work for the rest of their *lives*? There are consequences to the corners you cut, Tony.'

Tony flinched.

'I want copies of all this,' Ward gestured to the paperwork. 'Or the originals to take with me. Has anyone else fallen ill with possible exposure?'

Tony was quick to shake his head. All the colour had drained from him as he seemed to shrink into himself, shoulders hunching, tall spine folding.

'I hope that's true. You understand, we'll be getting the relevant authorities involved if we find out there's been any wrongdoing? You might be shut down for good this time.'

'Aye,' Tony whispered, his eyes slipping shut.

Ward stood to leave.

'I'm sorry, alright? We—I'll be more careful.' Tony looked up. His voice had a desperate edge to it. Ward could understand that. Tony had lost his mate regardless —and he'd lose his business and his life if the worst were true.

'Should have thought about that first,' Ward said quietly. Whether or not Tony Brown was responsible for

Paul Moore's death, enough people had already suffered. Tony should have already acted to protect his employees. Instead, he had failed them on multiple occasions. Ignorance was no excuse. DI Ward had no sympathy for the man.

He left.

CHAPTER SEVENTEEN

TUESDAY EVENING

Ward stretched his aching neck as he stepped out into the cool night air, his feet crunching on the gravel of the rural property's rough driveway. The warmth of the car was instantly snatched away, but at least it had stopped raining.

He was almost home, but first, it was time to collect his sidekick, Oliver the Beagle, from doggy daycare down the road. Ward couldn't wait to see his little buddy. With work's topsy-turvy nature, it had been a couple of days and he was grateful that the owner was happy to keep Olly at short notice overnight if needed. It turned out, her brother was a police constable, so she was at least familiar with the odd demands of the job.

Ward missed the mad energy of the pup and wished he had more time with him. He crunched down the gravel drive to the doggy daycare place—a farmhouse in the middle of rolling fields, folded in a nook between the hills.

There, the dogs had a playground filled with all sorts, from ramps to pipes and more, with indoor and outdoor spaces to play and sleep and eat and a few young employees as bouncy as they, to keep them walked and entertained. Heaven, for a dog. Better than being stuck at home, in any case. Ward felt a *lot* less guilty since finding this place for his sidekick to hang out whilst he was at work.

Olly had even managed to worm a way into the main house with Susanna, the cheerful, ruddy Yorkshire woman running the business. She had her own two dogs who seemed to have become Olly's new best friends and three kids who had taken well to the fun little pup. Oliver had it made, alright. Ward was convinced the dog preferred it there to his own home, even after such a short time.

Susanna opened the door at his knock and invited him in.

'Thank you again, Susanna. You're a lifesaver.' he said, stepping inside.

She was. He paid a premium for the overnights, but he was glad to do it knowing Olly was safe, warm, fed, and in good company.

'Aye, well, he's no bother, honestly. Sweet little lad. My nippers'd love for us to keep him, but you keep coming back.' Susanna flashed him a smile and waved him past, shutting the door behind him.

The scent of roasting meat enveloped Ward and his stomach growled loudly. 'Excuse me,' he said, his cheeks warming.

Susanna chuckled. ''Fraid you're too late or I'd offer you a plate of leftovers. My gannets ate the lot and your pup got the scraps. Come look. He's happy as a pig in shit, you know.'

Ward let out a guffaw of mirth as he beheld his pup full, bloated belly up and sprawled out on a large doggy bed before a wood-burning stove. 'Lord Muck!'

'Aye, tell me about it,' Susanna said, laughing. 'Already thinks he owns the place, you know.'

'I'm not surprised; you treat him like a king. He eats better than me! Olly,' Ward called to the dog, who immediately opened one brown eye, regarded him, then shut it again and moved not one inch.

'Oi, you little toerag. Home time. Come on!'

Olly tipped his snout away from Ward and towards the fire.

'Take it as a compliment on your fine hospitality,' he said weakly with a smile towards Susanna, who stood with her arms folded, propping up the door frame.

She grinned at him. 'Olly, come on now, pet.'

The dog was on his feet faster than Ward could blink, stretching out leisurely, before trotting to her side.

Ward shook his head. 'Traitor,' he muttered. 'I've a good mind to take back that bone I got you...'

'You couldn't say no to this face.' Susanna bent low to scratch Olly under the chin. He snuffled into her.

Ward muttered a few choice words under his breath at the cheek of the dog. 'We'll see you tomorrow. Thanks.'

Before Olly could react, Susanna scooped him up and passed him to Ward.

Olly whined and yapped at the deception. An armful of wriggling, irritated Beagle erupted and Ward clamped on, charging towards the door before the dog could escape and run off.

'Cheers!' he called out as Susanna held the door so he could bolt outside and then shut it behind him.

Ward clambered into the car with Oliver still in his arms, before releasing his hold once the door had shut.

The dog knew the game was up. He whined and gave Ward a full 'puppy-dog eyes' gaze.

'Don't give me that look. I feel wounded too, mate! I miss you and can't wait to come pick you up and here I find you, larding out, living the high life with the Wrights. What, are you too good for me now, pup?' he asked Olly seriously.

The dog replied with a sloppy lick to the nose, his tail wagging.

'Hmm. S'a good thing you're cute, you know,' Ward grumbled.

Olly leaped across to the passenger seat and laid down, looking up expectantly at Ward.

'Righto, home we go.'

Ward was glad. It had been another long day and he was starving. No doubt he had some making up to do with Olly too if the Beagle's allegiances had changed so quickly. Maybe he'd found a doggy daycare that was too good, Ward mused as he pulled out onto the main road.

———

Daniel had just turned onto his street when his phone rang, cutting out the radio as the Bluetooth hooked up. He glanced at the screen, expecting to be able to reject the call.

At worst, maybe it would be the DCI, but he wasn't getting Ward back in the office. Not today. Not a bloody chance.

It wasn't the DCI. Or a nuisance call. Or someone he could ignore.

Eve Griffiths flashed across the screen.

CHAPTER EIGHTEEN

'Detective Ward?' Eve's shaking, disembodied voice filled the car.

'Eve. Are you alright?' Ward pulled over, never mind that he was a street away from home. He rested a hand on Olly's neck to keep the pup quiet. He couldn't see her, couldn't hear anything but that edge of something awful in her voice and it made him lean forward in his seat, the belt tugging him back.

'Yes, no. I'm not sure. I—I'm at the gallery. I saw someone skulking about outside and I just...'

'Are you inside?' Something cold flushed through him.

'Yes, I panicked. I'm in the back.' He could hear the rich depth of her voice, on the precipice of tears and tight with panic, and it made something within him clutch tight too. 'I'm sorry, it's probably nothing. I shouldn't have bothered you. Never mind.'

'No! Wait.' The words burst out on instinct. 'Is the door secured—are you safe inside?'

'Yes, it's locked, I have the key.'

That was a relief—of sorts. 'I'll be there in ten minutes.'

'W-what? Are you sure? Is that okay?'

'Yes, I'm sure, it's fine,' Ward said. He spun the car into a three-point-turn to head back out, rumbling stomach forgotten. Conflict gnawed at him as he sped along the pitch-black back road over the hill to Wilsden.

It was none of Ward's business anymore, technically. He'd been pulled from the burglary caseload, after all, to attend Moore's unexplained death and there was the caseload on Varga heating up too... but he had given his card to Eve and he'd told her to call him *anytime* if she needed.

Duty warred with personal interest inside him as he gritted his teeth against the unwelcome thought that he was being unprofessional. That she ought to have rung 999 like everyone else and relied on them to advise her.

He was going because he cared and he damn well knew it. He cared about her and he knew if he didn't go, no one would. 999 wouldn't send anyone. It wasn't an urgent case—there was no threat to property or life. Police didn't get deployed for shadows and fear.

Yet, Ward wouldn't forgive himself if he'd gone home, sat and eaten dinner, and ignored her plight, if then... *What if?* That was an unwelcome torrent of thoughts. What if there was a threat? What if she got hurt? Something unpleasant tightened in his gut.

'It's no trouble, anyway,' he growled to himself. Olly rumbled next to him, but Ward couldn't tell whether the pup agreed or disagreed—or whether he was still disgruntled that he'd been pulled from the lap of luxury at Susanna's.

It was the slowest few minutes he could count, but eventually, he screeched to a halt outside the gallery. It was brightly lit against the darkness, that inner light illuminating the darkened street outside, as though Eve had purposefully put every light on that she could to banish the dark stain of what had happened and all the shadows that threatened. There was the red blink of a freshly installed CCTV camera above the boarded-up entrance.

'Come on, pup.' Ward climbed out of the car and Olly bounded down beside him, nose to the ground, sniffing. He cast an eye around, but the street was deserted. The damned drizzle had started up again and it was getting late. No one was out in the small village without good cause. And that meant no one at all was out, it seemed.

He knocked on the wooden panel, the sound hollow and booming. 'It's DI Ward,' he called, hoping she could hear him.

The door clicked and Eve pulled it wide open for him. 'I saw you on the camera,' she said, pointing up. 'Thank you so much for coming.' Pale and drawn, she looked upset, and yet determined, as though she wouldn't go down without fighting.

She looked down in surprise as Oliver bounded in at his master's heels. 'Oh! Hello.'

Oliver's tail thumped against Ward's leg eagerly as the doggy realised he'd found another soft touch. He looked up at Eve, full puppy-dog eyes engaged and she bent to ruffle his head, cooing over him, her distress soothed for a moment.

'Sorry. I was on my way home with him when you called. I'll make sure he doesn't break anything.' Ward hoped, anyway. He stepped inside. It was much warmer with the broken glass panel of the door sealed. The scent of artist paint laced the air—faintly nostalgic, a reminder of his own mother's painting habit when he was a young boy.

'No, I'm sorry.' Eve reddened. She carefully locked the door behind them and stood, arms folded around herself. 'I feel silly now. But I saw them and I've checked the CCTV. There were definitely people out there.' She cast a scared look outside, her gaze snatching and lingering upon the dark pooling shadows between the sparse streetlights.

Ward glanced outside too. He hadn't seen a sign of anyone. 'May I check the footage?'

'Of course.' She led them into the small storeroom at the back of the shop, where the smell of paints and varnish grew stronger. In there, several unfinished canvases were stretched out, with unframed works lined up neatly and partly framed works in progress.

Ward realised he'd stopped to stare at the place and picked his way around a stack of boxes to a small computer tucked into a corner. It whirred as angrily as DCI Kipling before he'd had any coffee. Grainy footage was already loaded and paused. He kept Olly close to heel and commanded the dog to sit.

Oliver plonked his bum down on Ward's toes. Close enough.

Ward leaned closer, trying to pick anything out of the indistinct black shadows on the screen—before he froze, realising they were almost shoulder to shoulder in the small space.

Not seeming to realise—or mind—Eve skipped to an earlier time and hit play. Those shadows bulged and moved, forming into two people-shaped blobs, who stopped to peer into the window a little too keenly, gloved hands up to the glass. They stopped and stared for a good minute on the timelapse, shifting around to find different vantage points to peer in. One disappeared down the side for a long minute.

And then, both of them legged it.

'I shouted through the window then, told them to clear off. That's why they ran. I could tell they weren't customers. I didn't know what else to do, but I was so scared they'd come back. I wonder if they're the ones who broke in.' Eve shook her head and clamped her jaw shut.

Ward stepped back. 'It may well be, or it could just be some kids with nothing better to do than loiter. It's impossible to say, but you did the right thing. I think you should still call 111 and log it. They'll give you a crime reference number. It's antisocial behaviour, perhaps, but if something happens, you at least have a record. Save this footage too—make sure it doesn't get looped over, alright?'

'Okay. Thank you.' Eve took a deep, shuddering breath.

'Do you want me to take a look around outside?'

'No, it's ok.' Eve was blushing furiously now.

'It's no trouble, honestly.' He sensed she probably wanted the earth to swallow her up right at that moment. He crossed to the door, turning the key in the lock. 'Oliver will stay with you. I'll be a minute.' He glared down at the dog. 'Stay. Behave, mister.'

Oliver's tail thumped the floor as it wagged.

Eve had already bent to fuss him and Olly leaned into her touch with all the cunning of a well-trained pup who knew *precisely* how to enamour a willing tribute.

Butter would melt with that pooch.

Into the cold night, Ward stepped once more. It was silent outside. He used the light on his phone to check the pavement, but couldn't see anything discarded, or any clues as to the identities of the lurkers.

Next, he checked down the side of the small building, a small alleyway as wide as his arm span that was a dead end blocked by a fence. It was cast in total darkness. He held up his torch. A trade bin, its lid closed, stood there. Behind it, nothing. On the ground, nothing, just cobbles littered with what few hardy weeds could survive there.

Ward scanned the deserted street again and headed back inside to find Eve scratching Olly's belly as the dog sprawled out across the floor.

'No sign of them, I'm afraid. I see he's made himself at home.' Ward raised an eyebrow.

'Oh, he's adorable,' Eve said, glancing up at him, a

smile beaming on her face. But then it faded, as she glanced past him, to the boarded-up door.

'Thank you for coming. I'm sorry. I don't know what I thought... I just...' Her voice dropped to a whisper. 'What do I do if they come back?'

Ward's shoulders fell. There wasn't anything he could say or do to make her feel better. He wondered if she knew that—whether she wanted solutions or the semblance of comfort. The nights weren't going to get lighter any time soon. It really was burglary season.

'Keep the CCTV running, keep the door locked when you need to, and remove all valuables. Maybe get a panic alarm, in case?' The solutions sounded lame as he voiced them. They were all rubbish. The truth was, nothing could really keep her safe, but the alternative, to hide away, was no alternative at all.

Eve nodded, her eyes falling to Olly once more. 'Thank you. I really appreciate you coming. I feel like such a fool—wasting police time.' She winced.

'You're not wasting my time.'

'I have to make it up to you. You've gone out of your way and you're not even on duty, are you? I'm sorry. I feel like you'll think I have my own personal detective on speed dial, which is absolutely not okay!'

'No need to apologise, honestly.'

'Look, it's late and you were on your way home—do you have any dinner waiting for you? It's probably ruined by now.'

Ward laughed. 'Hardly. It's just me, myself, and I,

and I didn't plan ahead. It's probably going to be beans on toast, truth be told.'

Eve laughed, a gentle tinkle. 'Luxury gourmet, huh? That still beats my burnt lasagna from last night. I didn't want to waste it, but I forgot it was cooking and by the time I remembered...well. It was an experience alright. I don't fancy it, to be honest. Can I treat you to dinner by way of apology for dragging you over here?'

The fading smile froze on Ward's face.

At his expression, her smile melted away. 'I didn't mean to overstep a boundary.'

He raised a hand. 'No no. I appreciate the offer. I do, truly. That would be nice, but I can't. I'm sorry.' He forced a grin, but her hand pulled away from Olly's belly. The pup whined at her to continue, but she stood, looking entirely mortified.

'Yes, of course. Right. I'll show you out. Thank you and I'm sorry, it won't happen again.'

Ward's heart sunk. The damage was done alright. He'd blown what chance he had, even if it was for the best.

'It's no trouble, I'm glad you're ok,' he said, forcing a lightness to his voice that he didn't truly feel. 'Come on, Olly. Home we go.' The dog trotted to him and he bent to give him a pat. 'Good lad. Right... if you need anything else, please ring, alright?'

She nodded, but he saw the rejection and hurt in her eyes. She wouldn't.

'Call 111 and log it—and save the footage,' he said

and stepped outside. *It's nice to see you*, he wanted to say. 'Goodbye for now,' he said instead.

He left and climbed into the car, sinking into his seat and bowing his head over the steering wheel. 'You're a bloody idiot, Ward!' he snapped at himself. 'You can't win either way, so what does it matter? Damned if you do, damned if you don't.'

It was against regulations to have any kind of liaisons with witnesses, but he knew it happened. It was uncommon, sure, but sometimes, police even ended up marrying members of the public that they'd met whilst working cases. Ward had always been determined never to cross that line. It had been easy when he was married, of course. But the divorce was almost finalised now. Was it that freedom that had changed his tune? His marriage had been going south for a while and he'd never had the inclination.

But then he'd met Eve.

Ward groaned, his hands tightening around the steering wheel and his forehead resting on his knuckles. Olly nudged Ward's hand with his wet nose, worming his way through the cage created by Ward's arms, so he could lick his master's cheek. He whined softly.

Ward straightened and his hand dropped to the back of Olly's neck. He gave the dog a good stroke, rubbing behind Olly's ears the way he liked it. 'Come on. I'm being daft,' he sighed.

Before he could lose himself in a negative spiral of self-critical thoughts, he fired up the engine and sped off in the direction of the farm shop at the top of Brighouse and Denholme Road a stone's throw from home.

Sod the beans on toast.

He wanted something nicer than that to eat, even if it would be a lonelier meal than the one Eve Griffiths had invited him to so seemingly innocently.

When they pulled up at the farm shop, it was almost closing time. He dashed in and headed straight for the chillers, still stocked with a range of locally produced ready meals from a local business. *Forage – food for your heart from your home*, a bright banner proclaimed over the chiller.

Ward chuckled to himself. 'Small world. Eh, that'll do,' he muttered to himself, scanning the shelf. *Let's see for myself what this is like.*

Five minutes later, after begging a bone from the butcher at the back of the shop for Olly, he left with a bag swinging from his hand and some much finer fare than beans on toast to look forward to. A slab pie with caramelised onion and brie mash. Finer fare than he'd had in a long while.

I need to go there more often. It was definitely better food than a processed supermarket spag bol.

Olly went wild when he entered the car, clearly smelling the treat Ward had hidden in the bottom of the bag, loosely wrapped in a plastic food bag.

'Aye, lad, aye, I'm going to win you back onside, eh? No more split loyalties with the Wright's, thank you very much,' he said, shoving Olly away as the dog attempted to scramble into the passenger footwell where he'd placed the bag of food. 'But you're going to have to wait for it, alright? I don't want cow and bone all over my car, thanks.'

———

The food lacked good company, but Ward remained adamant. He told himself he had refused out of professional courtesy—Griffiths was a witness in a crime. It didn't matter if it happened, if police dated civilians. Not him. He wouldn't cross that line. No matter how much he wanted to.

Yes. It was entirely professionalism. And not at all, not one teensy bit, cowardice. Nope.

CHAPTER NINETEEN

WEDNESDAY MORNING

I t had been an endless morning poring over health and safety records and combing through record after record and investigated lead after lead. Tony Brown certainly wasn't as squeaky clean as he'd first presented.

Cash-in-hand jobs, cutting corners... it was the tip of the iceberg. The man ran a profitable freight business and yet, he'd tried to cream even more off the top and several people had been hurt as a result.

Ward had spoken to Mark Baker first of all. Arsenic poisoning. Mark had considered it—it could well be the cause of death. Paul Moore's skin would have been expected to change colour, though he was not too sure about the specific qualities of the rash. It would need further research, he had told Ward. However, it was another line of enquiry to open and a promising one, but only the final toxicology reports would settle the matter once and for all.

'I'm pushing as hard as I can,' Baker had assured him.

Ward didn't doubt it. He'd thanked the pathologist and left him to his long appointment line of silent patients. The HMET department would have to wait and hope that those toxicology reports contained the answer.

Ward didn't know what he hoped—that it would be arsenic, or not. *What a bloody awful way to go.*

He had set in motion an investigation over potential arsenic spillage and poisoning. Knowing that it wasn't the first time something might have gone wrong, that it seemed some incidents had been covered up and that Ward had an unexplained, but possibly related, death on his hands. Ward didn't trust Tony Brown as far as he could throw him.

DI Ward sent in the CSI team immediately to glean what forensic evidence they could—assuming, of course, it hadn't been wiped or lost in the time since the industrial arsenic had passed through the property. They had trooped in, kitted out in so much protective gear that it looked like they were on a mission to Mars. DI Ward couldn't blame them. They were dealing with the nastiest of chemicals.

It had been to no end, however. Victoria Foster had found no sign of any spillage or contamination. Ward wondered whether that was because there had been none, or whether it had simply been covered up well.

They'd found nothing either in the company records —the ones in the books and the scraps of paper hinting at cash-in-hand jobs Tony had taken. However, Ward knew that was just the tip of the iceberg. If Tony Brown had taken a couple cash jobs and cut corners, chances were he'd taken a heck of a lot more than Ward and his team could find evidence of.

Ward considered that they might be looking at fraud and tax evasion charges on top of everything else. As if negligence and manslaughter weren't bad enough to be going on with. His gut instinct wasn't playing ball, but all logic was starting to point to Tony and something going terribly wrong, even if he hadn't intended for Paul to die.

Ward leaned back in his chair with a heavy sigh. Across the desk partition, DS Nowak raised her head to regard him with a cocked eyebrow, a question in her gaze.

Ward nodded. 'I think we've reached the line, Sergeant. I don't know that we've got enough to charge him yet, but we have more than enough to speak to him under caution. We need to bring in Tony Brown.'

'I'll put out a warrant for his arrest now, sir.'

———

'I might have something, sir,' Patterson said, grim-faced, from across the office an hour later.

Ward raised a brow.

'I've sent the screenshots to your inbox. Pulled from Paul Moore's WhatsApp. I've finally managed to get ahold of his wife. She gave me a list of possible PIN combinations, one of them eventually got me in. I thought I'd take a break from the Tony Brown stuff to have a look.'

Ward understood that. The health and safety stuff was *tedious*.

'There's a lot on there—personal messages and everything you'd expect, to be honest, but there's also an unknown number with some pretty nasty messages. There they are.'

Ward pulled them up on his screen and scanned through the thread. 'Do we know who this number belongs to?'

'Not exactly, sir, but I did read back through the whole thread and, piecing it together, it seems like Tony and Andrew weren't the only people that Paul Moore borrowed money from. He was in deep to a loan shark.'

'The type who'd send a message if they didn't get paid?'

'Aye, sir.'

'Though not with some kind of poison, right?'

Patterson scrunched up his nose. 'I don't think that's quite their style. That being said, the messages from Paul mention that Tony is his guarantor...that he'd pay up if Paul failed to make payment.'

'Shite,' Ward muttered. 'Any idea who Paul's in debt to?'

DC Patterson, joker of the department, went deadly serious. For once, that twinkle was entirely gone from his eyes and no smile tweaked his lips. 'I think it's Eddie Tyrell.'

'You're joking.'

'I wish I was, sir.'

Eddie Tyrell was known to them. Much like Varga, he had his own operation, though much smaller. He specialised in illegal cash loans that preyed on vulnerable victims and capitalised through high interest rates, extra payments, and enforcement to exploit any who engaged with him.

'Paul Moore was daft enough to get in with that crowd?' Ward shook his head and blew out a deep breath. How did Eddie Tyrell tie into it all? Moore had allegedly been poisoned. This wasn't the behaviour they'd seen before from Tyrell. Intimidate. Terrorise. Batter. That was more the man's style.

'This changes things. We need to find Tyrell. I don't know what the hell's happening here, but if Tyrell's somehow tied to Paul Moore, I want him found pronto. Get on that, will you, Patterson? And I'll speak to Moore's wife to see what she knows about all this.'

Patterson ducked behind his monitor as Ward pulled up Janice Moore's number and dialled.

It took three attempts before she picked up.

'Hello?' her voice was quiet.

DI Ward introduced himself.

'Oh, I'm sorry. I thought...' Her voice sounded wobbly—but what else did Ward expect? She'd just lost her husband after all. 'What can I do for you?'

'I want to ask if you know about Paul's financial situation. We were made aware that he had some informal loans from his friend, Tony Brown. Were you aware of those?'

She sniffed. 'Yes. I knew Tony had lent us money. He paid Tony back though, didn't he?'

'We're looking into that now. How about Andrew Collins?'

'Yes,' she said, more resigned this time. 'They fell out

over that. Paul was a stubborn old mule and he was making Andrew hang on. We argued over it, to be honest, but the man wouldn't be told.'

'Paul, you mean?'

'Aye.'

'Alright... And how about Eddie Tyrell? Do you recognise that name?'

'No,' she said immediately, but her voice shook again.

'Are you sure? You're not in any trouble right now, Janice. We want to build a picture of what happened to Paul and we need to know what was happening in his life to be able to do that.'

A rush of breath came down the line. 'I don't know his name but... Paul borrowed a huge amount of money from somewhere and they've been threatening us to get it back.' Her voice dropped lower. 'My sister doesn't know the trouble we're in.'

Ward gathered her sister was around to hear that.

'I couldn't believe what he'd done. I was so mad when I found out, but he told me everything would be ok.' Her voice broke as she started sobbing.

Ward let her continue, pressing his ear to the phone to make out the words. He fiddled with a pile of sticky notes on his desk, flicking through the pile, before clicking his ballpoint pen and starting to jot notes as she spoke.

'They came, the other night. Battered at the door. I know it was them. Shouting and screaming what they'd do if we didn't have that money back to them. I didn't know what to do.'

'Did they threaten you?' Ward frowned.

'I hid inside. They didn't see me. Did they kill Paul?' And then she was inconsolable.

Ward wished he had answers, but that was what he had to find. Had Eddie Tyrell killed Paul Moore and was he coming to collect his debt? Was Eddie Tyrell entirely unaware that his debtor had passed away? That wouldn't stop him going after Paul's next of kin to get back what he considered to be his, from what Ward knew of him.

'We'll look into it, Janice. Do you know any names or details for these people that Paul borrowed from?'

'No. Paul dealt with it all.'

Damn. 'If you can tell us anything else that might help, we'll look into this as a matter or urgency.'

But Janice Moore could tell him nothing else. Ward hung up to the sound of her muffled crying, feeling even more wretched at the situation, but at least now they had another solid lead.

Toxic spillage or loan shark? Ward didn't know which way to hedge. He'd not thought that poison was Eddie Tyrell's style, but he wouldn't put anything past the man. He'd have to be creative in his line of business after all.

Ward would have to pay him a visit and find out what Eddie had to say for himself.

CHAPTER TWENTY

WEDNESDAY AFTERNOON

It took a surprisingly short amount of time to track Eddie Tyrell down. Ward didn't give the man advance notice—he wasn't daft. It was a case of old-fashioned sleuthing when it came to catching men like Tyrell unawares.

Ward had tried his last known home address and, lo and behold, the man himself answered. It was a fairly unassuming, decent house in Eccleshill, the sort of normal place that blended in. It'd been extended with a dormer on the top and a small addition to the side and sure, it was private with hedges grown high to block a view from the road and nice cars parked on the drive, but it certainly didn't look like the type of house a minor crime baron owned. Tyrell was careful to at least appear semi-normal. Even though Ward was fairly sure that everyone round there knew what he did for a living.

Tyrell stopped dead at the sight of Ward.

Somehow, criminals instinctively recognised police. And vice versa.

'You police? Not interested. Come back with a warrant.' He made to shut the door and winced.

'No need to worry, Eddie. Just a few questions,' said Ward pleasantly, wedging his boot in the door to keep it open. 'Quicker you speak to me, quicker I disappear.'

Dark dangerous eyes glittered at him. Ward betted Tyrell wanted to make him disappear alright —permanently.

Ward hadn't expected to catch the man in a dressing gown and fluffy slippers—they didn't really enhance the man's brand, that was for sure—but he wasn't about to judge. Though, he wasn't a fan of what the gaping open robe revealed.

A massive belly covered in a tangle of black hair and *budgie smugglers* which left absolutely nothing to the imagination protruded from the wide gap in the fabric. Ward held in a shudder. Hopefully this would be over quickly for the both of them. Good lord, the man needed to put some clothes on.

'Fine. You got five minutes, then you're outta here, pal. I'm not in the mood today.'

Ward had no doubt they were *not* pals. And Ward wasn't in the mood either. Ward squeezed inside, noticing the cosh and baseball bat leaned upright in the corner beside the door, underneath a very fancy looking alarm panel. He could hear vicious barking coming from the back of the house and hoped those dogs' barks sounded worse than their bites. And that Tyrell had them shut away somewhere. Tyrell took no chances on his own security then.

Ward followed him inside into the carpeted hallway, noticing how Tyrell walked gingerly. Frankly, Ward thought, the man looked like he'd shit his pants. He narrowed his eyes.

Tyrell turned a few steps in, forcing Ward to stop dead so he didn't bump into that belly. The door was ajar behind Ward, bleeding heat outside. Ward wasn't inclined to shut it. The overpowering smell of cigarette smoke made him want to cough.

That's as much welcome as I'll get. Alright. I'll take it. He hadn't expected to be let in at all—maybe Tyrell had let down his guard. The man seemed unfit, though he didn't know why.

'What d'yer want?'

'You alright, Eddie?' Ward cocked an eyebrow.

His scowl deepened. 'None of your damn business. What d'yer want?'

'Alright. Keep your knickers on, sunshine.' Ward allowed himself a smirk—but he didn't look down. He didn't want to catch sight of Tyrell's meat and two veg again. Ever. 'Just want to know where you were on Sunday between say five and eight in the evening.'

'Nowt to do with you.' Tyrell folded hairy arms over that stomach and glowered at Ward.

'Paul Moore.'

Nothing. Not even a flicker of recognition. He was good alright.

'One of your debtors.'

Still nothing.

'I suppose you won't have anything to do with the fact that he's lying in the Bradford Royal Infirmary's morgue now, would you?'

Tyrell scowled. He didn't answer for a moment. Ward wondered if he was considering how best to reply. Or maybe he'd had no idea. Anything was possible.

'Nothin' to do with me. I was in hospital. BRI, as it happens.' He stared levelly at Ward.

'What for?'

Tyrell's jaw clenched.

'I don't care whether you'd had liposuction or a hip replacement, Mr Tyrell. I need to know where you were on Sunday between five and eight in the evening.' The only window he really had for a direct hit on Paul Moore, though it lurked in his mind that he'd need to back up the preceding few days too.

Tyrell glared at Ward. 'I was in from Friday morning. Haemorrhoids.'

Ward didn't know whether to laugh or wince at that. His arse felt sore at the mere thought of piles, let alone surgery for it. *Oof.* He kept a carefully neutral expression instead. 'That's minor surgery, isn't it?' DS Metcalfe had been in for the same issue last year, he recalled.

'Yeah, 'cept I had a reaction to the anaesthetic. Had to be kept in all weekend.'

Ward had to admit, he did look a little red and blotchy—that made sense.

'When were you let out?' He could verify for himself, but it always helped to hear it from the horse's mouth.

'Monday morning.'

Damn. 'I'll check that,' he warned.

Tyrell stared at him.

'What about your lads? Any of them getting up to things they shouldn't?' *Definitely. Not that he'll admit that to me.*

'I don't know what you're talking about.'

'Of course not. They've already been knocking round Paul Moore's haven't they, threatening them to get your money back? We know about that.' Ward didn't break Tyrell's stare.

Nothing.

'You may as well leave it alone. The man's dead. You won't get your money back now.'

Something twitched in Tyrell's jaw but he held his tongue.

'Look, you help me and I help you.' Ward folded his arms. 'I can pull you to shreds and investigate you down to the last shit your men took. Or, you tell me what I want to know and I don't have to trouble myself.'

Tyrell's scowl deepened.

If looks could kill.

'Fine,' Tyrell eventually bit out. 'Your body's nothing to do with me. Or my men. I have no interest in clients being unable to complete their side of our contracts. And I won't say anything else on the matter without a lawyer.'

Oh, he was good alright. *Clients. Contracts.* Such pretty words for such a despicable business. But Ward understood—Tyrell danced a fine line to not incriminate himself, despite them both knowing full well precisely what he was up to. He'd just acknowledged Paul was in debt to him, without ever uttering the words.

Maybe one day that investigation would happen. Ward liked to think it definitely would. They certainly had a growing file on Tyrell in HMET. But if Ward could get what he needed now and make Tyrell think he wasn't interested, well, happy days.

'And I don't suppose there's anything else helpful you can tell me?' Ward kept his tone light.

'No.' The Yorkshireman opposite him had turned even more dour. No doubt he was gravely unhappy to discover one of his 'clients' was now dead and that his money would now be a bad debt unlikely to be recovered.

'Right then. Well. If you think of anything else, give me a bell,' said Ward, handing Tyrell his card.

The man made no move to take it.

Ward slid it into the side table next to a key tree. 'I'll just leave that there then. Thanks for your time.'

He turned to leave, Tyrell watching him silently. Ward paused on the threshold, stepping back so a gust of cold wind blew in. He fixed Tyrell in a flat stare. 'I shouldn't need to say, but... Paul Moore is dead. You won't get your money back. Don't go after it.' *Don't go after his family. It won't do you any good. I'll be watching.* Tyrell would hear the unspoken warning.

Without waiting for a reply, Ward left, closing the door behind him.

CHAPTER TWENTY-ONE

THURSDAY AFTERNOON

'Have we picked up Tony Brown yet?' Ward asked as he entered the office for a late shift, having just dropped off Olly at his favourite second home on the way in. For once, he'd gotten home at a reasonable time the night before, had a full night's sleep, and had spent a leisurely morning walking Olly. He felt a good five years younger for it. Just a shame that he still felt around ninety.

Eddie Tyrell had turned into nothing they could follow. They'd verified his hospital stay, plus checked out his most prominent associates. Their phone and vehicle triangulations, plus other enquiries, had not placed them anywhere near East Morton on the night of Paul Moore's murder, or in the couple days preceding it.

Now, Tony Brown was their most promising lead. Ward didn't know quite what to make of that. On the one hand, it had seemed a sure thing that a connection with

Eddie Tyrell would lead to *something*. One didn't simply become involved with that man and escape unscathed.

However, the fact remained that Paul Moore had apparently been poisoned. It wasn't Eddie's style. It was, however, perfectly plausible that he'd been exposed to something either accidentally or deliberately at work— and it looked increasingly likely that was precisely what they were dealing with.

What had Tony Brown done?

'No, sir,' said Patterson, glancing up.

DC Norris stood at Ward's entrance and hurried across. 'A word, sir?'

Ward frowned at Patterson. 'Keep on it, alright? I want him in custody by the end of the day. Can you send out an officer to check his work and home address, please?'

'Already done, sir. He's not at either, isn't picking up his phone and the receptionist said he hasn't turned up at work today, but she doesn't know why. I can personally go if you want, sir?' Patterson sat straighter and edged out of his chair hopefully.

'Not a chance, lad, we need you here. There's still two boxes of records to go through to tag onto the delightful health and safety investigation we seem to have started, besides you have the rest of your caseload to bottom. It's a weekday afternoon. We'll give a squad car a reason to have a leg stretch. Reach out to Tony's brother, will you? He might know something.'

'Aye, sir,' said Patterson glumly.

Ward still hadn't made up his mind after the shotgun

incident with the farmer in Grassington quite how incapable Patterson was, in all honestly. The lad still had some making up to do to live that fiasco down.

'Have you chased Moore's wife for the bank details yet, see if we can trace his last meal?'

'Yes, sir, when I got the information for his WhatsApp passcode. I forgot to mention, with the Eddie Tyrell stuff going on. She's at her sister's in Scarborough now. Staying there whilst everything is sorted, she says.'

'Mm,' Ward said noncommittally. That made sense. Janice had found her husband dead at their marital home —that would leave a lasting impact on anyone. No wonder she'd wanted to leave...but especially so, if Eddie Tyrell's lot were threatening to batter the door down.

'Sorry, what is it, David?' he turned to DC Norris, who had waited patiently off to the side.

'Warrants, sir. I need your authorisation on them all and I need you to chair some meetings—'

Ward groaned internally. He bloody hated meetings.

'—on the tactical strategy for intercepting Marko later.'

Ward's interest wobbled into life. That sounded like a less terrible meeting, at least—he hoped.

'I'll be detailing all our intelligence for the traffic cops and they'll attempt to intercept tonight, since he usually makes a weekly trip this evening over the hills to Manchester.'

'Right.' Ward resigned himself to several lost hours sorting that out, even if it would be useful for Norris to run him, as well as everyone else, through the painstaking amount of detail he'd correlated on the individual they hoped to take down. Ward glanced at the clock. He was on a late shift, so it was already two. 'What time are you on 'til?'

'Five today, sir.'

'I'm on a two-ten. I'll take over point when you finish.'

'Cheers, sir.'

'Let's get this over and done with.' Ward dared not hope that it might succeed – that they might sweep the streets cleaner of one more of Varga's key men that very night.

———

DI Ward emerged from the meeting needing a *lot* more coffee. It was going to be a late night, even later than he had planned. He hadn't chaired the meeting. The DCI outranked him and had taken the prime spot. With Ward's current tenuous status, he hadn't complained.

Nothing was being spared on this intercept, not with such a strategic, high-value target to acquire, one who was responsible in part for millions of pounds of drugs on the streets of West Yorkshire.

There were to be teams from Yorkshire and Manchester's traffic units standing by, ready and waiting on both sides of the Pennines along the M62 corridor. Yorkshire police, taking point, were to wait near the top of the motorway before it crossed the border from Yorkshire into Lancashire. Exits and the risk to others at that time of night were most limited there, with the road network at its quietest. There, a tactical box, or whatever strategy was required, would be performed to stop the car in question as soon as it passed.

More than that, Authorised Firearms Officers were to be deployed, too, since the vehicle and its known occupants had weapons markers. At that, Ward had felt a rush of anticipation, the thrill of an armed job, before realising that most likely, he'd not be permitted to attend, given his recent misdemeanours.

He planned to petition the DCI all the same.

You don't get it if you don't ask, right?

———

'Come on, sir,' Ward pleaded after the meeting as the room emptied around them.

'Absolutely not.' The DCI's voice was hard as steel.

'I know I fucked up, sir.' It was as close to grovelling as Ward was going to get, but he'd do it to have a chance of getting in on this sting. 'It won't happen again. Put me right at the back. Heck, there's no guarantee I'll even be anywhere near where the action happens. You know how fluid these things are.'

'Still no. And watch your language.'

Ward glanced at the clock. They'd be getting ready to deploy soon—the interceptors and the AFOs. It was already pitch black outside, the sky lit orange with the glow of Bradford's streetlights.

Ward opened his mouth but barely got another syllable out before DCI Kipling rounded on him.

'I won't hear another word, DI Ward,' he snapped. A clear warning to Ward to remember his place—his rank, who he was speaking to—and not to push it. Not one inch more. 'Question me again and I will have you suspended.'

With that, Kipling stormed off, shoving through the double doors and onto the stairwell.

Ward leaned heavily against the wall in the empty corridor. He had failed. Annoyance surged through him, but only some of it was directed at the DCI. The rest was at himself. It was entirely his fault, the mess that he'd found himself in. It was of his own making. His own blind stupidity. Impatience. Arrogance, even.

He'd taken those shots at that Range Rover filled with the wild abandon of adrenaline and the laser-focus of revenge and retribution against Bogdan Varga. The decisions he'd made in those split seconds were decisions by a man filled with anger and fear. Not a detective of West Yorkshire Police, who ought to have acted with calm, measured logic, been able to analyse the risks appropriately and know that his wild actions were damned from the start.

DI Daniel Ward knew he didn't deserve to be there that evening to see what happened, let alone take part... but all the same, he wanted to see Marko put away.

However, he didn't even make it back to the office upstairs before a visibly irritated DCI Kipling found him again, charging down the stairs as Ward plodded up, in no hurry to execute the rest of his shift at his desk, knowing where he would rather be.

'It's your lucky day, Ward,' snapped DCI Kipling.

Ward didn't follow. 'Sir?'

'AFOs are vastly understaffed tonight—this bloody vomiting bug again.'

Ward's spirits rose and he clamped down viciously on that tiny spark of optimism that threatened to ignite.

Kipling muttered something harshly to himself under his breath. 'This goes against every ounce of better judgement I have, but you're needed as an AFO tonight. You're the only other body I have who's trained and vaguely spare, who's available to cover.'

'Thank you, s—'

Kipling didn't give him a chance. 'I'm warning you, Ward, you're on a short leash. Screw up tonight and you're done. You're on the back lines. Do I make myself clear?'

'Crystal, sir.'

'Kit up and get to the briefing room for final tacticals.'

'Sir.' Ward sprinted off before Kipling could change his mind. He'd never been more glad to not have to work his current case. Instead, it was downstairs to the weapons lockup to check out his kit and get tacked up.

DC Norris was already waiting down there, hovering in case he was needed. His intelligence gathering had proved critical to organising the operation. 'Sir?'

Ward grinned at him as he filled in Norris on what had happened, unable to keep in the relief and excitement he felt at getting a taste of something so high-octane. This was as close to touching Varga as they had come yet. He wanted to see it happen. Wanted to be part of the action. Wanted to make sure they didn't fail. It wasn't that he didn't trust anyone else to carry out the operation, more that he was so deeply embedded in it, that he needed to see it from end to end for himself, his team, and all the victims of Varga they acted for.

'Go get him, sir.' DC David Norris' voice was filled with quiet determination and hope—not for himself and the countless hours of work they'd spent on it, but for the victims they were already too late for, the ones yet to save, and the human cost of the darkness Varga and his associates spread that they wanted to exterminate once and for all.

CHAPTER TWENTY-TWO

THURSDAY NIGHT

W est Yorkshire Police had driven in convoy well early—though still after dark given the late month of the year—to the top of the westbound M62 between junctions twenty-three and twenty-two. It was the last point of major direct contact with West Yorkshire's towns before the motorway wound up over the hills, crossed Saddleworth Moor, and then descended into the county of Lancashire and onwards to Manchester and beyond.

Up there, the winds blew wild and the bare, desolate moors were scoured by the early winter storms. It was harsh, inhospitable, and unpopulated aside from a few remote farmsteads. The rural, remote nature of the place made it ideal for a stop.

At that time of night, the network was as quiet as it was going to be, the bulk of the traffic overnight freight rather than a blockage of commuters grinding to a standstill. There were few exits and it was a long stretch to the next junction, well past the locally famous house in the middle of the motorway, a farm that nestled on an island-like slit between the two carriageways, accessible by a remote lane and tunnel.

As far as they were concerned, the risk of collateral damage was low and the risk of failure lower still.

So Ward hoped, anyway.

With the weight of the bulky vest confining his movements and his Glock 17 strapped to him, Ward was stuffed in one of the vehicles alongside the rest of the AFOs he'd been placed with. They skulked out of sight up the westbound slip road onto the M62 above junction twenty-three. Waiting.

Ward's whole body seemed fired, on edge, ready to leap at the slightest sign of provocation, as adrenaline ran through him, that ever-present rush of anticipation mixed with fear that assignments like this brought. The unknown—both good and bad. He shifted in the seat again, his fingers laced together, thumb tips tapping together the only outward sign of that pent-up energy.

Sat in the front, DI Ward was lucky to have a better vantage than the rest of them. His eyes scanned the motorway ahead and every car that passed them on the slip road, glancing past the lorries and transport vehicles that passed, but hyper-focusing on every car, dismissing them one by one as he identified the make and model as not the one they were searching for.

The beginnings of a headache already buzzed, his eyes straining in the dark to catch every single vehicle that passed by. The shards of orange illumination from the lights on the slip road and motorway over-taxed his eyes.

Beside him, the driver sat silently, also scanning the carriageway ahead and periodically fiddling with his comms set, his tactical gear, and tapping on the steering wheel. A hum of chatter and then a ripple of laughter filled the vehicle from those in the back. About what, Ward had no idea. He wasn't a part of that bubble.

Ward shifted again, gritting his teeth. The waiting was the worst. The worry that it would all be for nothing. And the worry that it wouldn't. The thrill of the job wasn't always a high. Firearms brought danger and a very real threat—one none of them took lightly.

They were not the only vehicle waiting. It felt like the full force of West Yorkshire Police had been deployed. Further back at junction twenty-four, Ainley Top, and twenty-five, Brighouse and Halifax, and even as far back as Chain Bar at twenty-six, interceptors waited. Ahead over the moors, more units awaited. Beyond the border, Lancashire forces lurked too. The full corridor of the M62 would be covered that night.

They were all waiting for the call.

Everything hung on that moment.

Would the vehicle even pass? Was the intelligence correct? Would tonight be the night it just didn't happen for whatever reason? Would all the careful planning and logistical arrangements be for nothing?

Ward could hardly bear considering the possibility. Not after raising his hopes sky-high. This truly was the largest punt they'd ever had the opportunity to take against Varga and his operation.

Comms flickered into life. The message came through – the one they'd been waiting for.

Deploy.

They were on.

The atmosphere changed at once. Laughter and smiles died and the space seemed to instantly fill with a sharp focus as hands rushed to check kit, check weapons, check their own nerves. Ward felt no different. It was though an internal switch had been flicked.

A rush of pure fear raced through him, one that scoured anything else from his veins before he reined it in and wrangled it into submission, where it seethed inside him, roiling. He let it. It sharpened his nerves. That fear wouldn't stop him acting, but it would keep him alive, alert to any and every threat and nimble enough to avoid harm if he kept a level head.

Beside Ward, the driver's hands tightened on the wheel of the idling vehicle as they waited. The heavy armoured vehicle was no match for the interceptors. The call had come from junction twenty-seven where the vehicle had joined the network at Birstall. Interceptors would be filtering onto the motorway too, one junction at a time. Like chess pieces on a board, each taking their position, carefully, stealthily—until the moment to strike came.

For them, it was time to wait until the convoy caught up with them. Their armoured vehicle would filter in behind the main chase, joining others, before the stop was enacted. That was the theory, anyway. It didn't stop Ward's hands tightening on his thighs as he ran through every possible disastrous scenario that it could end in— and there were many.

Through the rushing in his ears, he could barely hear the driver as he responded to another message on the comms. The engine roared into life, the heavy vehicle seeming too slow as it inched ahead, crawling onto the slipway, but picking up speed. No doubt the driver had his foot to the floor. Ward glanced sideways. The man was as grim as they came, his lips pressed in a thin line as he leaned forward over the steering wheel, as though wishing he could urge it faster.

They pulled onto the carriageway, another armoured vehicle directly behind them, staying in the inside lane.

Ward turned the other way, glancing in the mirror to his side, grateful to have better visibility than the lads in the back—flashing blue lights lit up the sky.

There it was.

The Audi.

Norris' work had paid off. All those painstaking hours to be able to predict *this* place and time. The man didn't drink, but Ward owed him a bloody good reward for it because they'd have had no hope without his work.

The Audi soared past them, as seemingly effortless and honed as a whippet slipping around the tracks. It was gone in a flash. Their vehicle stood no chance. But the boys in blue did.

Pride swelled in Ward's heart as a line of interceptors raced past in the fastest cars the squad had on the books.

Up ahead, more blue lit the sky as those cars lying in wait at traffic points along the carriageway filtered on ahead of the chase.

At least, they were up to speed in the armoured vehicle, though it seemed too damn slow as they passed under the soaring arch of Scammonden Bridge and through the Deanhead Cutting. Then, they were out and the house in the middle of the M62 was a tiny pinprick of lights in the shrouding darkness of the moors.

It was a mess of blue, as half a dozen interceptors stretched back and forth across the carriageway, navigating with expert precision and in synchronicity to keep the car in their midst. Closing like a shark's jaw upon prey. Slowing that car down. Boxing it in to an inexorable stop.

Except that the Audi refused.

As the interceptors closed ranks, out it shoved, veering harshly to the right and sundering through the line of police vehicles, nudging one and sending it spinning into the central reservation.

Ward's vehicle, having caught up to the slowing box, thundered past that stopped vehicle, swerving to avoid debris littering the carriageway. It was a smoking wreck, the front driver's side crushed beyond recognition.

Other emergency services in the area would respond.

Ward's priority—the priority of every police body there—was to stop that car and apprehend the driver.

And so, their armoured vehicle raced onwards too. Ward watching, his knuckles white as he gripped the door handle, the sickening chase ahead, that game of cat and mouse, as interceptors fought valiantly to overtake and contain that tempestuous, volatile Audi as the scent of burning rubber filtered through the air vents.

One interceptor shunted the Audi—a tactical choice and a risky one. It pushed the car's back end out and the R8 screeched, swerving as its driver attempted to correct its course. The vehicle charged towards the hard shoulder and the barrier there, all too fast, for time did not slow as Ward watched, urging it to crash with every fibre of his being, a vicious pleasure manifesting.

But the vehicle corrected at the last possible second.

Off it sped again, crashing past the back end of another interceptor vehicle. Up ahead, the next junction, the last one before the Yorkshire-Lancashire border.

By now, the Audi's front end was ruined and in the flash of a beam of headlights, Ward saw how one of the front tyre arches had crumpled right onto the tyre. The Audi accelerated, but smoke billowed from that tyre as it caught on the bodywork. The Audi's charge stumbled to a pathetic limp.

Police vehicles pounced. Four BMWs converged on the Audi, boxing it completely and forcing it to a stop in a screech of tyres and a clash of bodywork. Still, the Audi would not surrender and the police vehicles braced alongside it as it attempted to shove its way out. More smoke belched forth from the wheelspin of the ruined vehicle. But it went nowhere.

Alongside on the hard shoulder, Ward's armoured truck lurched to a stop and in a second, his seatbelt was off, ready to deploy. He knew it would be carnage. The bastard wasn't going to come easily, he had made that plainly clear.

The moment the door opened, that wall of sound assaulted his ears and the stench of burning rubber was so acrid it made his eyes water. The baying howl of several police dogs joined the cacophony of shouting—and Ward's own pulse hammering through his veins felt loud enough to drown it all out. Ward leapt from the truck, his booted feet tramping on the cold tarmac alongside other AFOs who lined up with him, awaiting a command from their higher-ups.

The interceptors ahead had finally managed to wedge and pin the damaged R8 in so it would not escape. Or, Ward suspected, it had sustained so much damage it simply could not, since he doubted its driver would ever give up the fight given how fiercely he had attempted to evade capture. Police ragged at the doors, trying to pull them open in the confined spaces wedged between various vehicles, but they were locked.

'GET OUT OF THE CAR! OPEN THE DOOR! OPEN THE DOOR NOW! ARMED POLICE, OPEN THE DOOR NOW!'

Challenges shouted across the air, warnings—then glass shattered as the window went, put through by a baton with a few sharp, crunching hits. The first police officer stumbled back a half-second before the gunshot shattered the air.

It wasn't one of their own.

The driver had opened fire.

The officer's quick reactions—presumably seeing the

glint of a cocked gun deep in that car—had possibly saved his life. But he was still down on the ground awkwardly between several of the cars and did not rise. A second later, several officers bodily hauled him away, out of the line of danger, as others sheltered behind their cars.

Firearms brought a new level of danger and those interceptors were unarmed. A baton was no match for a gun. Ward's Glock17 was ready and in hand, the cold metal a reassuring strength against Ward's palm. Alongside him, AFOs readied at the barked command.

He raced to flank the vehicle with the AFO's in his vehicle, their weapons trained on the car, providing cover for another group who sprinted towards the driver's side. They didn't wait. Didn't give him a chance. The bastard, whoever was inside—and Ward prayed it was Havel Marko—had opened fire on West Yorkshire's force.

They were quick, brutal, and effective. Reaching deep into that vehicle and dragging the driver out, scraping him past the jagged glass and through that hole. It was a tangle of dark-clad bodies and Ward could hardly tell which limbs belonged to whom as the driver fought back and multiple AFOs engaged to subdue him.

Ward wanted to dive in. Every muscle itched to take point. But not only was it not his command, he had to behave or he was done for good. Every moment of forced stillness was torture as he watched them wrestle with the driver and then the passenger in the car.

AFOs slammed the driver down on the ground as Ward's team inched closer, spreading out tactically to cover all angles. All weapons were out and trained, but it looked as though, at last, the man was under control.

A gun and a switchblade skittered across the tarmac as the driver was relieved of them and they were kicked away to a safe distance. Arms were wrestled into position and they cuffed the driver behind his back, his face pressed into the tarmac, legs kicking futilely.

Already, officers were in the car. A cry went up and an officer passed out a savage machete that gleamed in the streetlight above them. The dogs were called forward as drugs paraphernalia was passed out next.

An officer popped the boot. Ward craned his neck to see in the torchlight as the officer passed over the contents of the boot—more bags for life, stacked with a shitload of money. Ward bet there were enough fifties in there to buy a street's worth of houses in Bradford.

He was on the way to a pickup.

A police van trundled up behind the wreckage, light inside spilling into the carriageway as the back doors opened, ready to receive their two honoured guests.

The driver turned his head and Ward stilled as his face came into clear view, lit by the back of the van. It was Havel Marko.

Marko watched them all contemptuously from the ground where he lay on the freezing, damp tarmac with his arms twisted and cuffed behind his back. He did not seem cowed in the slightest that they had him like that, nor that a dozen weapons were trained upon him, or that an officer's knee rested upon him to keep him down.

Ward drifted forward, shifting position with the

remaining AFOs as their targets moved. Dragged to their feet by officers, pushed towards the van, and half-lifted inside. The two men didn't come quietly, screeching swearwords in English and goodness knows what in Slovakian as they were shoved into the van.

Ward's pulse still raced—he could feel it inside his neck, so powerful was it. The very sight of that man's face. Knowing who he was. What he meant to Varga. To their investigation.

He was a key connection to *everything*. By all accounts, Marko was Varga's main man in West Yorkshire. He oversaw everything from contract kills to drug shipments, distributions to enforcement.

And they'd got him.

Ward couldn't help but feel a soaring triumph as the back door of that van slammed closed, sealing Havel Marko inside. Sealing his fate. Varga's castle of sand was truly beginning to crumble and Ward wouldn't stop until the tide of justice had washed it all away.

———

It was so late it was early by the time Ward tumbled into bed. Olly had stayed over with Susanna again. His apartment was silent, but his mind was busy.

Ward was exhausted, but although his adrenaline had run out, he still buzzed from the thrill of that mission. The tension and danger kept every nerve singing as it replayed over in his head, moment by moment, a slow-motion blow-by-blow, refusing to let him succumb to sleep.

They'd *got him.*

Although one officer had been shot, it was a relatively superficial wound—an upper arm injury that would heal well given time, according to the paramedics on the scene. That split-second reaction had saved the guy's life, or he'd have been shot in the face at point blank range.

Ward felt pumped full of victory.

I'd love to see the look on Varga's face when he realises we're closing in. Ward wasn't a vindictive man, but he wanted to see Varga's face when they took him down too. However, he knew the noose wasn't tight yet—they still had plenty of work to do.

It looked like they would easily be able to charge Marko from the evidence in the car and Norris' hard work, but Varga wouldn't be that easy. They had to dismantle the stack one card at a time, but it would take more than his crony falling to damn Varga.

With us closing in, he'll be more dangerous than ever.

Perhaps it was that which kept him awake. He had poked a beast and the beast wouldn't sleep until it had ruthlessly annihilated any who threatened him. By continuing to dog Varga's heels, Ward knew he was making himself and his team a target. That was the thought that kept him company in the darkest of nights and turned every small nighttime sound into a looming threat.

Give over, you silly git. Stop scaring yourself. We did

good. We got Marko. And we'll get Varga. Whatever it takes. We're so close...

Ward fell asleep at last to recurring dreams of that operation, and each time, Varga loomed out of the darkness ahead on the tarmac of the M62 with the promise of violence in his black eyes.

CHAPTER TWENTY-THREE

FRIDAY MORNING

When Ward awoke, he was tired and groggy from a lack of good quality sleep. It took a while for him to come around as nightmares overlapped with reality for a long few minutes in the dark of his bedroom, the November sun steadfastly refusing to rise until it was damned good and ready.

He hauled himself out of bed with a groan. Norris would oversee the evidence that day to process, question, and charge Havel Marko, but Ward still wanted in, despite knowing he had to get back to working the Moore case and questioning Tony Brown.

Varga pulled at him more. His long-time nemesis. His long-term evader. They were so close—closer than they had ever been—to reaching him and Ward didn't want to give up that hard-won ground, nor the momentum they seemed to be gathering with the help of *Prap*. Milanova on both sides of the British Channel.

Ward made it into the office, clutching an extra-strong coffee from a drive-through on the way. 'Patterson, where's Brown being held?' he fired at the young lad immediately. Better to deal with that first, then Ward could get right back to the Varga caseload whilst the iron was hopefully hot.

Patterson's owlish blink did not fill Ward with hope. 'Eh, sir?'

'Tony Brown,' Ward muttered as a throb burst through his head, a fresh headache threatening out of sheer exhaustion.

Patterson's face was utterly blank.

Ward turned the full force of his morning pre-coffee ire-filled glare on the young DC.

'Er, right, sir. No, Brown hasn't come in yet.'

Ward frowned. 'What? Why the hell not?'

Patterson explained that they hadn't managed to find him anywhere.

Ward suppressed a curse and dumped his coat on the back of his chair. 'It's been *days*. Plural. That's not good enough.'

'I'm sorry, sir, I don't know what to say.'

'Don't say anything; get your arse out there, Patterson, and find him. Priority numero uno. He's wanted in connection with a suspicious death, possibly murder or manslaughter at this point.'

And if he's disappeared, well, that makes him look even more guilty, Ward didn't add. That ought to have been blindly obvious. 'Turn over every stone he could be hiding under and don't come back without him, you understand?'

Ward watched as Patterson legged it out of the office, the thump of his footsteps quickly muffled to silence as the door swung shut behind him.

Ward stayed stock still, staring at that door, coffee in hand. It was a distraction snagging at his train of thought devoted to Varga. What did it mean if they hadn't found Tony Brown by now? Already, his mind whirred into action, formulating plans. If he'd fled, they'd need to access bank records and telephone records to track him down. It didn't look good for Tony either, if he knew he was wanted in connection with something this serious and he'd bailed.

Where was he? Had he fled? Was he guilty of some wrongdoing? At best, was he responsible for his friend's death? At worst... murder?

DS Nowak waltzed in. 'What's up with Jake?'

Ward filled her in.

'Oh no. Sorry, sir. I didn't keep tabs on it yesterday, I had another case to run. I assumed he'd been brought in and processed already. Apologies. I should have chased.'

Ward grumbled that it was alright. It wasn't her job to babysit Patterson. If anything, it was his—he had been distracted by Varga, as per usual, and another ball had dropped.

Professionalism warred with his personal vested interest. At least with no sign of Tony Brown, they couldn't process him, which meant Ward was free to question Havel Marko. And he rather thought he preferred that by a long mile.

'I'll leave it in your hands,' he said to Nowak. 'Put out more feelers to family and friends—anywhere Patterson hasn't already hit—his brother, partner, friends, work, any known associates we can use to try and track him.'

'Of course, sir. On it.'

Ward hadn't even put his coffee down. He didn't, taking a swig as he raced downstairs to the custody suites. He had a date with Havel Marko that he didn't want to miss.

―――

DI Ward and DC Norris sat knee to knee in the interview room. Before bringing in Marko, Ward wanted to speak to *Prap.* Marika Milanova. Beside him, DC Norris was armed with a stack of paperwork—research, evidence, questions—and he flicked through it, the papers gently rustling.

Milanova picked up the call and her face filled the screen—a videolink to her office in the Organised Crime Bureau department of the Slovakian Police Force head-quarters in Bratislava.

'*Ahoj,* Detective Ward, Detective Norris,' she greeted, a Slovakian twang to her accent. '*Ako sa máš?*' *How are you?*

'Vel'mi *dobre – a ty?*' Very *good – and you?*

'*Dobre.*' She raised an eyebrow expectantly at his emphasis. Ward liked Milanova. She was interested in one thing. Business. She didn't care for pleasantries. He wasted no time.

'We have Havel Marko in custody.' He allowed a smug smile to creep across his face as he mentally relived the moment where the arsehole had been pressed to the cold tarmac and cuffed.

Both brows raised then and she took a second to respond, her eyes glittering with renewed interest. 'How? What happened?' She leaned closer to the camera and tucked a stray strand of dark hair that had escaped from her ponytail behind her ear.

With every word Ward spoke, detailing that thrilling chase and the work to get Marko, her own smug smile grew.

'Excellent,' she said when he'd finished, sitting back in her chair, arms folded across her chest. 'I wish I had been there. What a moment.'

'It was very satisfying.' Ward chuckled.

'When you're done with him, I'll be putting in a request for extradition. He has a list of charges to face here too. I've been after the *prasa* for a year.' Ward assumed that *prasa* was some kind of insult. His basic self-education in Slovak hadn't included much swearing. 'He's been dodging arrest with bribery.' She scowled.

Ward's lips thinned. He didn't envy her that; having to fight the inside and the outside all at once. 'When we're done, he's all yours.' Marko would end up in a British prison but when he was finished, maybe there'd be a term at a Slovakian one too to add on to it.

'This is sort of why I'm calling,' Ward said, shifting in

his chair. 'We wanted to see if there's any intelligence we can pool on Marko—yours might help us, ours might help you.'

Milanova nodded slowly, considering. 'Yeah. That makes sense. What *isn't* he wanted for? There are arrest warrants and charges for him in connection with dozens of offences here. Money laundering. Theft. Bribery. Assault. Drugs. Guns. Whatever you can think of, he has probably done it.'

'He seemed like a real nice guy.' Ward remembered the string of curses—English and Slovakian—that Marko had thrown at them during his arrest.

Milanova pulled a face. 'He's a...' She huffed, entirely mirthlessly. 'I should not swear. This is a work call. But he's an evil *čurák*. He deserves nothing less than the worst of words, he is the worst of humanity, along with the likes of Varga. He's not been seen on our patch for a while. I think he's been over with you for some time.'

'That aligns with what we think,' Norris chipped in. 'Based on the surveillance we've conducted and our investigation, he's been running county lines drugs for a few months here.'

Milanova was already nodding. 'Yes, yes, I have not heard anything of him since before summer in Bratislava. This is unusual. It makes sense if he is in the UK. Other players are in the game here right now for Varga. There was a big bust-up here in...' She paused for a second, thinking. 'May, I believe. Maybe June. Organised crime, turf war, between Varga and another gang coming over the border from Hungary. Marko was heavily involved—

we have him on outstanding charges for seventeen offences just in that week alone.'

'No wonder he left.'

Milanova shook her head, her jaw clenched. 'He must have fake documents to leave the country without us knowing.'

It would be another line of enquiry for them to follow. 'The drugs den he uses here will be dismantled and we have some personal effects in evidence. I'll be sure to send you everything we find.'

'*Vďaka*.' Thanks.

With little else to share, they wrapped up. Ward was itching to interview Marko now.

'I wish I could be there.' Milanova's tone was filled with vicious longing. 'Get him, eh?'

'You bet we will.' Ward grinned at her before he terminated the call.

———

Havel Marko sat before them. He towered to Ward's height, but unlike Ward, he was built like a brick shit-house. No wonder it had taken so many bodies to subdue him.

Beside him, sat a tiny woman—an interpreter—dwarfed by his size. She did a relatively good job of appearing unruffled, but Ward didn't miss the way her eyes kept flicking to Marko and she sat on the furthest point of her chair away from him.

Marko had declined a lawyer, but Ward soon understood why.

'No comment,' he spat in a heavy Slovakian accent to everything Ward asked of him—if Ward even got a reply at all. Mostly, stony-eyed silence was the best he got.

Norris ran through what they had on him—from the night at the warehouse, where the fire had raced through the building in an attempt to destroy the bodies and evidence left behind. How his blood had been present in the getaway vehicle—the Range Rover that had been dumped and unsuccessfully attempted to be set on fire—and his prints all over the steering wheel. An oversight that HMET had seized upon.

Ballistics had made a belter of a discovery too: several of the bodies in that warehouse had been killed by gunshot wounds.... and lo and behold, the bullets matched precisely the model of gun they'd seized from Marko during his arrest.

He had nothing to say to that either, merely flexing his bulging folded arms and clenching his jaw tighter still, his dark eyes promising death and destruction to Ward.

Ward had to admit, much as he felt smug as fuck that they'd got the bastard, he was glad the behemoth was chained to the metal table. And that the table was bolted to the floor. And that the chairs were pinned down too. No wonder Varga had a right-hand man like Marko. He had a half-decent brain and very decent brawn. A solid enforcer and second in command.

With no actionable feedback from Marko over the

warehouse incident, Ward shrugged and raised a brow to Norris. 'Onto the finale, then?'

'Aye, sir.' Norris pulled out the reports from the previous night. He went through everything, from the false plates the Audi carried, to the money they'd found, the weapons, the traces of drugs, the paraphernalia, his associate in the passenger seat... and to it all, Marko said nothing.

'Do you have nothing at all to say?' Ward challenged. 'You won't even stand up like a man and own what you've done?' His lip curled in disgust.

Marko stirred at last. His attention had been on Norris. Now his head turned to Ward. He fixed Ward with a stare and the corner of his lip tweaked up in a cocky smirk. 'Mister Varga sends his regards, Mister Ward.'

Ward narrowed his eyes. 'What's that supposed to mean?'

But the man only smiled darkly at him.

Ward straightened, smoothing his face. 'Fine. Play it however you like. We have the evidence and you'll be going inside for a long time, Mr Marko. We hope you enjoy your time spent at Her Majesty's pleasure. And that's *Detective* Ward to you.' He smiled, but it was empty and Havel Marko's widening smirk attested to the fact his suspect knew it.

Mister Varga sends his regards. What the fuck is that supposed to mean?

He tried to brush it off as Norris wrapped up the interview—reading out charges and confirming with the interpreter that they'd been understood—but the casual targeted threat seeped beneath his skin, leaving Ward unsettled.

Was it the idle threat of someone who had nothing but barbed words as their weapon and no other way out? Or was it a credible threat?

They had Marko banged to rights, surely? With a list of charges as long as Ward's arm—and that was merely the ones from the previous few months, not including the ones Milanova wanted to slap Havel Marko with and anything else they could link to the man—Marko wasn't worming his way out of anything.

Marko would try to weasel out of it, but that was alright. Good luck to him with the evidence they had. Because as Norris threw Ward a satisfied look as Marko was led away in cuffs, they knew they'd got him. And with him, they'd also secured a foothold into Varga's empire.

Yet, in that moment, as they watched Marko walk away flanked by two officers, Ward felt more uneasy than victorious.

CHAPTER TWENTY-FOUR

H e'd been ill for a day or so now, but food poisoning had never felt this bad.

Tony Brown groaned. *So weak.* It hurt so much. It clawed through him, every tear excruciating. He rolled in the bed, but it didn't matter. No matter how he moved or writhed, he couldn't chase away that pain. God, it felt like he was dying. Never mind that Zoe would have called him dramatic—that was how bad it hurt, the very truth of it.

His guts were on *fire* and not like after a curry. This was deep inside him, a burning pain so great it took his very breath away as it radiated out through every bone, muscle, and sinew. He was so weak he couldn't even stumble to the bathroom anymore. The last time he'd had to drag himself there—arms and legs shaking, on all fours —and back again. That had felt like climbing a mountain, never mind getting back into bed.

It definitely wasn't food poisoning. He knew that

now. No food could make him this ill, could it? He hadn't eaten anything out of the ordinary, after all. There must have been something. He'd checked all the records, spoken to everyone—no one had reported any spillages at the firm, either on or off the record.

His thoughts hazed again. What had he just been thinking about?

Tony moaned as the pain seared through him again. It left him quivering, even though each twitch hurt. He'd been laid up for over a day now. He'd ignored the braying at the door—though perhaps that had been in his head—whenever that had been. Zoe had a key and he didn't give a shit about anyone else. He wanted her to come home, look after him, even though he knew that wasn't gonna happen. Not with the barney they'd had before she'd left.

Still, he waited and hoped—not like he was capable of anything else. She didn't return, though. It was dark, then light, then dark again. He'd lost track of it all. And it scared him. He felt weak as a baby and as helpless as one too. The thirst was making him delirious, but he didn't even have the energy to haul himself up to the sink to refill the drained glass beside his bed.

He reached for that glass, hoping to find even a drop in the bottom, but his arm spasmed. His hand collided painfully with it, swiping it off the side table and onto the floor. The fine glass cracked.

Tony groaned and then struggled to draw in a breath as he recovered from even that simple act. He'd been too sick to even speak to Zoe the last time she'd called. He hadn't picked up the phone.

Damn it. She'd probably thought he was ignoring her. She probably hated him even more now. Was she due home today? Or maybe tomorrow? He couldn't work it out anymore. Either way, he was desperate to see her. Desperate for her to look after him, to reassure him that it was going to be alright, because he'd never felt this bad in his life.

Regret curdled in his stomach. Regret for a lot of things. Particularly one.

He'd run from that guilt for a lifetime, making sure it never caught up with him. Sometimes, he could even fool himself into thinking he didn't feel it anymore, shrouded in the trappings of a happy and successful life and pretending not to see it lurking in the corner.

Every breath felt like inhaling slow, viscous treacle. Every movement felt like he was weighed down. Fresh new spasms assailed him, even though he felt like he couldn't control his own limbs, so weak were they, clumsy and beyond his reach.

He couldn't breathe, Tony realised. Not properly.

Panic soared in him.

His heart rate notched up another level, frenzied in his chest, with the fear of it. Fear of whatever this was. Fear of his own mortality.

Darkness frayed the edge of his vision as he tried harder to suck in another breath. Everything blurred. That darkness crept in, inch by inch, across the dim, curtained room, blotting out the pale light filtering in from outside through the crack he'd left.

He just needed to hold on for Zoe to get back, to look

after him and then everything would be alright, he reassured himself foolishly. But he knew something was wrong, that he was in trouble, and that if he closed his eyes he wouldn't wake up again.

Tony Brown's last thought was inescapable... he knew he deserved it.

CHAPTER TWENTY-FIVE

FRIDAY AFTERNOON

Ward's whole body sung with triumph, energising every step as he strode back to the office from the interview room downstairs. They had enough to reach the charging threshold and Marko would be remanded in custody. They had him and he couldn't worm his way out.

However, Ward's satisfaction vanished as soon as he saw DS Nowak dashing towards him, her face blanched white.

'Sir!'

'What is it, Emma?' Something cold curdled the satisfaction in his belly.

'Patterson's called it in. Tony Brown's body's been found.'

Ward stilled. 'Beg pardon?'

'Yes, sir,' she said quietly.

Ward fell into step beside her as she explained. 'Brown's girlfriend arrived home just before Patterson turned up there and they found Tony Brown's body upon entering the property. Up in the bedroom, Patterson said, in er... well, I won't repeat what he said. But, um, in a pile of unpleasant bodily functions, shall we say.'

'How?'

'Patterson isn't sure yet. He said we'd best go take a look.'

'Aye, that'd be best. Didn't you speak to the girlfriend?'

'Zoe? No, I couldn't get ahold of her whilst I was trying to pin down Brown. It makes sense—she would have been travelling home from up North. Patterson says she's been away for a few days on some girl's break or something.'

'How long's he been there?' Ward could have groaned. Of course, they'd sent someone to the house. Perhaps Tony had already been dead for goodness knows how long. No wonder no one had answered the door. His car was probably tucked away in one of those garages. To the casual onlooker, it would appear that no one was home.

It had been a few days since Ward had seen him and his receptionist hadn't seen him either. Being dead would be a *pretty* good explanation for not showing up to work.

Without the correct warrant, one to search Tony Brown's home, they would never have known. It was lucky Brown's girlfriend had turned up to allow Patterson access to the property. Though, less lucky for her.

Now though, they needed to find out what had happened. Why was Tony Brown deceased and how had he died? Was it a coincidence? Ward's thoughts strayed to Paul Moore. He didn't believe in coincidences. Two friends dead in such a short time span? Workplace poisoning seemed all the more likely now. Was this a horrendous accident, or something more sinister?

It certainly seemed something more than an unlucky chance.

Besides which, Ward considered the guilty web Tony was ensnared in. *Could he have taken his own life?* People had suffered horrendously as a direct result of his actions. Tony hadn't seemed the type, but then, people rarely did. People hid their true feelings well, until sometimes, it was too late to help them. *Was Tony trying to make it right, escape his guilt?*

All Ward knew, was that now they had two dead men and even fewer answers. Ward had nothing but possibilities until he saw the crime scene and Tony Brown's body. He grabbed his coat and headed straight out.

CHAPTER TWENTY-SIX

FRIDAY LATE AFTERNOON

W ard arrived at Tony Brown's house in Riddlesden just as an ambulance was leaving, turning onto the narrow lane and trundling down the hill to Airedale Hospital, no doubt. DC Patterson was present, his Fiat Punto parked wonkily on the drive, next to a Mercedes A-Class. Ward swung into the last parking space that the ambulance had presumably just vacated.

Patterson guided a woman back inside. He turned at the noise of Ward's car and paused, relief washing over his face as he realised who it was.

'Sir' Patterson greeted.

Ward introduced himself.

'Zoe. Ms Zoe Coates,' Patterson offered. When the lady didn't stop, drifting into the house through the open door, he said, 'We'll be in in a moment, Zoe. I'll catch my colleague here up, alright?'

Zoe gave him a watery-eyed stare and a nod before she vanished inside.

Patterson waited until she disappeared before letting out a great sigh. 'Right, sir, it's not pretty, so I hope you didn't eat. He's upstairs in bed. Well, kinda. Halfway. Sorta. We're dealing with the usual sort of um, evacuations,' Patterson said delicately. Ward knew what that meant: the bowels had emptied soon after death. Fairly standard. Never pleasant.

'Plus, it seems there's been some accidents as he's tried to use the ensuite loo, as if he couldn't quite get there. I haven't disturbed anything, but it's kinda like what you described at Paul Moore's, sir. He's dead, but I can't see any obvious reason as to why.'

'Does he have any rash that you can see on his skin? Any mottling, discolouration, anything like we saw at Moore's?'

'No, sir, not that I could see.'

'Hmm.' That didn't mean anything without an autopsy, Ward supposed. Tony could have had a slightly different reaction to exposure than Paul had had, assuming the cause of death was the same.

Don't assume anything, he reminded himself. It was a rookie mistake. It still could be a coincidence that two friends had died within a week of one another. Ward still didn't have any evidence of any chemical spillage, accidental or deliberate, at Brown's haulage firm.

'Anything else?' Ward asked.

'Afraid not, sir. I've been taking down all the details, sorting out the ambulance, and making sure Ms Coates is alright. It was quite the shock.'

Ward was impressed at his thoroughness. 'Well done, Patterson. Good thinking on your feet.'

The lad beamed.

'What happened? Run me through it.'

'Well, we arrived at a similar time. I'd been braying on the door for five minutes when she pulled up. I explained briefly why I was here once she'd identified herself and she seemed shocked, like she had no idea what had been going on.

'She mentioned she hadn't heard from Tony for a couple of days. Not unusual in itself, but that he'd ignored her calls now for a good day and she wasn't too happy about it, sir, no indeed. I think she'd been steeling herself to come back from her girl's trip and have a right go at him for it. So she was more than happy to let me inside. I mean, us wanting to speak to him was only fuel on the fire at that point. She was going to give him an earful alright.'

'Lucky Tony.'

Patterson snorted mirthlessly. 'Not so much. It's a bit drastic to get out of an argument by dropping dead.'

'I don't recommend it.' Ward allowed himself a wry smile. 'Since you seem to have a rapport with her, you take point on having a *chat*. Find out whatever you can that might be pertinent. We really are clutching at straws for Moore right now, so if they're connected, hopefully, this will give us the lead we need for Moore and if not, well, we have to get to the bottom of this one too. I'll take a look at the scene and get CSI and the mortuary lined up.'

'Yes, sir. Thank you.' Patterson puffed slightly at the key responsibility he'd been given on a murder scene.

Ward hoped he'd done the right thing. The lad was daft as anything and Ward swore Patterson left his brain at home some days, but he had good instincts and, when he was paying attention, a great eye for detail, especially numbers.

Ward headed straight upstairs as Patterson followed Zoe into the kitchen. The sound of his soothing talking filtered up the stairs to Ward who padded silently up each step. The smell of excrement and death—that weird, unique smell Ward could never quite describe—strengthened as he hit the landing. It was light, the spotlights overhead casting the minimalist white walls into bright surroundings. At the end of the hallway, a door was open ajar—the rest were closed.

On instinct, Ward crossed to it.

He nudged the door wide open. It snagged, brushing on the thick-pile cream carpet of the bedroom inside. The scent of death rolled out. Ward steeled his stomach and breathed through his mouth as he slipped on shoe covers —internally berating himself for not doing so sooner—and stepped in.

Tony Brown lay half in and half out of the bed. His legs hung off the side and his bare torso, rolled onto its side, resting on the pillow. The duvet had snagged around his midriff and his arm wound tightly around his middle, as though he was cradling his stomach. Perhaps he'd been trying to get out of bed but hadn't quite managed it, or perhaps he'd fallen out and couldn't manage to clamber back in.

Dirty washing was strewn around the bedroom, boxers and tops, adding something sweaty and musky into the mix. Ward resisted the urge to throw open the window and let in some of the blessedly cold, fresh, clean air from outside.

Light flickered from behind him. Ward turned, careful not to step away—the fewer steps the better so he disturbed the scene as little as possible for CSI—to see a flat-screen TV hung on the wall was on but muted. A re-run of Never Mind The Buzzcocks had just started. As Ward glanced around, he saw the TV remote on the bedside table. He tipped his head to one side to look at the empty glass on the floor.

Dropped? Knocked off? He couldn't tell.

Ward risked a step closer. Tony's face, turned into the pillow, was only half visible. His eyes were closed, his face slack.

There were no wounds—like Paul Moore, it seemed he had just dropped dead. But the man Ward had seen the other day had seemed fit and healthy, without any pressing issues to his health. *Is it a toxic leak at work?*

Ward couldn't see any other explanation and he couldn't help but link the two men's deaths. They seemed too similar—unexplained deaths, on the face of it, without obvious causes... the sole link being their shared workplace and its patchy-as-hell track record for safety. Perhaps Tony Brown's negligence had claimed him too.

But Tony couldn't have died of exposure... Ward's mind suggested insidiously. *He wasn't there*. Their research in the office had indicated that Tony Brown hadn't been anywhere near the hazardous substances. Besides which, if there had been a leak, wouldn't other staff members have fallen ill? And so far, all staff had reported being fine.

What's not adding up? Ward asked himself, but he couldn't answer.

Ward took another look around the room. Some of the washing had been slung across the back of a dressing table chair—men's clothes, chinos and a shirt, nothing of Zoe's. Smarter than what Tony wore to work —had he been out somewhere? *Maybe they're his golfing clothes.*

He took a quick look in the ensuite—there was piss everywhere, like Tony Brown hadn't been able to get himself to the toilet—and headed back downstairs, glancing in each room he passed on his way. There didn't seem to have been any visitors, or signs of breaking and entering.

He made a few quick phone calls whilst in the downstairs hallway, mindful to be quiet so he didn't add any more distress to the lady, arranging for the house to be scoured by CSI and for the body to be collected and taken to the mortuary for a postmortem.

Ward stuck his head in the kitchen, where Patterson was serving Zoe a cup of tea across the island.

'I just, I wish I'd known!' she sobbed. 'I would have come home sooner if I'd realised he was ill. What if I could have helped him? He didn't pick up my call...' She subsided into a fresh round of tears at the thought, her earlier rage having vanished in the face of her unexpected loss.

'I know, it's so hard, but you mustn't blame yourself, Zoe,' Patterson said soothingly.

She sniffed loudly.

Ward cleared his throat and slipped inside. It was a neat and tidy house on the whole. The most out of place thing was a stack of dirty dishes in the sink and an opened letter tossed on the counter.

'Help me,' mouthed Patterson, his eyes nudging sideways to the crying woman.

Ward suppressed a smile at Patterson's discomfort. It was all part of the job, comforting relatives and witnesses of all dispositions.

'If there's nothing else, we'll be off,' Ward prompted.

Patterson latched on gratefully. 'Yes, sir, I'm all done here. I have everything we need.' He tapped on his pocketbook and picked it up, slipping it inside his jacket pocket.

'Thank you, DC Patterson,' Ward said. 'Ms Coates, our Crime Scene Investigation team will be along very shortly. We ask that you don't disturb, touch, or move anything until they've gone. Transport will also arrive soon for Tony, they'll look after him.' He smiled sympathetically and handed her one of his cards.

'If you think of anything else, please ring us. We're sorry for your loss.' The words rang hollow as they always did.

Ward stifled a yawn as he and Patterson stepped outside. He was cripplingly tired after the sting operation the previous night and the long day. They could do nothing more for Tony Brown, or Paul Moore, today, at least.

He sent Patterson straight home, promising the lad his extra hours back as time off. Goodness knows when, like. But it was better than the alternative—there was no more paid overtime and the lad couldn't work for free.

That was the downside of being the DI. Ward worked it all anyway, regardless of getting paid or not. Above all, the job came first and it got done. He'd haul himself back in tomorrow with another fresh body to investigate.

How had Tony Brown died?

CHAPTER TWENTY-SEVEN

SATURDAY MORNING

Ward woke aching and feeling older than his age. Something deep in his bones that sleep—not that he got enough of it—didn't seem to fix. He downed a porridge pot for breakfast, the watery contents at least warm in his stomach, the cinnamon and honey adding some kind of taste to the otherwise bland food. Then, it was the usual—doggy daycare for Olly and work for him. Never mind that it was a weekend. That meant nothing to front line public services.

———

The heating in the office was now entirely broken, it transpired. He slipped his coat back on five minutes after dropping it in its usual spot on the back of his chair, regretting that for a change as he shivered along with the rest of the team in the frigid office. Somehow, they'd gone from a tropical summer to an arctic blast.

The first email Ward saw in his inbox was a message from the DCI assuring them all the engineers were downstairs fixing it at that very moment, and that no, it wasn't cold enough for them to legally be able to go home.

With his breath practically frosting in front of him, Ward phoned Baker to tell him another body was headed his way.

'Morning Mark, did you get my present?'

'Your present?'

'Another fridge-filler for you? One Mr Tony Brown?'

'Ah, yes.' Mark chuckled. 'You do know how to treat a lad, Daniel. Anything I ought to know about this one before I take a look? I presume that's why you're ringing, anyway.'

Ward winced. 'Sorry. Mind on the job, you know how it is. How are you?'

'I jest, I jest,' Mark said airily. 'Fine, thanks for asking. I know you all work your socks off.'

'Not in this weather,' Ward grumbled.

Mark laughed. 'Quite, quite.'

'Well, Mr Brown was friends with Paul Moore, who came in the other day. Brown is Moore's boss, as it happens and we're currently investigating the firm for leaking toxic substances. They have a pretty terrible track record. Right now, I don't know if it's accidental or deliberate, but I believe they were both exposed to the same substances... it seems the most likely connection anyway, since there's nothing immediately obvious that's caused either or both of their deaths.'

'Hmm. Troubling, indeed,' mused Baker.

'The thing is,' Ward added, unable to not mention it, 'I'm not sure Tony Brown could have been exposed to the same substance. The evidence we have suggests it's unlikely, but they're both dead and pretty inexplicably.' He sighed heavily down the phone.

'I know what you're saying. It seems like it could be, but also doesn't seem plausible.'

'Exactly.'

'And you don't want to shoehorn it into an answer if that's not right.'

'Aye.'

'I know what you mean. You mentioned the arsenic, but the more I think about it, the more I'm uncertain that Paul Moore was exposed to that particular substance. Some of the physiological responses I saw don't seem consistent with that. Be that as it may, that is the more likely explanation.'

'What else could it be?'

'I won't know until the tox reports come back, Daniel. I simply have a hunch that it's something else, but what that other substance could be, I truly won't know until I have those chemical analyses back. Until then, I'm afraid I can't answer you, I'm sorry.'

We're investigating blind without that information.

Ward could hear the edge of frustration to Baker's voice. More than wanting answers for DI Ward, Baker wanted them for himself—Mark Baker was a perfectionist and a seeker of truths—having one evade him was the epitome of a problem.

Mark added, 'Well, leave it with me—or, him, rather.

I'll take a good look and expedite toxicology samples to get to the bottom of this for you.'

'Appreciate it, Mark.' Ward hung up.

'Sir?' Patterson chimed in, popping up behind his desk, a huge black bobble hat bouncing on his head, a matching thick scarf wrapped around his neck.

Ward did a double-take.

'My mum bought it, alright?' Patterson muttered, a slightly sullen scowl flashing across his face.

Ward bet he wore it to work and nowhere else. That Patterson wouldn't be caught dead seeing his mates whilst wearing that.

'Cute,' Ward said, winking.

Patterson glared at him.

In Ward's hand, his phone vibrated into life, ringing again. He glanced down absently and frowned. *Baker's calling back?*

'Hang on,' he told Patterson and took the call.

'Daniel?' asked Mark, with a strange tone in his voice.

'Yes?'

'Hmm, did you know perchance that Tony Brown's brother is also in my fridge this morning?'

'Uh, come again?' Ward managed to say, because he had to have heard Mark wrong. He beckoned Nowak over as she slipped into the office with a stack of papers in her arms. She drifted towards him, eying the phone he held up to his ear.

Mark elaborated, 'A body came down from upstairs on one of the wards. A Mr Lee Brown. The familial resemblance is uncanny or spookily coincidental.'

At this rate, it looked as though they might have another case to dive into before they'd even properly opened the last one. *Drowning under dead bodies. What on Earth?*

'No,' Ward managed to finally say. 'That's Tony Brown's brother, alright. What happened?'

Beside Ward, Patterson waited, shifting his weight from foot to foot, unable to stand still with his impatience.

Mark cleared his throat and there was silence punctuated by the occasional scuff of paper. 'It says on his notes that he arrived last night by ambulance. Collapsed complaining of a headache. Profuse vomiting. He didn't recover and died in hospital. Suspected poisoning, according to the paramedics.'

Ward sank into his chair. *Shit. Shit shit shit.* Three dead. All possible poisonings. 'Anything else?' he managed to croak.

'I think three unexplained dead bodies is quite enough for you this morning, by the sounds of it, Daniel.'

'Right.' Ward exhaled deeply. Thoughts swarmed— pure chaos and no answers, only questions. 'Do your thing, Baker. Let me know what you find.' *We'll be doing the same.* Desperately. Now that they had three bodies. All suspected poisoning. Each presenting slightly different symptoms. Ward was reeling. They *had* to be connected now.

Ward hung up and stared blankly at his computer screen.

'Sir?' Patterson was still there.

Ward blinked, reality coming into focus again. 'Ah, sorry, Patterson. What is it?'

'Um, I think I found Lee Brown, sir,' said Patterson, but the young lad looked sheepish, glancing at Ward's phone.

Ward suspected he'd overheard enough from his half of the conversation to piece it together. He dropped his head into his hand. 'I think Baker might have beaten you to it, son.'

Ward couldn't even figure out where to begin, blind-sided by another death. Now three running parallel, to investigate and somehow connect.

Ward had that nagging sixth sense deep in the pit of his belly. The one that said he'd been barking up the wrong tree. Tony Brown hadn't been there to be exposed to the arsenic. Perhaps Lee Brown had, but the symptoms he'd reported were subtly different to those of Tony and Paul. Ward had been trying to make that fit because it was the most convenient and obvious answer... What if... what if it was something else?

They were all friends... That would be one hell of a coincidence... but what if it wasn't?

'Patterson, I want full background checks on Tony Brown. The works. And make sure you've finished on Paul Moore—did you look into his bank yet?'

'Yes, sir. His wife sent over the most recent few statements from the joint account and I've gained access to his personal account. About to start looking at them now.'

'Good. DS Nowak?'

'Yes, sir?' Emma peered over the separating screen between their desks. He filled her in briefly.

She groaned.

'I want full background checks on Lee Brown. We have to find a link between the three of them, other than their friendship. Until we receive the toxicology reports back, we likely won't know a cause of death for any of them, since they definitely shouldn't have dropped dead and their deaths sound incredibly unpleasant.

'I'm betting they're not natural... but I'm not sure we can put them at the same exposure, since they seem to have had different symptoms leading to their deaths, from the skin discolouration on Paul Moore to the vomiting in Lee Brown, to the lack of either in Tony Brown that we know about.'

Ward had a growing feeling that they hadn't been exposed to the same substance at the same time and the different times of death signalled to his instincts that they'd been exposed at different times. Although, the Brown brothers could have been exposed at a similar time due to the advancement of their symptoms and the closeness of their deaths.

'We might have to look more seriously at murder,' he mused aloud. 'Three friends are dead. Different times. Different places. Very similar MOs.' He shook his head. '*Poison.*'

What did that mean for their investigation? It meant that a murderer might be running rampant in their patch. And if so... why? Who? Was anyone else in danger?

CHAPTER TWENTY-EIGHT

SATURDAY EVENING

They were all due a break. It had been an exhausting month—though that was hardly out of the ordinary—and there was one event in the HMET calendar that the team had been looking forward to for weeks.

DS Scott Metcalfe's (unofficial) fiftieth birthday party.

They'd all been invited to the official one the next day, of course, by Scott's wife Marie, at the Metcalfe's local church hall, but sandwiches and cake wasn't exactly HMET's style. It wasn't Metcalfe's either, truth be told, but Marie ran the couple's lives and social calendars, so what Marie wanted, Marie got. Not that Scott minded, he doted on her in his own gruff way.

HMET had preempted the get together with one of their own at one of the bars in the Sunbridgewells underground development near Centenary Square.

'Happy birthday!' they all roared, raising a pint to

Scott Metcalfe, who grinned as he lifted his own in thanks.

'Happy hundredth birthday, old man,' quipped Ward with a wink, nudging Scott with his elbow.

Scott quaffed a gulp of his beer and rounded on Ward. 'You cheeky bugger!'

'Sorry, is it ninety-ninth? I can't remember how ancient you are these days.'

'You wish you'll look this good at my age.'

'I think I'm doing fine.' Ward eyed Scott's growing beer belly-cum-shelf pointedly.

'More cushion for the pushing,' grumbled Scott.

Ward nearly inhaled his pint as he snorted with laughter. 'Christ, I don't want to imagine that. It'll put me off my beer. Give me nightmares!'

Scott chuckled.

Ward glanced around the table—the whole team was there. Even the DCI had come for one, single drink, though he didn't join in with the team banter and sipped his half-pint looking altogether a million miles away deep in thought.

'Are you alright, sir?' Ward asked. It never hurt to reach out, even if none of them had any kind of friendly relationship with the DCI. He was so far removed from their day-to-day, it felt like a gap too big to bridge.

DCI Kipling looked up. 'Ah, yes thanks, Ward. Just a lot on at the moment.' He looked worn out, truth be told, and the dull lighting threw yawning shadows that didn't help his visage.

Ward knew the feeling. The DCI didn't invite any further conversation, so Ward left it at that.

Beside him, Metcalfe and Shahzad seated on his other side around the long trestle table were laughing at something, whilst opposite, Nowak and Patterson were deep in conversation.

'Penny for your thoughts? What are you two scheming away at?' Ward sipped at his pint, enjoying the hum of noise around them, a positive buzz filled with the start of pre-Christmas cheer that his life seemed otherwise sorely lacking.

Nowak grinned and grimaced. 'You know me, sir. Work. Can't stop thinking about this case—well, *these* cases now, I suppose.'

Ward raised an eyebrow at Patterson. 'And you too?' Truth be told, he hadn't thought the lad so conscientious. It was a pleasant surprise that DC Patterson was finally beginning to knuckle down and pull his weight rather than being the department's clown and loose cannon.

'Yes, sir. We're pooling our knowledge, seeing if there's anything that we can piece together from the research we were doing on the Brown brothers today.'

'Good thinking, but you can leave it until Monday, you know. They're not going anywhere.' It was a one-way trip out of the pathology lab, after all.

'I know, sir,' said Nowak. Ward recognised the wrinkle in her nose, the slight frown of her brows. It was the same niggle he usually had. Like a dog with a bone, the pair of them couldn't drop it until they had answers.

'Alright, I'll bite. Did you find anything useful?'

'Not yet, sir, no. We had other cases to work on today, but on Monday, rest assured, this'll be our focus. We'll get to the bottom of it.'

'Aye, that we will.'

Ward eyed them both. 'So switch off for tonight, alright? Tonight's about Metcalfe and letting our hair down. You both need it too.'

'Yes, sir.' Nowak grinned at him.

'You're not going to let it go are you?' Ward raised an eyebrow.

'No, sir,' they both chorused.

Ward chuckled. 'Well, at least I couldn't ask for better detectives to work with—you included, Patterson. There must be pigs flying outside. Nowak's rubbing off on you.'

Patterson shot him a half-hearted glare. He was used to the ribbing by now—and still living down the shotgun debacle.

'Speech, speech!' Shahzad interrupted them, laughing, from the other side of the table.

'Alright, alright,' grumbled Metcalfe, his cheeks reddening. 'I don't want a fuss, like.'

'Ah,' Shahzad brushed him off. 'Chief, you know we wouldn't survive without you. You're a dad to us all and we appreciate it, whether you're telling us our fly's down or helping us with a case.'

'Hear hear!' said Ward with the rest of them. 'You know it's true, Scott. I wouldn't be half the detective I am now, without you. You taught me everything I knew back then—in the very distant past—' That earned a chuckle,

'—and I hope I can be as good of a role model to this numpty as you were to me.' He gestured to Patterson and winked.

Patterson grinned back.

The DCI delivered a completely dry monologue to ruin the jovial mood and then the chatter started up once more as the DCI departed for an early night and Ward got in another round to liven them all up.

'Will you two pack it in, eh? Don't think I don't know what you're doing?' he warned Nowak and Patterson who huddled together in the corner as he returned with a drinks-laden tray.

Nowak looked up, but the mirth was gone from her eyes. 'Sir, I think Patterson might have found something useful.'

Ward frowned. 'Eh?'

Patterson held up his phone, and a picture of two very familiar men stared back. 'I thought I'd have a quick look, see if any of them had public social media. Well, Lee Brown has an Instagram account. We're looking for something that could link them, right? A few days ago, Tony and Lee went out for dinner together. What if this was the evening they were exposed to whatever it was that killed them?'

Ward examined the picture. The two men leaned close together to get into frame. Both smiled, a ruddiness to their cheeks suggesting they were already deep into a decent evening together. Nothing showed in the background and the post didn't have a location tagged.

The caption read a simple 'dinner with my bro'

which was hardly helpful. Both men were dressed in polos and Tony wore a smart jacket—one that, now that Ward thought about it, he'd remembered seeing strewn on Tony's bedroom floor amongst the dirty washing. Could this image be a lead?

He felt cold all of a sudden, even though the underground pub was warm and edging towards stuffy as the number of bodies in there grew. He looked around at his colleagues sat around the table, chatting merrily, aside from Nowak and Patterson who stared at him with the same serious intensity he knew he reflected onto every case. Part of him wanted to race back to the office and tie it all up too.

'It'll have to wait until Monday,' he said eventually, sighing and leaning back in his chair.

Nowak and Patterson shared a glance and nodded.

'I know. I feel like that too. I want to get it sorted as much as you both do, and we will. Let's wait for answers from Baker's postmortems on Tony and Lee on Monday. We'll pull together all the background information, last known movements, build a picture... Something will come together. I know it. Three deaths now. They have to be connected, by a workplace accident or something else. We will find the link.'

It was a promise to them as much as it was to himself.

'Cheers to that,' said Nowak, lifting her glass.

Patterson took one last look at the happy Brown brothers on his phone before shutting down the app and picking up his own glass to join them.

CHAPTER TWENTY-NINE

MONDAY MORNING

W ard was back at the office raring to go on
Monday morning. He'd spent Sunday morning
nursing a sore head after the night with HMET for DS
Metcalfe's birthday and the afternoon chasing Olly out
on Ogden Moors above Thornton for a much-needed
walk for them both.

It was a chance to clear his head too. The divorce
hadn't been on his mind much lately, caught up with
everything else, but he'd received a letter from the solici-
tors at last that said everything was progressing.

In a few short weeks, he'd be officially divorced and
single again. It was a strange feeling that opened a greater
well of emotion than he wanted to deal with. One step at
a time, trudging over the soft, springy peat moor, he'd
banished the wound of it, with Olly galloping happy
rings around him.

Monday came all too soon for his body. He was tired
from the ever-increasing deficit on his reserves. Mentally

though—and emotionally—he was happy to throw himself back into it, if only to avoid the complex feelings that the solicitor's letter had excavated. Especially, now that they had three unexplained and increasingly suspicious-looking deaths with no concrete leads to show for it.

It was bad news that awaited, however, in the form of the CSI's final reports on the Paul Moore scene and the Brown Haulage examination.

'It's not arsenic, Victoria says,' Ward murmured to Nowak beside him. Patterson stood at his other side, so he heard too and the pair looked up at his words. 'Couldn't find a dang trace there. Let's put aside the fact that Tony Brown wasn't around when the arsenic was being transported—a huge hole if ever there was one—there's simply no trace of any chemical exposure of any kind at that firm.'

'Hmm,' said Nowak, and Ward could hear the scepticism oozing from that one word. 'That doesn't mean it was never there, simply that, if it was, it was well-cleaned.'

'Aye, but there'd be traces, surely. Few people can do such a good enough job that CSI can't find *something* there.' It was the nail in the coffin for Ward. 'I think we have to bin that theory. The workplace is a red herring. Yes, it connects them significantly, but it's not relevant to their deaths.

'From your reports into Moore's personal life, Nowak, and your early work on the Brown brothers, it appears that they were in good standing there. No personal or professional grudges, that sort of thing. No motive from anyone else there. I don't think that's a coincidence. I think we're finding nothing there because there's nothing to be found.' Ward sighed and his fingers tapped on the desk, drumming away for a while.

'What next, sir?' Patterson asked.

'We widen the search,' Ward said. 'I hate to admit it, but maybe we latched onto the toxic spill at work too much. We need to go back and review all the information we have.'

'What's that report?' Nowak asked, tilting her head to glance down at the other report in Ward's inbox.

Ward opened it and quickly scanned through it. He shook his head. 'I'm not sure it's of any significance. Not yet, at least. The contents of Moore's last meal—the one plastered all over the floor—is detailed. Chicken, a mix of vegetables, potatoes, berries, some perhaps wine-based gravy. Pretty fresh, ingested in the few hours before his death as it wasn't heavily digested at the point it was vomited. Victoria's sent a sample off for toxicology reports. It'll be a while before we get them back. Could be something, could be nothing.' Ward felt deflated.

'Jake, add that to your list, would you?' Nowak called over to Jake who was already at his desk and diving into records.

'Hmm?'

'See if you can figure out where Moore's last meal came from.' She smiled down at Ward and shrugged. 'Might as well dot the i's and cross the t's even if it's a dead end.'

'Aye, right you are, Sarge. Have you checked our databases for all three men yet?'

'Not yet, sir. It was on my list of jobs to do this morning.'

'Right. I'll take that then. Basic background check, I know, but it'll free you up to deep-dive into Tony Brown. I'll take Lee Brown and pull the background stuff.'

'Cheers, sir.'

'Teamwork makes the dream work, as they say.' He forced out a grin that was more enthusiastic than he felt. 'Between the three of us, we'll get there.'

He hoped.

'What about Eddie Tyrell, sir?' Patterson asked. 'He has a motive for harming Paul, perhaps murder. He was in debt to Eddie, and his lot don't mess about.'

'I agree. It's just the poison that throws me off that theory, Patterson. These people are the type to break bones, smash stuff up, intimidate, why would they kill someone? They'd never get their money back then.' Like Andrew Collins had said about his money.

Ward sucked the inside of his cheek. They had precious few other options. 'Chase it up anyway. Nowak?'

'I spoke to Tony's girlfriend again. It turns out the two of them had an argument before she left on her trip. He had a voucher for some fancy restaurant and he'd promised to take her, but instead, he decided to take his brother whilst she was away because he couldn't be bothered cooking and they had last-minute availability. She was *livid*.'

'That could be the picture we saw on Lee's Instagram, then,' mused Ward.

'Yes, it probably was. I don't know where—still looking into that. I've searched through Tony's personal effects and the CSI report but there's nothing detailed, nothing in his wallet, that sort of thing.'

'Alright. We can put a pin in that. Might be something in their phone records to clarify where they went. Is this relevant?'

Nowak frowned. 'Well, I'm not sure, but perhaps. Tony complained the next day that he'd got food poisoning after the meal. He messaged, that is, they didn't speak. He said that he'd sacked off going to work and was complaining of tummy pain, muscle pain, and weakness, shaking... he thought he'd had a really funny reaction to the food the previous night but he'd not eaten anything weird. A steak, he'd told her, with some salad garnish thing.

'Zoe didn't reply. She was too mad at him and thought he was rubbing it in that he'd not taken her, so she ignored the message and his phone call. She felt guilty later when she hadn't heard anything else, but when she called back, he didn't pick up, nor the next morning either.'

'Right, okay. So we know they ate together, which is probably the same time the two brothers were exposed to whatever killed them, either before, during, or after this get-together.' Ward's head hurt.

He continued, 'I've followed up with Lee's next of kin—no significant other—and they can't account for any of his last movements. I've requested his phone be down-loaded so we can examine that for anything pertinent, plus CSI has been for a preliminary investigation over the weekend too. They've found vomit consistent with his symptoms on route to hospital in his home and nothing much else there. His personal effects are downstairs in evidence and I'm about to go take a look for any other information I can glean.'

Nowak shifted. 'Did you run the background checks? I haven't seen anything come through.'

'Ah.' Ward winced. 'Sorry. I got bogged down in chasing this and that. Let me look now.' He scooted his wheeled chair closer to his desk and with a few fast taps and clicks, accessed the PNC database. He searched for Tony Brown first, narrowing the results down as there were a few hits until he found one with matching details.

He scanned down the record briefly, until his attention snagged on a criminal record entry at the bottom. It was familiar—chillingly so.

'Is that what I think it is?' Nowak leaned closer over Ward's shoulder.

Ward didn't answer. He had an uncomfortable hunch. Instead, he pulled up Lee Brown's record too and navigated to the criminal record section.

The same detail had been entered there. The same criminal record—one they had seen before.

CHAPTER THIRTY

THURSDAY LUNCHTIME

Nowak shared a glance with Ward and Patterson. 'How is this possible?'

They all stared again at the screen. *Not guilty*, it said, next to a historic charge of rape. Such a serious offence that even despite the not guilty verdict, it had never been expunged from the men's criminal records. In the eyes of the law, it was innocent until proven guilty and the three men had not been able to be proven guilty... so they had walked free, no doubt, however, with the marked shadow of that hanging over them for many years after.

Ward did not need to check the dates—it matched perfectly to the entry on Paul Moore's criminal record. The three had been charged with the rape of Elizabeth Munroe and found not guilty. Ward browsed through his history to find the newspaper articles. Why had their names not been mentioned? Had he forgotten? Surely, with the coincidence of that—or lack of—Ward would have instantly mentally flagged it when Tony and Lee

Brown had become involved in the Paul Moore case, as a matter of curiosity if nothing else.

He managed to find one of the articles and scanned through it. Then he understood. The men had been minors—under the age of eighteen at least—when the offence had been committed and when the case had gone to court. Their identities had been safeguarded because of that—in the eyes of the law, they were children at the time.

Men enough, thought Ward darkly. *Seventeen is old enough to know right from wrong... particularly where that crime is concerned.*

'I don't believe it,' said Nowak. 'What does this mean? Is this connected to our case? Did they do it?' She knew if it were still on their records after all these years what it meant. Some crimes were too serious to wipe after the statutory period had elapsed, even when a not guilty verdict was recorded.

'Their friendship is the common denominator in that case and it seems to be what most closely connects them in ours,' said Ward. 'But beyond that...'

'Could they have enemies from this?' Patterson said.

They stopped to consider.

'It was a *long* time ago,' Ward said, chewing on his lip. 'If anyone wanted revenge, they'd have acted sooner, I'm sure. Besides, their victim is long dead. They have more pressing concerns, at least in Paul Moore's case. I know we haven't had much time yet to delve into the Brown brothers. The loan shark, for example, and his tiff with Andrew Collins—they're more likely to have been a threat to him these days. The three of them have otherwise clear criminal records. From that, we can surmise they *probably* didn't have any other run-ins with the law. Certainly not ones so serious.'

'And we know it's not the workplace,' Nowak chimed in. 'No safety issues or spillages of toxic and hazardous material there that we can see. CSI turned the place upside down and we've been through all their records.'

'Aye,' agreed Ward.

As Patterson and Nowak mused between them, Ward dug into the historic case. More press articles and some court documents that he was able to access.

From what he read, the young woman, Elizabeth Munroe, had accused the three young men of attacking her on her way home from work one night. She alleged that they'd taken turns assaulting and raping her in an alleyway before leaving her there, injured. Ward already had a sickly metallic taste in his mouth at the thought of it —to suffer so horrendously, to feel so powerless, how scared she must have been.

Elizabeth Munroe had sought medical treatment after the attack, the brutality of which had left her with injuries both external and internal. Not to mention the psychological trauma which would have gone entirely untreated in those days, though a small mention was made at the distress suffered at the hospital emergency department, where the young woman was treated without any compassion or warmth, and instead dismissed with callous disregard by both medical staff and the police to whom it was reported.

Ward knew how it was back then. Things had become much better since, but they *still* fell woefully short of what was needed in terms of support for victims of serious sexual assault. No doubt, with such a taboo on the subject of rape and the abhorrent trend of victim-blaming and shunning, placing blame on the victims, not their attackers for provoking what had happened...

Ward was surprised Elizabeth Munroe had managed to get so far towards a court case. The personal emotional cost would have been great, not to mention the sheer diffi-culty of managing such a feat.

Her father had been a headteacher, Ward recalled seeing in one of the press articles. Ward wondered if that was why it had ever got as far as a trial—that Mr Munroe had had enough clout in the local community to try and find some justice for his daughter.

Lizzie had gone to school with all three lads as a child. It was a small enough community that everyone knew everyone back then and Ward's heart filled with deep pity as he read a portion of the transcript that he could access. Elizabeth had had no trouble identifying her attackers even in the dark. She knew their voices. Knew their build. Worst of all, they had identified them-selves inadvertently to her in goading each other on.

Even that wasn't enough to get a conviction—Eliza-beth Munroe had little on her side in the way of evidence. Internal injuries could not prove who had attacked her after all. It had been terribly difficult to bring a case like that to court successfully in those days. Rudimentary DNA evidencing meant they simply didn't have the tools and techniques available as they did presently, to accurately identify a perpetrator. Ward's stomach curdled, his growing appetite was gone and he no longer wanted his lunch.

The case had gone to court, Elizabeth Munroe had suffered the indignity of it and the three men had been found not guilty, mainly down to the witness testimony of one person in particular, who had given the men an alibi that was unable to be proven or disproven, much like the rest of the case.

Somehow, Ward knew whose name he would find before he scanned for it. Andrew Collins. His heart sank anew. What had Andrew Collins done?

Ward had already convinced himself that the lads were guilty. Had Andrew Collins lied in a court of law to protect his friends? To ensure they walked free from something they should have been punished for?

It seemed even more likely in the face of what had happened next. Elizabeth Munroe had taken her life shortly after that trial... Ward knew what that meant. Her name had been dragged through the mud and any reputation she'd had would have been in tatters. She would have been a social pariah. Her word discredited. Her name forever tarnished and stained by what those men had done to her—never mind that she was the victim and they the guilty.

In the eyes of the court, with that not guilty verdict, her entire experience had been deemed invalid. Ward suspected with every instinct that they were, in fact, guilty, and that now he knew Andrew Collins had been involved, possibly to lie on behalf of his friends so that they would be proven not guilty... It made him sick to his core to think about it. Elizabeth Munroe had *died*.

She had died and they had lived. Gone on. Forged lives, families, careers, whilst she faded from time and memory, her spirit gone and the life she had deserved so cruelly snatched from her by the haunting torture of what she had endured. They had reaped all the parts of life that she should have experienced and never had the chance to do.

His heart was heavy as he searched for Elizabeth's family. Her father had passed away a number of years ago and her mother still lived, but when he looked up her details, it seemed the telephone number registered to her was that of a nursing home. She would be old and frail now, Ward reckoned. He wondered if she had ever stopped grieving for the child she had lost and what her daughter had suffered. What she as a parent had been unable to protect her from.

At least, Ward thought, he didn't have that pain. He had no living children—though he and Katherine had tried, but they always ended in miscarriages—and he'd never had to endure raising a child only to lose them. Losing them before you even got to meet them was hard enough, he couldn't even imagine their pain.

One sibling was listed, a Rebecca Munroe. And little other family besides that, without going into Elizabeth's parents' siblings and lineage. He could have followed the trail further, but was there any use in investigating? It had been so very long ago.

The men had been found not guilty and it seemed everyone had moved on with their lives in whatever ways they could. There'd been no connections between the victim's family or her attackers in the years since, that Ward could see on any criminal records—no attempts at revenge. Elizabeth's parents would be long beyond that now.

We've already wasted enough time on dead ends, Ward berated himself. Between the loan shark and the toxic spillages at Brown's haulage firm, both of which he'd been so sure would yield results, they'd reached nowhere at all.

How the hell did these men die, and why? he screamed silently to himself once more. What was he missing? His irritation was budding into anger—at himself for not being able to see the connection, at the world for seemingly withholding the *something* he needed to crack the case.

Unease at discovering the historic connection between the men laced through his unsettled feelings. Not guilty did not mean innocent—why else would Elizabeth Munroe have taken her life? It left such a distaste in him, he didn't want to pursue the case with that feeling so raw. But what did any of that matter in his search for answers about their deaths and justice for them, if it was so needed?

They deserved the same thorough investigation as anyone else, surely, no matter if they had done something so terrible and walked away unpunished for it in the past. That had no bearing on this, he told himself again, but he still wasn't buying it as his moral conscience wrestled with his professional duty.

No matter what these men had done in their past, he had to see their case through to its finish, with nothing spared to find answers, much as he no longer wanted to find justice for them.

CHAPTER THIRTY-ONE

MONDAY AFTERNOON

W ard had wolfed down his lunch regardless of how nauseated he felt after digging through the Munroe court case. Afterwards, the three of them reconvened once more around Ward's desk.

'Right.' Ward sighed. 'Last movements. Let's run through their last movements again, see if we can see any other common denominators off the bat before we delve more extensively into each of the Brown brothers.' That would take significantly more man-hours than he wanted to devote to the case.

'We still don't know if this is accidental or deliberate, so let's keep an open mind. Patterson, what do we know for Moore?'

Patterson cleared his throat. 'Paul golfed with his friends and colleagues. Tony Brown, Lee Brown, and Andrew Collins every week. The day of his death, Sunday, he had a typical day at work with nothing out of the ordinary noted by his colleagues or friends and no unusual duties, aside from the day itself being overtime in the busy run-up to Christmas.

'He seemed fine at golf, where three of them—Lee Brown being unavailable due to work commitments—attended the driving range. They then had a pint at the local pub, where Paul and Andrew argued about money that Paul owed Andrew, before making an onward journey separately to their homes. When home, it appeared that Paul Moore consumed some dinner from an unknown source and died shortly after. He was discovered very soon after death by his wife, Janice Moore, who had been at work.'

'Right. So the food is an obvious question,' said Ward, 'but we need to wait on the tox reports for the precise poison that killed him and to know whether the food was contaminated with that same toxin from the sample that CSI sent off.'

'Yes, sir,' Patterson replied. 'The golf argument led us to a money dispute with Andrew Collins and also to debts owed and threats made from Eddie Tyrell, a loan shark who isn't unknown to us. Andrew Collins doesn't exactly have an alibi—he was at home after golf. As for Tyrell, I wouldn't put it past him, but he's more into broken bones than poison and if he killed Paul Moore, he'd never get his money back. There were significant hints of a contamination incident at Paul's workplace, but we haven't found anything to support that theory.'

Ward turned to Nowak. 'What about Tony Brown?'

Nowak cleared her throat. 'Tony Brown. He was an old school friend of Paul Moore and his employer. Paul worked for Tony as a driver. Tony was found dead on Friday by his girlfriend Ms Zoe Coates at his home when she returned from a long-distance trip. She had been unable to get in contact with him for forty-eight hours and his workplace also reported he'd been absent for the same period.

'According to Ms Coates, Tony had visited a restaurant with his brother Lee on Tuesday evening—she's unsure where, only that Tony had promised to take her there as a surprise and it was the source of a falling out between them. After dining there, Tony reported feeling ill the next day and complained that he had food poisoning to her. She did not hear from him again and he was later found deceased. Baker estimated that he could have been dead for up to a day before he was discovered.'

Ward stirred. 'And last of all, we have Lee Brown, Tony Brown's younger brother. Also worked at Tony's firm. As we know from Zoe, he likely dined out with Tony on Tuesday. He has no significant other, children, et cetera that he lives with to verify his last movements. He called 999 to report severe food poisoning on Thursday night. He was rushed to Bradford Royal Infirmary by ambulance and died shortly after arrival in the early hours of Friday. Paramedics report it was likely he ingested some kind of toxin from the symptoms he exhibited.

'Initially, we pursued the arsenic spillage at the haulage firm—or some other contamination. Given the firm's poor safety record, and that the three men worked together there, it seemed as likely a place as any for them to be exposed to whatever toxic substance killed them. That being said, they were not congregated in the same place to have been in contact with the same contaminant at the same time. Nor are their symptoms entirely identical.'

'Should we pursue the food then?' Nowak asked, frowning.

'I think we have to.' Ward sighed. 'It seems a pointless exercise, but Tony and Paul fell ill a short time after eating together. It's possible, though stretched, given Paul's total lack of connection with that as he was already dead, that this could be a lead.'

Secretly he hoped it would lead them to something more fruitful though the chances of that were also slim. It would have needed to be a fast-acting toxin on all counts, or a very high quantity of one. Besides which, as yet, they had no way to tell where the food had come from without deep-diving into the brothers' financial records to hopefully be able to trace the transaction.

It was an even bigger goose chase than the bloody hazardous waste spills, Ward thought. That the safety record at their workplace hadn't turned up some further incident that involved them all had entirely stumped Ward as that was the theory he'd been banking on.

Good thing I'm not a betting man. I'd have lost that one.

Ward stirred. 'That reminds me, I still have to go through Lee Brown's personal effects in evidence. They'll have been logged by now. Perhaps there'll be something on his phone.' Ward hoped so. They had sod-all else.

Ward's phone buzzed in his pocket. He slipped it out. 'Alright, Mr Baker?' He gripped the table, his knuckles white, as Mark replied, his jovial voice stripped and dark.

'Daniel? I have Paul Moore's toxicology report.'

'What is it?' Ward knew instinctively that Baker had Big News. He slipped the phone onto the desk and switched on the speaker mode. Baker's voice boomed across the office.

'Paul Moore died of poisoning, alright, but it's not something I'd have ever expected to see. He was poisoned with belladonna.'

Silence greeted him.

'Bella-what?' Ward asked, frowning.

'*Atropa belladonna*, more commonly known as belladonna, or deadly nightshade, is a highly poisonous perennial herbaceous plant. It's toxic when ingested and if left untreated, or ingested in large quantities, is fatal.'

'So... Paul Moore ate a *plant*, is that what you're saying?' Ward shared an incredulous look with his two equally baffled colleagues.

'Well, yes and no. Yes, in that it's the toxin in his system. No, in that I can't imagine he plucked it from the earth and started munching away. We're not really in the growing season for it now, aside from growing it inside a greenhouse, perhaps as a garden plant.'

Greenhouse. Ward's first thoughts were of the greenhouse in the corner of Paul and Janice Moore's garden.

Oblivious to the chill slowly spreading through Ward, Baker continued. 'The whole plant is poisonous, but especially the berries and they're dangerous in that they look very innocuous—small, black things like a dark blueberry—and taste very sweet. You wouldn't know until after you'd ingested them that there was a problem, really. A couple is enough to kill a small child.'

'And what about a grown man?' Ward asked.

Baker's breath huffed down the phone in a rush of static as he considered. 'Perhaps half a dozen? A dozen? I can't say I've ever studied it. Either way, even a few would make one seriously ill. I can't imagine anyone ingesting the rest of the plant—it's a dark purple flower, green stem, nothing that one would eat in the normal course of day-to-day nutrition, for certain.'

'I don't understand where he would have come across that—the plant, or the berries,' Nowak said, thinking aloud.

'What about his wife's greenhouse?' Ward said.

'Of course...'

'We need to speak to Janice Moore right away. Is there anything else you can tell us, Mark?'

'That's all I have for now, Daniel. All I can say is that it's definitely not arsenic or another substance that would be found at Moore's workplace, as you'd theorised. It's *Atropa belladonna.*'

Before Baker had even hung up the phone, Ward was swiping for his car keys and slinging on his jacket. Whether Janice Moore was home or not, he was going to look in that greenhouse.

CHAPTER THIRTY-TWO

B elladonna *poisoning.* The more Ward thought about it as he made the trip to East Morton, the more far-fetched it sounded—like the plot of some kind of obscure, Sherlock Holmes-style crime novel, as opposed to the modern-day suburbs of Bradford Metropolitan District.

DI Ward slipped into the deserted garden on the corner plot, his car silent on the now-empty driveway. He knocked on the door and waited. Knocked again—and waited. A third time.

Nothing.

Janice Moore still wasn't home, it seemed. *Well, I didn't come all this way for nothing.* Had she fled to escape Eddie Tyrell's threats, or because she was guilty of Paul's murder? Ward wasn't certain what to think anymore.

He marched across the decking to the greenhouse. Green clogged the windows so much he couldn't see inside—living things curling up the sides of the cobweb-filled and dirt-stained glass, as though each tendril was feeling for a way out. The door was unlocked and creaked as he opened it. Stepping inside, it was so late in the year that it wasn't that much warmer inside.

He peered at the tangle around him, not having a clue what any of it was. The greenhouse was an arm span wide and twice as long, lined with shelves on both sides. Some pots and trays were neatly labelled with herbs and other plants Ward had at least heard of. Others weren't, and their inhabitants were an unruly mess of green leaves. Few things sprouted flowers or fruit and Ward supposed that was down to the time of year and the chill in there. He wouldn't want to grow out here either, he reckoned.

Flicking to the search engine on his phone, Ward pulled up a picture of belladonna flowers and then the berries, comparing it to everything in there. Nothing matched—no flowers, the leaf shape or colour, and certainly no berries.

Ward chewed the inside of his cheek. There had been some house plants inside, he recalled. A massive cheese plant and some other small green things... nothing that had flowered. He would have remembered the dark, bell-shaped blooms with their delicate caps of green, now that he stared at the detailed close-up picture on Google.

There's nothing here.

Ward racked his brains as he raced back to the office. He checked with Patterson en route on whether the bank had turned anything up—had Moore or his wife shopped anywhere unusual before Moore's death, somewhere they could have possibly traced that toxin back to? But Patterson hadn't found anything untoward, and no evidence of the last takeaway Moore had eaten, suggesting he had made a cash purchase.

Patterson had checked with Paul Moore's wife and she'd had no idea where he'd bought the meal. Ward recalled seeing some form of berries in the vomit from Moore's last meal—could those have been belladonna berries? Damn it, nothing added up and nothing seemed to answer any of it—three different men, three different times and places, dropping dead. The only connections they had—work, friendship, golf, and the historic marks on their criminal records—led nowhere for Ward.

The gnaw of anxiety wormed through him. He steeled against it. He *had* to crack this case. With three men now dead, even more so... but for himself too. The DCI would see him finished if he fudged it up.

———

When Ward made it back to the office, he dug straight into the evidence dump on the system for Lee Brown's personal effects. He flicked through carefully taken photographs of each of his personal effects, from the old, battered Tissot watch the man had worn, to the leather wallet that had sculpted itself to the shape of his back pocket, to the collection of notes and receipts inside, each meticulously unfolded, smoothed out, and photographed back and front.

A familiar logo caught his eye—an F with two leaves sprouting from the top bar.

Forage. The very same company that Ward had purchased from indirectly at his local farm shop. He'd right enjoyed that meal—good, hearty food. The place must be good if it was so popular that he couldn't seem to escape it.

Ward squinted. The receipt was dated a couple of days before Tony and Lee Brown had passed away—for drinks only. The day before Tony had reported feeling ill to his girlfriend, Zoe. Ward wondered if they'd split the food. Tony was the boss, after all, and likely more affluent than his brother, perhaps more generous too. Who knew? He never would, without them to speak to.

Ward sighed and shifted, leaning back in his chair. Either way, he'd have to call the restaurant now. Even though the lady on the phone when Patterson had called had confirmed that a man—Paul Moore, they knew—had called, but that she hadn't delivered to him, being outside the area. Now, two dead men had drunk at her restaurant, and Ward presumed, had eaten too, given the anecdotal evidence they had. It was too much to completely ignore, likely as it was that it was yet another dead end.

Of course, the friends would talk and recommend the place between them if they had planned to visit. That much, at least, was plausible. It didn't point any fingers at the culprit responsible for their deaths, though. Ward wondered about the toxicology reports on the Brown brothers... they'd be waiting a while on those too. Baker reckoned by the differing symptoms, that the three men had ingested or been exposed to different poisonous compounds. Had someone targeted them, perhaps whilst they were together at that restaurant? It didn't make any sense. Ward ground his teeth in frustration. A throb pulsed behind his eyes, another pounding headache threatening to erupt.

Nevertheless, Ward looked up a number for the Forage restaurant and called it, hoping that it would be open late afternoon for the early evening trade.

'Forage, how may I help you?' a friendly female voice greeted him.

Ward introduced himself and asked for the proprietor. 'This isn't anything to worry about—a few routine questions to trace the last movements of two men. I believe they visited your premises on Tuesday. A Tony Brown, and a Lee Brown.'

'I see.' Confusion coloured her tone. He thought from the timbre of her voice, that she sounded like a middle-aged woman, but he could tell little more than that. 'I own the restaurant. Let me check our bookings, I can tell you if anyone had a reservation under either of those names and pull up the table bill if they did.'

'What's your name, please? For our records.'

A slight hesitation. 'Becky Callahan.' He recalled the name—DC Patterson had also checked in with the same lady, as it happened, when following up Paul Moore's phone history.

'Thanks.' He waited.

'Yes, I can see we had a reservation made under the name Mr Brown on Tuesday. They had a gift voucher, actually, so their food was deducted from that and extra drinks paid for on top.'

That explained the receipt in Lee Brown's wallet then.

'Have any patrons reported any sickness or issues on or around that date?' Ward kept his tone light, casual. He didn't need to alarm the woman yet.

'No, definitely not. We've never had any issues like that,' she sounded flustered. 'Is there a problem?'

'Not necessarily. We're looking at all possibilities. I had one of your meals myself, it was delicious,' Ward said, attempting to put the woman at ease. He pulled up the website on his computer and browsed the menu. 'You use local ingredients, right?'

'Yes,' the woman latched on quickly and Ward could tell she was passionate about the subject as she gushed. 'It's so important to live sustainably and healthily and that's really our mission here; to provide top quality food. That's my dream—to show folks that local, sustainable, healthy living is possible.

'We grow a lot ourselves and all of our suppliers are within a twenty-mile radius, so that we can ensure welfare and growing standards are high, food is organically reared, and has the lowest possible carbon footprint. Why, I can probably tell you which field your steak was raised in, if you asked.' She chuckled and then coughed. The sound was muffled for a few seconds as she continued. 'Excuse me.'

'Admirable.' Ward smiled. It was, really. In a culture of capitalism, profit before planet and people, it seemed a race to the bottom sometimes—the cheapest prices, the most value, no matter the cost to welfare or climate. It was heartening to hear about a local business taking their responsibility as global citizens seriously. 'You grow yourselves, did you say?'

'Oh, yes. I have enough land to grow all the vegetables and herbs we need, which forms a huge part of our menu.'

'Fruits as well?' Ward's thoughts lingered on those berries in Paul Moore's last meal.

'Some,' she acknowledged. 'Great conditions here for blueberries, raspberries, and blackberries, for example, but I can't grow citrus to save my life this far north, I'm afraid. That's about all we have right now. Oh! And tomatoes, though I don't want to argue if they're a fruit or vegetable.' She laughed again and Ward found himself smiling, warming to her personality.

'And you know the provenance of everything you serve? Nothing that could have been contaminated from other sources? Or inedible plants mixed into the menu?' He kept his tone light.

'Oh no, absolutely not. Like I say, I can tell you which field your steak was raised in. It's the same for the produce we use—all locally grown and sourced. Top-notch professionals. There's no margin for error in the food industry, not where safety is concerned.' She sounded almost offended at the suggestion and Ward wondered if her tone was intentionally polite to rein in her indignation at that insinuation.

'Alright, thank you. You don't happen to recall

anything about those two guests I mentioned? Anything off in their behaviour? Did they meet anyone, or did anyone approach them, for example?' He described them briefly for her benefit.

'Ah no, I'm afraid not. I'll have been in the back cooking. We're busy on Tuesdays and Wednesdays, as we run our early-bird deals those evenings to drum up mid-week trade and looking at the bookings, we'll have had a high table turnover. My staff would have mentioned anything untoward to me about any of our patrons.'

'Right. Please, will you send me details of whichever staff members would have served them that evening? I'll still need to check.'

'Of course.'

Ward gave his email address and phone number and she promised to send them the next day when she'd had a chance to double-check the rota.

'That's all I need for now. Thanks for your time.'

'Feel free to stop by for a meal,' she said suggestively and he could hear the warm smile in her voice.

He might just, he considered as he hung up. His attention free, he scrolled down the menu. Each dish sounded more delicious than the last, from a beef Wellington with some creative stuffing, to a chicken with...

Something in Ward stilled. He read the menu, but he might as well have been reading the report from Paul Moore's autopsy and the crime scene reports. The contents of his stomach, which had been shared so generously with the kitchen floor. An oven-cooked organic chicken breast with garlic served with wild berries and a red wine *jus*—which Ward assumed was a posh word for 'gravy'—and some rosemary roasted potatoes...

...how did they match up so perfectly?

But then, Patterson had, of course, taken the take-away's word at face value when he had initially spoken to them following Paul Moore's death. The lady had told Patterson that they hadn't delivered to Moore's area and so an order hadn't been taken.

But what if the woman had been *lying*? They hadn't considered that. Not at that point, when she'd been an innocent source of potentially useful information—a lead that had gone nowhere.

Then, Tony and Lee Brown had each complained of food poisoning after dining there... and then died. Ward had no answers but more questions still and nothing to link them together. Nothing but this.

Ward immediately dialled the restaurant back. The honed instinct within him blared that this was *something*, something he ought not ignore.

No one picked up.

He tried again.

No answer.

CHAPTER THIRTY-THREE

'Shit shit *shit!*' Ward cursed under his breath as he scrambled on his keyboard for answers, wondering if his wild theory was right.

'Alright, sir?' Nowak popped her head up over the divider between their desks.

'No.' He briefly explained. 'I'm pulling her up on the PNC now, see what I can find. Get her on social media, will you? I need to find out if there's any connection between her and our three victims.'

However, by the time he had finished speaking, he had already found it. He dug deeper to check—date of birth, hunting out the relevant birth certificate to check parentage.

'I've got her on Facebook if you want to see, sir. Private profile though, but it has a profile picture...' Nowak trailed off at the strange look on Ward's face. 'Sir? What is it?'

'No need. The lady who owns Forage...is Becky Callahan. No connection on the face of it and yet *everything* to do with it all. Her maiden name is Munroe. Given name Rebecca Sarah Munroe.'

Understanding flashed across Nowak's face. 'Elizabeth Munroe's sister.'

'Aye.'

'Do you think...?'

'I think I do.' Ward shook his head. 'It still doesn't make sense—it's been so long—but it all checks out. Paul Moore rang them—it's only her word that says he didn't order—but the contents of his stomach match almost exactly to one of the items on her menu.

'I bet if we checked triangulation on her phone and her employees, one of them would have made a delivery in the area of Moore's home that night. We already know the Brown brothers ate there and she herself confirmed that, soon after which, they both fell ill and died.'

'And now she's not picking up the phone,' Nowak added quietly. She had already risen, her deft hands winding a scarf around her neck, before she reached for her coat.

'We need to find her. Now. Patterson?' he called across the room.

Patterson shot up like a meerkat. 'Yes, sir?'

Ward filled him in quickly. 'I need you to find Rebecca Callahan. Trace her phone, her car, whatever you can. We'll head to the restaurant and her home address to see if she's there. We have to speak to her urgently in connection with all this.' She was the missing link. Ward felt it in his bones.

And with that, Nowak followed him outside into the early dark of the November evening to find their possible murderer with nothing more than hunches and instinct to go on.

CHAPTER THIRTY-FOUR

MONDAY EVENING

Andrew Collins was a strapping man who could take care of himself in a fight. But as the cold wind blew in the open garage door, causing the shutters to rattle, he jumped all the same. He couldn't fight shadows and threats with muscles, after all, could he?

A hail of rain peppered the roof like bullets, sending his insides somersaulting. He cursed himself under his breath. 'Don't be such a bloody drip, man.' He steeled himself against the creak of the open door to the small cubby he used as his office at the back of the garage. Forcing himself not to turn and look.

'There's nothing there,' he muttered to himself. Fear wasn't an emotion he was comfortable feeling. 'Don't be daft!'

And yet, it was hard not to jump at every shadow. Three of his friends were dead now, in freak poisonings... freak poisonings that weren't anything to do with Tony's sloppy safety record at work, it seemed, because on the grapevine he'd already heard that the police had turned the whole place over and found the square root of knack all.

If it wasn't to do with that, well... That deep fear that had lain dormant inside for so many years reared, uncurling until it was so large it overshadowed his waking thoughts and his nightmares. He couldn't help but think it was a hitlist... and be paranoid that it was to do with the rape case.

They *had* done it, after all.

His friends hadn't admitted it at the time, but he knew now that they were guilty. They had fobbed him off, told him that they needed him to vouch for them or they'd be sent down and that they didn't deserve any of it. He'd been a good mate—the best. He hadn't questioned it. That was what friends did, right? Backed each other up. Especially when they claimed to be innocent.

He'd known, even then, that something was off. He hadn't known what. He wondered if maybe they'd groped her, or if it was a bit of fun gone wrong—he'd not known and they'd refused to say, claiming that it was all a huge misunderstanding. He'd known in his gut that it wasn't quite right and he'd been a damn coward in facing up to that.

Andrew Collins continued working away under the bonnet of the car, each turn of the wrench angrier and more forceful and fear-filled than the last.

It had been Lee Brown who let it slip years later that they had all been guilty. That had floored Andrew. Even though they'd cleaned up their acts, fearful enough of the law catching them again to try anything, and not put a foot out of line since, he felt like a bloody idiot for not realising. He'd decked Tony for that. Tony, the ring-leader. Tony who had always got them into trouble as lads—and then managed, always, somehow, to talk them out of it.

Andrew Collins felt as guilty and besmirched as the three of them. He had provided the alibi that had cemented their not guilty verdict after all. That they'd all been together on the opposite side of town at a pub where others could vouch for seeing him, and they had techni-cally joined him later on. After they'd raped the lass. It was enough of a link that it had exonerated the lads at the time.

He had got them off the hook—and the bastards had been guilty, every one of them. It didn't matter to him at all that they'd got on the straight and narrow. They had done it. Raped a lass only just older than his own daughter now. Worse still, they'd used him to get away with it. He was still angry about that, he realised, as he clenched his jaw. He didn't think he'd ever forgiven them for that.

They were all blokes, but they didn't ever really talk about it. Not really. They'd papered over it in all the years since. Tony had always been extra generous with Andrew when it came to pints, or pay-day loans, or this favour or that. Andrew knew it was because he'd bailed them out. That Tony owed him. And Andrew Collins had never called in that debt, not really.

Could he ever? It wasn't as though any of them could

undo what they'd done to that girl. He certainly felt like he could never undo his part in it. He carried the guilt of it even now. He'd tamped it down over the years but out it surged, heavy as the day he'd realised the truth. It felt as though a weighty presence bowed his shoulders. Something watchful and waiting that trailed a cold idle finger down his spine, setting his nerves on edge. Death was coming for him too. He could feel it.

He jumped as his phone rang. The sound blared across the radio that he had turned down for fear that someone would sneak up on him working. His heart hammered and he forced himself to calm. 'Good god, you're a bloody coward,' he growled to himself. Who was he scared of?

He didn't know who was responsible for his friends' deaths and that was the unknown that terrified him. How was he supposed to look over his shoulder, not knowing who he was looking for? How was he *not* supposed to look over his shoulder, knowing what they had all done— and what he suspected they had died for?

He wiped the oil off his fingers, smearing another level of black onto his overalls and fished his phone from his pocket.

Charlotte. His daughter. Andrew and her mum had split years ago. He'd had knack-all custody, but in her teenage years, Charlotte had started to visit him more— mainly when she clashed with her mum. Teenagers. He mentally rolled his eyes.

What did she want now? Probably another tenner. God knows what she'd done with the one he'd given her yesterday. She burned through his money faster than a tank of petrol, which was saying something these days.

'*Dad.*' Her voice was a pleading whine. Not the sassy, attitude-laden caw he was used to.

The tone set him on edge even more. 'Charlotte?'

And then, 'Dad, help me, *please.*'

His whole body tightened. Fear lashed within him. 'Honey, what's up? Where are you? What's wrong?' His grip tightened around that wrench as though he could protect her. In reality, he was miles away from wherever she was.

'Home,' his daughter choked out. 'She says she's going to kill me if you don't come, Dad.'

Scuffling sounds came down the line before he could reply, like the phone had been taken away.

'*Dad!*' Charlotte's scream came from a distance, and then the line went dead.

CHAPTER THIRTY-FIVE

Panic exploded in Andrew Collins.

Andrew abandoned the car he was working on, leaving it unlocked, bonnet up. He didn't care—not one shit did he have to spare as pure terror raced through him. The sound of Charlotte's voice repeated on a loop in his mind. *Dad! Help. Please. Dad!*

He raced for his van keys, hanging on the hook in the office and sprinted out. He'd never been so lax, but it would take too long to shut the roller door, so he left it open to the elements, the radio still buzzing away on low volume in the background. Lights on. The full takings of the garage up for easy pickings. For once, he didn't care.

Who knew how much time he had? He was so far away. His mind raced, calculating. How many minutes would it take him to get home? Ten? Twenty? *Too many*, came the agonising answer. *More than you have.*

He couldn't bear to think about it. What might happen to Charlotte if he didn't get there in time? Who had her? Who was going to hurt her? What had she become mixed up in? He didn't have any answers. He had to see her, to know she was alright

His hands fumbled, almost dropping the key as he jammed it into the keyhole and unlocked his van. He clambered in, shoved the ignition on, and screeched away. For a second, he bounced around in the dark of the bumpy car park before remembering to turn his lights on as he zipped through the open gates. He didn't bother getting out to padlock them like normal.

Andrew pulled onto the main road, cutting off a car whose driver had to lamp on the brakes to avoid him. The blare of a horn followed him as he accelerated away, not apologising with a flash of his hazards or a wave. What did it matter? Every action cost precious seconds and as he sped to double the speed limit on the thirty-zone road, he still felt as though he was crawling.

The roundabout was blessedly traffic-free in the right-hand lane as he navigated onto the Keighley bypass and floored it, the roar of the road noise in his ears drowning out, for a blessed few moments, the sound of his daughter's fear. He lived in Ingrow, on the other side of town and as he hit the Toby Carvery roundabout, peeling off to cut through the lower end of Keighley, he also hit the last glut of rush hour traffic that clogged the streets.

His hands were a drum on the steering wheel, his whole body bouncing in the oil-stained seat, pounding with nerves and fear, as though his agitation could somehow part the wave of traffic before him and let him through. Of course, it didn't. He crawled, one agonising foot at a time past the train station and supermarket, through to the Worth Way and South Street junction.

Now that he had slowed down, his radio could be heard again. Merry Christmas songs jingled away, the chipper beat an anathema to him. Andrew smashed a hammy fist in the general direction of the on/off button. Whether he hit it, or busted the radio, he didn't know or care, but it shut up at least.

Though now, he could hear her more clearly again. *Dad.* He saw her wide, warm eyes, tear-filled and staring up at him pleadingly, his mind doing its best to torture him.

Up through town he wound at an agonisingly glacial pace until, at last, he floored it through a red light onto South Street out of Keighley and up to Ingrow. Just before the old train station tucked away at the bottom of Ingrow hill, he peeled off right, earning himself another honk for diving through a too-small gap between oncoming traffic.

The spire of St John's Church carved through the orange glow of streetlights beside him as he turned up the hill into the maze of streets. His house was next to the graveyard, as it happened, an end of terrace. He didn't mind the quiet neighbours—but now it meant there was no one there to help his little girl.

His street. At last. It was unlit and the streetlights of the maintained road were swallowed up by inky blackness. The small outside security lights from the church didn't stretch across the graveyard. His van bumped and jolted down the potholed private dead-end road, but he didn't slow and didn't brake, hurtling to a stop at the last second. His spine crunched as he overshot. The van shuddered up onto the old stone kerb and came to rest cock-eyed, half on the road and half off.

Andrew Collins didn't care how shit his parking was. He had to know if his little girl was alright. He leapt out and slammed the door behind him, not bothering to stop and lock it. He took the three steps up to the front door with one leap, slamming his palm onto the cold stone bricks to stop himself from crashing straight into the door. His heart thundered, his breath seemed too loud, and he felt unwieldy and huge and clumsy—and entirely out of his depth—as he ragged the door handle.

Locked.

Andrew fumbled for the keys in one of his overall pockets, and dropped them. He swore viciously, scrabbling to pick them up. He jammed them in the door and he turned, pushing down and in on the handle so hard that the door bounced back off the inside wall as it opened with such force, nearly taking him out.

'Charlie!' he called, his voice hoarse, his throat dry with panic.

'Dad!' came the reply from the the kitchen. The two-up-two-down Victorian terrace felt even more cramped than usual as he squeezed through the cluttered hallway, causing an avalanche of mess behind him with his wide shoulders knocking everything down.

'Don't come any closer,' a harsh female voice rang out.

Andrew skidded to a halt. Obey or fight? His daughter was in there. She was threatened. Every instinct screamed for him to charge, attack, defend her. But by doing so... he could endanger her further.

His healthy breathing stalled utterly as he saw the silver glint of a knife in the light of the kitchen beyond, held up by a disembodied arm.

He edged closer.

Enough to peek around the door frame.

His daughter sat at the tiny table. Her hands were both palm-down on that scratched-to-hell old wood. She was shaking so much her loose hair quivered, dancing in the air as it hung to the sides of her face. Tears had tracked dark streaks of mascara down her face.

That knife was all too sharp and all too close.

Andrew edged closer still, as quiet as he could be with his massive booted feet and bulky profile in that narrow, crap-filled hallway.

The woman standing behind his daughter wore a face lined with premature age—an odd contrast with the sleek, full head of hair pinned back in a bun. *A wig*, his brain supplied, though he didn't quite know what to do with that information. He didn't recognise her, wig or not. Who the hell was she? Why was she here? What did she want?

He met her furious gaze.

'Who are you? What do you want?' he demanded, his tone as hostile as his body was rigid, prepared to explode into movement at the slightest provocation. He didn't dare rush her. Not with that knife. Not yet.

More questions bubbled on his tongue, but he held them back and forced down the erupting panic at the sight of his terrified daughter.

'I want revenge, Andrew Collins, before it's too late,' she said. Her voice was soft and yet it cut through the small kitchen clearly, carving through the rush of his pulse in his ears.

'I don't understand. She hasn't done anything, she's just a kid.'

His daughter looked up at him, indignant fire burning in her eyes. He willed her to keep quiet, that her teenage insolence wouldn't put her in further harm's way.

'Not her! *You*,' snapped the woman, brandishing the knife towards him.

'I don't know what you're talking about,' Andrew said. He carefully raised his hands in a placating gesture. The space was small. If his daughter wasn't there, he'd have rushed the woman. He was twice her size. Even with the knife, he was sure he could overpower her quickly enough to limit the damage.

But with Charlotte between them, Andrew Collins swallowed his prickly pride. 'Listen, we can work this out. Whatever it is you think I've done, it can be fixed.'

'No, it can't!' Her voice was as scathing as her glare. That knife wobbled in her grip, the five-inch blade splashing reflected light onto the tiled wall. She looked his age, but so frail. Her forearms were bone-thin and the skin of her face pallid.

He could definitely take her if he got the chance, he reckoned. She'd snap in his grasp.

'You can't ever bring Lizzie back.' She bared her teeth at him.

The bottom fell out of Andrew Collin's stomach. *Lizzie.* He hadn't heard that name in thirty-odd years. *It can't be.*

CHAPTER THIRTY-SIX

'Oh yes,' said the woman, grinning viciously. 'You might have forgotten her, but Elizabeth Munroe has haunted my steps every day since the day she died.'

'You're...you...' Andrew gaped, unable to formulate words. It was happening. His worst nightmare. It was true. 'Who are you?'

She seemed to take personal pride in the way Elizabeth's name punched the height and vitriol out of Andrew Collins, raising her chin and sneering at him. 'I'm her sister.'

'You killed them. Paul, Tony, Lee.' Cold seeped through him.

'Aye.' That sneer widened. 'They thought they were untouchable. Thought they'd earned their freedom or forgiveness. Thought they'd got away with it. I know what they did. I made them pay.'

'How?' he asked, though he dreaded the answer, for surely it would be the method of his own demise too, if he wasn't careful. He dared not even say *poison*, not with his daughter there. She didn't have a clue what was happening. He saw it in her wide eyes. They were fixed upon him, silently begging him to protect her, get her out of there, get this knife-wielding nutter away from her.

Andrew Collins wished it were so simple.

If this woman was Lizzie Munroe's sister and she'd done away with Tony, Lee, and Paul—seemingly with no intervention from the police—he and Charlotte were in greater danger than he cared to admit.

The woman cocked her head to one side, pausing before she answered. 'Poison. Poison they'd never see coming. Poison they paid me for the privilege of eating.'

He didn't understand. What on earth was she talking about? He resisted the urge to look around the kitchen. The only toxic substance he had was the bleach upstairs next to the loo—he wasn't about to drink that. Who did she think she was?

The woman slipped something out of the pocket of her long cardigan. 'For the first one, I did him with belladonna. The berries are so sweet, and so deadly. I hope he gobbled them up like a greedy little piggy. The next, poison hemlock.' She held up the item in her hand. 'That's this beauty.'

It was green-stemmed, with pretty bursts of tiny, delicate white flowers. The kind of plant that flowered every summer in the verges lining country roads and fields, he thought.

'A little bitter, I'll admit, but with a matching flavour palette and served so nicely, well, it's ingested before one even realises. There's no cure for that one. And the last one, well, he went thanks to deadly webcap. A mushroom that you'd mistake for any other.

'They're a delightful bunch. Vomiting, nausea, dizziness, paralysis, and oh, the *pain*. Pure agony, intensifying over days and hours until the body can take no more. It shuts down. Once you're on the way, you know the end is coming and you can't stop it. Just like my Lizzie. I wish I could have been there in their final hours to enjoy their suffering for myself.'

He saw the glow on her face, that faraway look in her eyes—as though she was imagining it—that told of her pleasure at knowing their end was slow and hard. Her smile faded and her gaze darkened as her focus returned to him.

'It can never erase what happened to Lizzie. It can never bring her back, undo her suffering, or our loss... Their suffering isn't a patch on what she endured, but I can hope they hurt long and slowly before they met their end. They deserved every bit of it. Her death is on their hands—and it's on yours.'

'I didn't know, I swear.' But even he knew he was lying—his gut instinct had told him at the time that he'd been covering something up. He'd known something was off. He'd been in denial that his pals were monsters.

They had all joked about screwing around back in those days. It had been a race to see who could get laid the fastest, the most often—all notches on their bedposts as they turned from boys to men, and half of it bullshit and bluster. He hadn't wanted to believe they'd been capable of it. Until it turned out, they very much had. And he had got them out of a prison sentence with his testimony.

She knew he was lying too—somehow. Her face darkened, her sneer turned into a snarl. 'My sister *died* for your lies. She couldn't bear the shame and guilt of what they'd done. It *tortured* her and she couldn't take it anymore. She took her own life. You know who found her? *Me*.

'I'll never unsee that as long as I live. It haunts me every night when I try to sleep. Knowing that she's gone and that she suffered so much that she couldn't bear to live anymore is pain enough—' Her grimace then, as though she did feel the grief of that cleaving her in two, made the threat of her diminish, seeming human and frail again, that knife in her hand momentarily forgotten. 'Knowing that you all lived and walked free... That has driven me all these years. I had to make sure she got justice one day, since the courts were never going to do it for us.'

'I swear I didn't know—not at first.' Andrew rubbed a hand over his face, never taking his eyes off his daughter. 'Not until many years later when they let it slip. I couldn't believe it myself. I'm sorry. I truly am. I didn't dare come forward. I didn't want to lose everything I had because of what they did.'

Anger flashed through her again. 'And what *you* did, Andrew Collins. Whether they were innocent or guilty, you never should have knowingly lied in court for them!' Her fingers tightened around the stem of the plant at her side and the knife in her other hand rose again.

'What do you want?' he asked desperately. 'Please don't punish her. It's not her fault. I'm sorry, I promise. What can I do to make it right?' It was as close to grovelling as he could get and he'd go down on his knees if he thought it would help, cramped hallway or not. Not that he wanted to—he'd be far too slow if that woman decided to knife his daughter. He'd never be able to stop her in time. A fresh wave of panic thundered through him.

The dark answer came. 'I want justice for Lizzie and since the courts will never give it to her, I'm taking matters into my own hands.'

'Why now?' Andrew dared to ask. 'It's been so long.' He had watched over his shoulder for so many years and nothing had ever come of it. He had grown complacent, in reality, forgotten sometimes even, about it all. He had sometimes wondered if it dogged their footsteps—Paul's, Lee's, Tony's—like it had his. They had all seemed to live their lives with no shadow hanging over them about what had happened.

'That's none of your concern. You're next on my list and I want you all *gone*. You all killed Lizzie.' She raised her chin. 'So, I have a choice for you: be a coward again or step up to the plate and take justice like a man.'

Something cold curled through Andrew at her words. His glance flicked to that knife. His tongue darted out to wet his lips and he swallowed. Evaluating again—was she capable of taking him down? Was he capable of taking her down?

'What do you want to do?' He kept his voice as calm and even as possible, for his daughter's sake. Tears slipped once more down her cheeks, falling onto the table below her chin. Her hands were now fists clenched on the wood. 'Let's not be hasty. My daughter doesn't need to be any part of this. She's just a girl and she's done nothing wrong. Please, leave her out of it.'

More than anything he didn't want Charlotte to be harmed, but neither could he bear the thought of her having to watch him suffer in some way.

'I intend to. No more girls or women should suffer at the hands of you men.'

'But she will suffer if you hurt me. I'm her dad.'

'It's too late for that. Nice try, though. This is still on you. What I want you to do is very simple.' She smiled serenely.

Andrew tensed. Was she going to ask him to stab himself? He ran through his options mentally. Maybe if he tackled her... Even with Charlotte between them, he stood a chance. *Maybe*.

'What?' His heart pounded so loudly, his pulse thundering through his ears, that he saw her lips move but he didn't catch the words.

'Eat it.'

'I... What do you mean?'

Slowly, the woman raised the plant and placed it with precision on the table between his daughter's clenched fists.

'It's that simple. Eat it.'

CHAPTER THIRTY-SEVEN

A ndrew gaped.

'It's poison hemlock. A nasty death, granted, but no less than you deserve. Eventually, it'll paralyse you right to your lungs and your body will shut down. There's no cure. Once it goes in, well, you're off to the morgue.' She looked happy about that.

'*No.*'

The woman stirred. She pointed the knife first at him and then at Charlotte. 'Either you eat it... or she does.'

'Not happening.' Never mind that she wielded a knife so close to his daughter, she was clearly insane if she thought he'd do it. He had to tackle her.

She saw him tense and drifted closer to Charlotte. That knife closed in on his daughter. The blade wove between Charlotte's loose hair, teasing out a strand. The woman pulled back on the knife, taking that hair with her. It rippled off the smooth side of the blade in a waterfall.

Charlotte whimpered.

'Do you fancy your chances?' She cocked her head at him. 'If you won't eat it and she doesn't, what do you think this is for?' She wiggled the knife. 'I'm a desperate woman, Andrew. The difference between you and me, is that I don't have anything else left to lose.'

Andrew swallowed as that knife closed in on his daughter's neck. Too close. He was in sweet agony already, frozen in the face of that terrible choice. Save himself... or save her? He couldn't do it. He *couldn't*. He didn't want to die... but Charlotte. The way she glanced up at him, her lip trembling, her body frozen absolutely still in her fear that the slightest movement would see that knife plunged into her...

This had to end.

'Alright.' His throat was so scratchy his voice came out hoarse. 'Alright...' His shoulders slumped.

Hers rose. She knew she had won.

'You promise if I do this, she'll be unharmed?'

'I promise.'

Andrew edged into the kitchen and reached slowly towards the table, not wanting to startle the woman with any sudden movements. He felt alternately flooded with heat and frozen with ice, that fear charging through him. His hand shook as he took the plant from the table.

His fingers itched at the touch of the stem. Was that his imagination? His whole body wanted to reject that thing violently. He trembled as he forced his arm to draw back, overriding his own good sense.

An inch at a time, he raised it to his nose for a quick

sniff. Sour, almost urine-like. Unpleasant. Its stench warned him not to eat it—not like he would be so foolish as to try.

'Do it,' the woman urged.

The world continued on as normal outside, unaware that in this small dwelling, his entire world was so close to shattering. Traffic noise was a low grind outside, a constant symphony punctuated by a lone siren that rose above it.

For a second, it was a ray of hope before he ground it to pieces, not wanting it to break his resolve. It was a police car unaware of his plight. Or an ambulance going to the hospital without him. Not like they would be able to help, if what the woman said was true, that this was an incurable poison.

He could not help but examine it. It was a plant. How could this have taken down Tony? It scared him that he didn't understand this hidden world. Those tiny white flowers didn't look as though they held such a dark secret.

Thinking about it wasn't helping. He swallowed. He didn't want to do this, but he couldn't see his daughter hurt. That would be even more unforgivable than the guilt he had borne for knocking on thirty years now over this whole pile of shite. He glanced at Charlotte, and it was impossible not to take in that knife too, hovering so near to his girl's throat.

Her watery eyes were fixed on him.

Andrew brought the plant to his mouth. Those delicate flowers brushed his lips with soft velvet kisses. He shuddered with revulsion. And forced it in, past his incisors.

It was on his tongue. His hand shook so much, he could feel the poison hemlock dancing in his mouth.

Bite. Just bite, he urged himself.

And yet, he hesitated. Was he a coward for it? Or was his overriding sense of self-preservation stronger than his desperate shards of honour?

'Do it!' she barked, and that knife wavered as she edged closer to Charlotte. 'Last chance.'

It snapped something within him.

CHAPTER THIRTY-EIGHT

He couldn't do it. Andrew Collins spat the plant out explosively and launched himself at the woman. In the tight space, his hands collided with her shoulders almost immediately. The pair of them crashed into the wall behind her.

Charlotte shrieked and pushed herself to one side away from them, half falling off the chair into the wall. As she slid to the floor, kicking the chair out, its legs tangled with Andrews. He tripped, and swore as he went down too.

It gave the woman the gap she needed as Andrew withdrew, trying to stay upright. She slashed out with the knife.

He raised his hands before him. Blazing pain erupted across his outstretched palms.

Charlotte's screaming drowned everything out as the young woman scrambled under the table and fled into the hallway. Andrew didn't care. She was behind him now.

He was a physical barrier between her and this madwoman.

The woman slashed again, forcing him back and then a gust of freezing air blasted in as the side door opened behind her, sweeping away the stuffy warmth that had accumulated in the small kitchen.

Behind him, Charlotte's shrieking mingled with the sound of sirens bleeding in from that open doorway.

Andrew advanced on the women then dove backwards to cover Charlotte as she flung the knife at him with vehement force, a snarl locked on her face.

It crashed onto the tiles on the counter behind him and bounced onto the floor with a clatter. The door crashed shut an instant later, bouncing so hard in its frame that it didn't catch and jumped open once more.

He was a cage over his daughter. She sobbed on the floor as he hunched over her on all fours, shielding her with his body. Expecting at any moment to feel that knife searing into his back.

His hand throbbed where it had been slashed. Dark blood oozed out, smearing across the vinyl floor, and across him, his daughter's clothes... Gods, it was a mess. Under the table, the crushed, twisted plant remained. He kicked it away viciously, as though it too were a threat that could attack them at any moment.

It took a long moment to realise there wasn't another blow coming, though the tension in his body didn't ease. She was gone, that crazy, revenge-bent woman, and she hadn't come back. Maybe she wasn't coming back.

The knife lay on the floor behind his foot where it

had fallen. They were damn lucky not to have been caught by it at all, but adrenaline surged so high he couldn't tell if anything else was hurt—even his palm was a hazy kind of pain, half-numbed in his state.

Andrew grabbed the knife and leapt to his feet, lurching to block the open side door with his body, just in case. The door banged into the wind as he strained his eyes to see into the inky blackness. Over the low wall to the side of the house, across a narrow path that ran from his street to the next, was the church graveyard. Swallowed by darkness, he saw nothing. With those sirens so loud and close, he could hear nothing too.

Was it the police? Were they here for her? Were they here for him? The unwelcome thought intruded. Perhaps they knew what he had done. If the adrenaline hadn't been running so high, he'd have feared that.

Andrew swallowed. Brandishing that knife at the dark hopelessly. He retreated inside, shutting and bolting the door, before turning to his daughter.

He helped her to her feet, smearing her with the dark crimson of his blood from the wound on his hand. 'Are you alright?'

She sobbed in his arms.

'Charlie, are you hurt?' He needed to know she was alright—and then he could collapse.

'She didn't touch me. I was so scared!'

'I know, I know,' he said soothingly. 'You're safe now, love, I promise.'

Braying erupted as someone hammered on the front door.

His nerves erupted again and he swiped the knife from where he'd dropped it on the side, pushing Charlotte behind him again, but as he glanced down the hallway, he saw the flash of blue lights illuminating the living room through the front window.

Police.

Pain throbbed in his hand. Andrew glanced down at himself. He was in a right state. Spattered with oil as usual, the black of it staining his blue overalls, but now smeared with dark blood spots too. He discarded the knife, grabbed the tea towel half-hanging off the side and wrapped it around his injured hand, before wiping his face with his other sleeve in case there was blood there.

Someone brayed on the door again, with indistinct shouts from the other side.

'I'm coming!' he called, striding past Charlotte and kicking dislodged things out of his way in the hallway to get through.

The door was still unlocked. He opened it to the sight of two lit-up police cars outside and one white Golf blocking in his van. Inside the vehicles, watchful officers waited, the whites of their eyes lit blue every other beat of the lights. All of them had eyes on him.

Two detectives stood on the steps. He recognised the bearded gruff chap and the young woman he'd already been hounded by. Wrapped up in warm, smart coats, they were a world away from the mess he wore right now. His skin crawled for a shower, to cleanse what had happened. His tongue tingled and he was already paranoid he had poison coursing through him.

The sight of them got his back up at once. His already fraught nerves couldn't take any more. He tensed, his body recoiling to the thought of being cornered and captured by them, locked up for all of this when he was still on an instinctive high to protect himself and Charlotte. He couldn't do that from a cell.

Both detectives raised an eyebrow at his ashen face and shared a glance.

'Is she still here?' the man asked.

A wave of relief threatened to overwhelm him. *She.* They were here for her. They knew, somehow. They weren't here for him—yet. He sagged against the door frame, that adrenaline starting to give way to shock. 'She's gone. Graveyard.' He waved his towel-wrapped hand in the general direction.

The male detective's glance snagged on the towel.

Andrew hid it behind his back as he realised that blood was starting to soak through. He still felt wired enough not to trust that he was to remain a free man.

'I think we'll need to come in,' the detective said lightly, throwing another knowing glance at his partner.

Andrew left the door hanging open and trudged back into the house, ushering Charlotte away from the scene of carnage and into the living room.

Aye. I think you might. He only hoped they'd be leaving with the woman in cuffs and not him.

CHAPTER THIRTY-NINE

W ard could practically feel Nowak's eyes burning
into his back as he stepped into the terraced
house after Andrew Collins. Blood and muck-stained,
wild eyes, nostrils flaring—Andrew Collins looked mad
alright, like he'd been through a right ordeal. They
needed to find out exactly what had happened, whilst
outside, the police who had accompanied them spread
out to search for Rebecca Callahan.

It was carnage in the hallway. Piles of boots, shoes,
coats, boxes, and detritus had toppled over the floor in a
wave of mess that required Ward to glance at his feet to
pick a path through.

'In here.' Andrew's gruff voice directed them into a
calmer looking living room at the front of the property—
though not before Ward got an eyeful of an equally
chaotic kitchen at the end of the hallway, with a chair on
its side, the table nudged out of place, and the floor
covered in more blood.

What the bloody hell's happened here? Ward thought. 'Take a look in there and get CSI on their way pronto, please, Sarge,' he directed quietly.

If he was being honest, he was half expecting her to find a body in there. He'd stay with the chap in here and extract what had happened—and try not to get himself killed if the man was on a murdering spree. They had stumbled into the scene of a violent crime, that was for sure.

He wasn't sure who on earth had instigated it yet, but Rebecca Callahan had been here, he surmised. And from that, he knew that the team's instincts had been dead on. Andrew Collins had been in danger and it seemed that he had just fought for his life.

Andrew paced to the window and back to the sofa, unable to sit down. Ward saw the edge of tension in him. Understandable. The man'd be on high alert—especially with his daughter there, Ward assumed from the teenage girl curled up on the couch, her knees drawn to her chest.

He made no move to sit down next to her, instead, folding himself into a corner as best he could to avoid Andrew's pacing in the tiny room.

'What's happened here then, Andrew?' he said as mildly as he could.

Andrew turned on him, pinning Ward with the full force of a wrathful glare.

'Are you alright?' Ward frowned as he caught sight of Andrew's hand wrapped in the increasingly bloodied towel. 'Do you need a paramedic?'

That threw Andrew off. He glanced down. 'Oh. No.

Maybe. I don't know. She knifed me. Fucking hurts.' He unwound the towel, grimaced at what was revealed and wrapped it back up. 'I'm not leaving my daughter. Not with that bitch out there.'

Ward fished out his phone and flicked to a photo of Callahan pulled from her ID. 'Is this the woman you're referring to?'

'Uh...yeah. Different hair though. She was wearing a wig. A brown one, in a bun.'

A wig. Weird. But then, maybe she had disguised herself to avoid them.

He excused himself for a second to nip outside, update the copper on the doorstep, and radio the officers searching for her. She wouldn't slip past them again, he hoped. They'd narrowly missed her, it seemed.

'Is this your daughter?' he asked as he re-entered the living room.

'Yeah. She threatened her. Threatened us both.' Andrew's hands shook as he folded his arms, clamping his hands under his armpits, probably to stop them.

Ward took her name and age, examining her visually. 'Are you hurt?'

Charlotte shook her head, glaring up at him with teary, swollen eyes rimmed with smudged black eyeliner and mascara that had run down her cheeks in a splodgy mess.

'What happened?' he glanced between them.

'I got a phone call,' Andrew said roughly. 'From Charlotte's phone—she was terrified. The woman had her here, threatening her with a knife, telling me I had to come home or she'd be killed.' He growled out that last word like a curse.

Ward scrawled in his pocketbook in the absence of Nowak, who he could hear speaking in the kitchen, presumably on the phone to CSI.

'Right, okay. I think we need to backtrack. Charlotte, I know it's extremely traumatic and I'm sorry to have to ask, but I need you to answer a few questions so we can understand what's happened here. Is that alright?' He waited for her nod before he continued. 'Thank you. How did you meet this woman?'

Charlotte sniffed and dragged a hand under her nose. She seemed to shrink back under her long curtain of dark hair. Andrew crossed to her, still bouncing on every footstep, a bundle of pent up energy. He sank onto the couch beside her and wrapped her under his uninjured arm.

She had stopped crying, the tears drying on her cheeks, but she huddled under there for a long moment.

Ward waited, hovering awkwardly in the corner with nowhere else to sit, backed up between the TV and the window.

In a halting voice, she finally spoke. 'A lady knocked on the front door. I wasn't going to answer, but the knocking kept coming and I thought it was someone important. I didn't know her, but before I could close the door she told me to wait. Um, she said she was sorry to bother me but her car had broken down outside and she didn't have a phone... could she possibly use mine to call someone?'

'You shouldn't have let her in!' Her father glared down at her.

She shrunk further under his arm.

'I'm sorry, Dad. I wouldn't normally, I know, but she seemed so nice and upset and it was cold and dark. She was only wearing a cardigan and honestly, she looked so old that I thought she might die on the step if I didn't let her in.' With a slight roll of her eyes, Ward saw a hint of the teenage attitude starting to bleed back into the lass.

Then, that faded as the girl relived the horror of what had happened. Her voice dropped to a whisper and Ward had to strain to hear her. 'But then when I let her in... I invited her into the kitchen, it was warmer in there. I was getting my phone out of my pocket to give to her and next thing I know, she had one of our knives in her hand.'

She faltered, falling silent. Her dad squeezed her in a one-armed hug. He looked pale and drawn, his stare slightly glassy as though he too was reliving the horror of what had happened to them both.

'Go on,' said Ward. 'You're doing great.'

'She made me sit down at the table and ring Dad. I don't know how, but she knew his name... I realised that she'd come on purpose then, but I didn't know why. I was so scared. I didn't know what was happening. I rang Dad like she asked me to.

'She made me ask for him, tell him that—' Her lip trembled and her shoulders shook as she started sobbing. '—that if he didn't come home right then, she'd kill me and she had the knife, I didn't know whether she was being serious or not, but I was so scared.'

'I came straight home,' said Andrew. 'Did she hurt you at all?'

'No, Dad. She made me sit at the table. She wouldn't tell me anything and I didn't dare ask, she just said you needed to be there. When she took the phone off me and hung up, I didn't know if you were coming.' Her sobs intensified until her words were almost unintelligible.

'Sh-she said you'd come. She d-did. And I wanted to believe her b-but I was so scared you wouldn't and what she'd do to me. She had that knife right there n-next to me and she made me sit with my hands on the table. She said if I tried to get away, she'd hurt me and not to try it. I didn't dare move. Not until you c-came.'

'I'd never leave you, Charlie, you know that. That was the scariest moment of my life.' He bowed his head, pressing his lips to the crown of her head, silent for a long moment. 'I got here as fast as I could. Didn't lock the garage up or anything. Ah, shit,' he added, groaning with the sudden realisation that he'd left his work premises open to any opportunistic thieves.

'What happened next, then?' Ward prompted. The garage was nothing to do with him, not whilst they had a murderer on the loose. No one had come in yet to let him know Rebecca Callahan had been apprehended. The seconds and minutes ticked by, and with each one, the growing fear that she'd vanished and they'd lost their only lead on her whereabouts.

Andrew filled in what had happened next, telling a

harrowing tale of how the woman had admitted to murdering his three friends with a creative variety of natural, plant-based poisons and then, how she had threatened him. Of how he had very nearly condemned himself to death at her threat that either he or his daughter would die and that to save her, he'd have to damn himself.

'Did she say why she wanted you dead so badly?' Ward asked as Andrew trailed off after telling Ward how he had managed to fight her off—sustaining the cuts to his hands in the process—and how she had then fled into the night before the police's arrival.

'No,' answered Andrew, after a pause that was awkwardly long.

That was alright. Ward had other ways to draw it out. 'So let me get this straight. Your three friends are done in. She's coming for you to finish the job. She knows what you did, doesn't she?'

Andrew stayed silent, his hooded eyes as guarded as his still tongue.

'She's Elizabeth Munroe's sister. Her father's dead, her mother's ailing... Perhaps she felt like if she didn't get justice now, she never would.'

Andrew's jaw twitched. Ward wondered what he wasn't saying.

'They did it, didn't they? Paul, Tony, Lee.' He was being careful with what he said in front of the teenage girl. She didn't need to know how dark the world could be at her impressionable age.

Eventually, Andrew nodded.

Ward took a deep breath in and out. 'And did you know when you defended them?' That was the crux of it for Andrew, he reckoned. His testimony had seen them walk free. Clearly, to Rebecca Callahan he was as guilty as his friends if she had tried to kill him.

'No,' Andrew said in a low voice. 'I swear it. I thought something might be off, I admit, but I trusted them. They used me and stabbed me in the back. I only found out years later that it was true after all.' He clenched his jaw again and anger darkened his gaze.

'And you didn't come forward.'

'No,' he ground out. 'Would you? I was married then. We had just had Charlotte. When the girl died... I didn't think it could get any worse, or that I could make it any better. I carried the guilt with me more than what I think they did, to be honest, and they're the ones that did it. Tony never spoke about it, or Paul. Lee mentioned it in passing, years later—that was when I realised. I put it together and I knew what they'd done then, and that I'd lied to protect them and they were guilty all along. But no, I didn't come forward. Why should I have ruined my life for what they did? Ruined her life?' He gestured to his daughter. 'I couldn't raise her from prison.'

She looked up at him wide-eyed. 'Dad, what are you on about? What did you do?'

'It's nothing, love, don't worry about it,' he reassured her, but his eyes remained locked with Ward's. He knew Ward held the power over his future. Ward felt it settle heavily on his shoulders. What should he do? He knew now why Andrew seemed cagey with them before. He had been hiding something—this.

Ward knew what was right. Andrew Collins had committed a crime. No matter how much later, by the letter of the law, he should be tried and punished accordingly for any crime he was found guilty of. And yet, Andrew was a man, much like him. He'd gone on the good faith of his friendship. That had been a mistake. He'd tried to protect his daughter later down the line, by not ending up behind bars. Who wouldn't try to protect their kids?

Ward's humanity was his undoing sometimes. The law was black and white. Humans were shades of grey. It was never as neat. How many lives would be ruined as a result of Tony, Lee, and Paul's actions on that night long ago? What happened had torn apart Lizzie Munroe's family for a lifetime, and now it tore apart the lives of her attackers with her sister's revenge.

Ward couldn't say in good faith that he wouldn't arrest Andrew Collins right there and then... but he also had no desire to break apart *another* family on account of all this mess.

Nowak poked her head in from the kitchen, breaking the awkward silence that had fallen between them. 'Sir?'

'Aye, Sarge?'

'CSI will be here within the hour. I've retrieved a sample of what looks like poison hemlock and a bloodied knife. We should be able to pull prints from the knife at least.'

'And the back door,' Andrew said suddenly. 'She must have touched that.'

Nowak dipped her head. 'Of course. They'll give the place a thorough going over. I haven't disturbed anything so Victoria and the team can conduct a proper examination with this being a violent crime. No word from outside yet.'

'She's gone.' Ward sighed heavily, his shoulders slumping.

'It looks like it, sir. They've swept the streets and the graveyard.'

They needed to find Rebecca Callahan even more urgently. She had admitted to Andrew Collins of murdering three men and arrived at his house with an intent to murder him, not to mention holding an innocent girl hostage.

He turned back to Andrew. The fight seemed to be bleeding out of the man and his face sagged with growing relief as the adrenaline faded and the shock set in. No doubt he would be relieved he had survived with nothing more than hopefully a minor, if not nasty, hand injury and that crucially, his daughter was unharmed.

'Are you alright?' Ward asked as Andrew Collins grimaced, squeezing his injured hand tighter in the sodden towel.

'Hurts like a fucker,' Andrew said through gritted teeth.

'We'll get you seen to.'

'I'll call the medics now, sir,' offered Nowak.

Ward flashed her a grateful smile. 'Andrew Collins...

you know what I have to do now.' He took no relish in it. It was his job and his duty.

Andrew nodded. 'Get it over with.'

Arresting him would still be a relief compared to death by an incurable poison, Ward reckoned. Not that he expected Andrew to thank him for it.

'Andrew Collins, I'm arresting you on suspicion of perjury and perverting the course of justice. You do not have to say anything, but it may harm your defence if you do not mention when questioned something which you later rely on in court. Anything you do say may be given in evidence. Do you understand?'

Andrew met his eyes. He sighed. The fight seemed to have left him. 'I understand.'

'My colleagues'll take you to the station.' He needed to trace Rebecca Callahan as quickly as possible.

'What about Charlotte? I don't want to leave her here alone, not after... and my garage. I need to lock up.'

Ward shook his head. 'You'll have to send someone else, I'm sorry. My hands are tied. Can you call her mother?' He tilted his head towards Charlotte.

Andrew let out a frustrated groan. 'I'll never hear the end of it.'

'Dad, what's going on? What've you done?' Charlotte looked between them.

Andrew forced a smile onto his face. 'Nothing, love. Look... just... go home to your mum's, please. I'm sorry. I'll call you as soon as I can and explain everything, alright?'

Charlotte's face clouded, but she nodded.

Ward saw what she wasn't saying. She was confused, scared, traumatised—and hiding it behind a moody exterior as she huddled back into the couch, already busy on her phone texting away like mad, the backlight of the screen illuminating her face from below, washing out what little colour she had on her red, splotchy, tear-and-mascara-stained face.

'Shall we?' Ward looked up at Nowak who hovered in the doorway still. Impatience niggled at him. Every moment they lingered was a moment Rebecca Callahan disappeared further into the darkness outside.

She had failed at her murder attempt. Who knew how desperate she would be. Who knew who would be next on her hit list. Ward didn't want to find out too late on either count.

'Let's.' The smile Nowak gave him was a grim one, full of promise. The Sarge loved a good chase too.

CHAPTER FORTY

'Right, Patterson,' Ward fired over the Golf's Bluetooth. With no leads, they were sat outside Andrew Collin's house still, waiting to at least figure out which direction to start travelling in, if nothing else. 'We have to track Callahan. I want any phones registered to her triangulating in real-time, as well as her vehicles flagged on ANPR. If she's moving or still, I want to find her.'

'On it, sir,' Patterson replied.

'We don't know where she's headed next or who she could be targeting. Is there anyone else connected with the case?' Ward asked. 'She's dangerous, possibly armed. She's failed this time but succeeded three others and she'll probably try again.'

Nowak stirred in the darkened passenger seat. 'I don't know anyone else she could be going for now. Maybe she'll give up and go into hiding? She must know we're on her trail by now.'

'Patterson?'

Patterson murmured much the same as Nowak. 'Sorry, sir.'

Ward sighed.

From the warmth of his car, they watched as a police constable led a handcuffed Andrew Collins away and held the door open for him to climb into the back of a marked police vehicle.

Shouting erupted as a woman pulled up, got out of her car, and started hurling goodness knows what verbal abuse at Andrew—they couldn't hear anything but muffled shouting from inside the vehicle. Half in the car, Andrew started yelling back at her.

Charlotte ran over from where she'd been waiting on the front steps of the house, standing between them and raising her hands, shouting at them both to stop. She gave her dad a long hug—one that he couldn't return in cuffs— before running to her mother and doing the same.

A police officer drifted over and from the hand gestures involved, Ward could surmise that Charlotte's mother was getting royal orders to piss right off and stop causing a scene.

Whatever Charlotte's mother thought of Andrew, it clearly wasn't much, but Ward found himself with a measure of respect for the gruff man now. The man had done wrong, but he knew it and from the sounds of it, he had worn the guilt for years. He had protected his daughter when she needed him most—had stood in the line of harm himself to make sure she was alright. What more could a child ask of their parent?

Ward had to acknowledge that at least the man's soul still had some decency left in it and wasn't entirely stained with the crimes of his past. Ward didn't believe that once a sinner always a sinner—not always. The man might always be damned for what he had done, but he wasn't above redemption.

'Families, eh?' Ward muttered. *Nothing but trouble.* His own was no better, not really. He made a mental note to text his brother when this case was all wrapped up. He hadn't heard from Sam in a worryingly long time. The lad was a constant source of worry for him. Even if Sam hated him, Daniel Ward had to check that he was alright. They had no one else to look out for them, after all.

'Yup,' Nowak agreed. 'She could be at the restaurant. How about we check there?'

'Or her home address. If she knows we're on her trail, she might return there to pick up a few bits before disappearing off-grid.' It did happen. They didn't know if she'd be spooked, panicked, or even smart and level-headed. Only that they had to work fast—and they'd struggle going in blind.

'Good point, sir.' Nowak mulled for a moment. 'Home.'

'Home it is.' Ward put the car in first and pulled out. 'Patterson, you check out the restaurant. Full search for her on the premises. We'll cover her home address. Make sure I'm updated the moment there are any hits on ANPR or mobile, alright?'

'Yes, sir!' Patterson's voice was infused with eagerness

as the young lad realised he got to leave the office to join in the hunt too.

Ward raced through darkened and quiet Keighley in the direction of Allerton where Rebecca Callahan resided.

Where would she be, home, restaurant... or somewhere else? And would they find her before something else terrible happened?

Now that Andrew Collins was in police custody, he was protected... but what if there was someone else Callahan sought that they didn't know about? Ward didn't want to be too late to find out.

CHAPTER FORTY-ONE

'She's not here,' DC Patterson reported.

Damn it, Ward cursed. He and Nowak were almost at Callahan's house which wasn't too far from the restaurant in Allerton where Patterson was calling from. Ward had a growing feeling that he couldn't ignore—one that told him they'd find the house empty too.

'I had a good look around, sir. I couldn't find her anywhere on the premises. Staff reported that she hasn't been in today, but that she does have appointments on the same day every week—today—so they didn't think anything of it.'

'Appointments? What for?' Ward frowned, trying to think what it could be. *Medical? Legal? Therapy?*

'I asked that!' Patterson sounded a little too pleased with himself for such basic detecting. 'And, uh, they didn't know. She's been going for months, that's all they could tell me.'

'Right,' said Ward through gritted teeth, annoyed that

his spirits had risen even a smidgeon at the thought Patterson might have gleaned something useful there. Whether the appointment was real or a lie, Ward had nothing to go on either way. He sighed. 'Right. Thanks, Patterson. Let me know if you come up with anything else.'

They soon arrived at Callahan's house—a small cottage swamped in darkness and surrounded by a wild garden with hedges so high the place couldn't be seen from the lane. It looked as though it had been swallowed by nature, but the number on the gate was, sure enough, the one they were looking for.

Ward and Nowak left the car, the soft thump of their doors closing the only sound to break the still winter night, like it too, held its breath with them. The closest streetlight's aura stretched to the front gate, a black wrought iron thing nestled between two dry stone walls, a hedge growing out and curling over the stone.

Torch in hand, Ward pushed through the gate—the smallest creak giving away his passage—and padded down the paved path inside. The wild garden was dead in November, empty stalks and evergreen leaves crowding the darkness, with no flowers to be seen when Ward swept his torch over the space. In summer, he reckoned it would be beautiful, bursting with life.

And poison, he reminded himself with a shudder. Who knew how many of these plants would be deadly or dangerous. He glanced at some hacked back bushes suspiciously—not a clue what any of them were.

The cottage itself lay in darkness with no internal

lights on. The path led around the side. He motioned for Nowak to follow him and passed into even deeper shadows in the lee of the cottage. The path led to the rear of the property, where several greenhouses nestled together at the other side of a patio crowded with empty flowerpots.

Ward crossed to the first greenhouse—stepping over a trailing lead—and unlatched the door. It didn't open fully, clanking as it hit a pot behind the door. Ward squeezed in, torch held high, its small beam swallowed up quickly by the tangle of greenery within. It stretched the full height of the glass structure on both sides, shelving providing a home for multiple layers of pots and trays.

It had been freezing outside and it was hardly warmer in there, though the trail of extension leads now made sense. A small electric heater whirred away. A futile exercise against a winter night.

Ward shivered as one overhanging green tendril caught the back of his neck, caressing like a finger. He leaned closer to the shelves, because in and amongst the tangle of green, he'd noticed upright lollipop sticks stabbed into each pot. Labels. Each of them, nearly annotated with a Latin or English plant name.

There were ones he recognised—hemlock, belladonna, foxgloves—and Latin names he did not. He peered closer at the hemlock. It was a visual match for the plant Nowak had found at Andrew Collins' property.

'Look at this, Nowak.'

He could even see where it had been freshly cut off at

the step and he wondered if the offcut at Andrew's house had come from this plant. He shivered. It was likely. There were more cuttings too as he cast the torchlight deeper onto the shelves. How many people was Rebecca Callahan intending to poison? Had she already taken out a few that they didn't know about?

Nowak peered at the plants too as he continued to look around. He wondered what else grew there and how toxic some of the other plants could be that he hadn't even heard of. Were there such things as airborne toxins from plants? The air burned his lungs with each breath, now that he thought about it, even though it was probably entirely his imagination. The freezing air outside had already been painful to breathe in and that was nothing to do with poison.

He was out of his depth and didn't want to learn the hard way that he'd made a foolish mistake. Abruptly, he hurried both of them outside. 'That's enough. We have what we need in there. CSI will like to take a look at that, I reckon.'

What on earth is Rebecca Callahan doing? From what he'd seen, she had enough toxic plants in there to wipe out a village. Was she planning on it? It was now starting to make sense, at least, as Rebecca herself had admitted to Andrew that she'd poisoned their meals—and that they'd even paid for the privilege.

Ward's stomach somersaulted at the thought that he too had eaten her food. Locally grown, yes, sustainable, yes... also potentially packed with deadly toxins. He'd been berating himself for surviving off of quick oven meals for months now. In that moment, it was an easy vow to swear off it all. *Goodness knows what I'm putting into my body. It could be literal poison and I wouldn't know until it was too late.* He felt sick.

'Are you alright, sir?'

Ward glanced at Nowak. 'Just rethinking a few life choices,' he mumbled.

That was it. Fresh cooking. He was back on it. Even if he was shit at it—perhaps he'd take a class or watch a YouTube video. Even if it was as simple as beans on toast with cheese sprinkled on top, or perhaps sausages if he was feeling adventurous. Heck, he could manage that. At least he would know what he was eating then.

Maybe whilst he was at it, he'd get his arse back to the gym. He'd wavered alright, in the months sorting out the divorce and the move, allowed himself to stagnate and distract. That and the ready meals had piled on the pounds and he bet he was carrying a lot less muscle and a lot more fat in there than he realised. He resisted the urge to poke his softening belly and grimaced with embarrassment, glad that the darkness hid his warming cheeks.

Instead, he followed Nowak to the back of the house. She peered through the glass panes of the back door. All the windows appeared latched and when she tried the door handle, it was locked.

He tried the same at the front, but that door was locked too, the house in darkness, unoccupied and no answer to their knocks. Unsurprisingly.

Another dead end. Urgency gnawed at Ward. *Where the bloody hell is Rebecca Callahan?*

Back in the warm car, he called Patterson. 'Any update on the ANPR, son?'

'It's just come in, sir.' Patterson sounded breathless. 'Her vehicle flagged over near Skipton on the A629.'

Ward's heart sank. They were miles away. 'Do you think she's heading into the Dales?'

The town of Skipton was the gateway to the Yorkshire Dales. After that point, there were no concentrated habitations, no towns or cities, only endless rolling hills, moors, crags and peaks, with villages nestled in the valleys. Little to no ANPR or police presence and a dearth even of mobile masts to triangulate by. If she went into the Dales they'd be looking for a needle in a haystack. Their chances were already slim. Now they shrank further still.

Patterson couldn't answer.

Ward fired the engine into life. 'Well, we might as well head up that way anyway. Alert local units. Hopefully, by the time we catch up, we'll have her next step locked in, or she'll pop up somewhere.' He sounded more confident than he felt.

'Yes, sir. Her mobile signal is moving consistently with the car, so hopefully, we'll be able to track one or the other.' It seemed Patterson was feeling optimistic. Or desperate.

Next to Ward, Nowak clung onto the door as he accelerated down the winding country roads with his lights on full beam, cursing that they were so far behind.

By the time they hit Keighley Road heading out to Skipton, an update came through from the control room directly this time. Rebecca Callahan's vehicle had now changed course. It wasn't heading out past Skipton west into the Dales. She had veered east down the Wharfe Valley, down the A65 that led to Ilkley, Otley, and beyond.

'I want all available units in the area,' growled Ward. Every marked car was fitted with ANPR. If she was there, she'd be found quickly, he hoped—if they had enough units to flood it. She was wanted for three murders, a fourth attempted, and goodness knows what else. She was their top priority now.

By the time they reached Ilkley, her car had already flagged down the valley at Burley in Wharfedale.

She's still on the move. And damn it, we can't do anything but chase.

'Can we get units there? Where are they?' Ward asked, coming through the other side of Ilkley. He was minutes out from Burley.

'A good ten minutes out, sorry, sir,' came the reply from the control room. 'We have units coming from Harrogate, Keighley, Menston, and Bradford.' Burley in Wharfedale wasn't exactly conveniently located close to any metropolitan hubs.

'Any more hits?' ANPR from fixed cameras would be few and far between without any units on the roads.

'I'm afraid not. From the timestamps, I believe the vehicle would have passed into Otley by now, but it's not triggered any of the units there.'

'Can you triangulate the mobile phone signal for me, please?' Ward was fast approaching Burley in Wharfedale—did he head past on the bypass, or remain to search in the locality? Anxiety coursed through him. His fingers drummed on the steering wheel as they wound down the road towards the roundabout. Second exit onto the bypass. Third into Burley in Wharfedale.

'Of course, sir. I have it right now. Ah, it seems to be stationary actually.'

'Where?'

'In Burley. Hang on. There are eight masts covering the area, but only three, maybe four, with half-decent signals. I'm trying to get general coordinates for you now.' A rush of static blared through the speakers as the operator sighed down the phone.

Ward pulled to the side of the road in the layby before the roundabout and waited for further direction. 'Can you pull up Google Maps?' he mouthed to Nowak.

She nodded and grabbed her phone out of her pocket.

'Right, sir. The mobile is not currently in Burley. It looks to be above it somewhere out on the moors.'

Ward frowned. *Why would she be up on the moors?* There was little enough out there and less on a cold November night. *What's up there?*

'Do you know where the Hermit Inn is, sir?' the operator asked.

'Aye.' A little pub tucked in a nook on the road that wound from Ilkley up onto the moors. There were routes up from other villages like Burley in Wharfedale too.

'Well, if you're following the road to the moors, it

looks to be past there. A little bit further than Burley Woodhead.' A small hamlet nestled almost at the top of the hills before grass fields gave way to tangled heather.

'There's nothing out there,' Nowak said. Ward frowned and glanced at her as she thumbed around her screen on Google Maps. She jabbed her finger at the screen and shoved it at him, her eyes wide. 'What about this?'

In the middle of the map, just off the road, was a marker for *Heather Hospice*.

'A hospice?' Ward raised an eyebrow, momentarily confused, and then concern flooded him. 'A hospice...' Full of people who would be in no fit state to defend themselves. He swore under his breath.

'We don't know who's on her hit list next, but I'm betting they're there,' he said to Nowak. To the operator, he said, 'All available units to that hospice, please. We'll meet them there.'

With that, he swung a right on the empty round-about, raced down Main Street and flung the car right onto Station Road.

She was there—so close—and Ward had a deep, sinking feeling that they would not be able to stop her before she had claimed her next victim.

CHAPTER FORTY-TWO

On the top of the moors, it was pitch black. No streetlights lined the barren tarmac and only the light of Ward's headlights raking around the corners gave any clue as to their surroundings. It was a new moon and the stars above gave precious little help to light their way.

'Here, sir,' said Nowak quickly. 'A hundred yards on the right, give or take.'

A track cut the line of coniferous trees, so slim that they would have missed it save for the white, oval-shaped sign, which contained a sprig of heather and the words, *Heather Hospice*, that stood where it met the road.

Ward turned into it. The track was unlit but ahead, warm lights bloomed, hidden from the road by that line of conifers and a slight fold in the land. He followed the track into a small car park where the hospice building stood.

'There. It's her car!' Nowak pointed.

Sure enough, that was her plate.

Ward parked and they scouted out the vehicle. It was deserted and locked, with nothing of note on the inside, bar the usual detritus of a car from an ice scraper to a stray hat. He tried the boot. Also locked.

'Let's go. We might not be too late.' Ward's heartrate had risen a notch. What were they walking into? What would they find? What was Rebecca Callahan's next move? Who had she come to take out now?

Ward marched to the old farmhouse with Nowak, passing an old barn door that had been turned into a giant window. Inside, a dimly lit living space looked like a warm retreat from the icy weather outside. A few residents sat tucked up in armchairs wrapped in blankets with drips stationed around them, the equipment flashing with little lights. Some were watching a flickering TV in the corner, others read, a few slept. Ward couldn't see Callahan inside.

The crunch of every footstep on the tarmac seemed too loud to him, his senses alert for the smallest hint of her presence. Ward opened the door marked 'Reception' and stepped into a burst of warmth. Inside, the calm atmosphere jarred his senses. Were they aware she was here? Had she entered the building? He hadn't seen any other noticeable entrances on the approach, at least.

Through another set of double doors lay a reception desk. Backed by artfully half-plastered and half-bare Yorkshire stone, with plants scattered about and plush chairs, it was inviting and calm. And stiflingly hot. Ward opened his jacket and Nowak shed her scarf.

'May I help you?' asked the young woman on the

desk, peering over her computer monitor. 'I'm afraid we don't have visiting hours right now, are you here to see someone specif—' She shut up at the sight of Ward and Nowak's warrant cards.

Ward browsed to a picture of Rebecca Callahan on his phone. 'I need to know if you have seen this woman, we think she's just arrived?'

'Oh yes, Becky?' The woman's mouth pursed and her brows furrowed as she looked between them in confusion. 'I don't understand.'

'We need to see her at once. There's a risk to life.'

Her eyes widened and she stuttered an unintelligible response. Ward could tell she hadn't been trained for this.

'Do you know where she'll be?' If this woman knew her by her nickname... that meant *something*, though Ward didn't know what.

The young woman nodded, apparently lost for words.

'Take us to her at once,' he said.

She scrambled to her feet. 'Um, yes, uh, this way please,' she said, her cheek's reddening. 'She'll be in her room.'

In her room? Ward wondered as a piece of the puzzle clicked into place.

The woman led them through that warm living space, where an episode of *I'm a Celebrity, Get Me Out Of Here* played, with Ant McPartlin and Declan Donnelly's latest chipper gag going down to some scattered chuckles. On to another corridor where closed doors

were marked with permanent room numbers and tempo-
rary name cards.

The woman stopped outside room ten and dithered
awkwardly, her hands twisting together. 'She's in here.
Should I knock? I can't let you go in. This is her private
space.'

'She's a patient?' Ward asked. He had to ask. He had
to know. Maybe now, it all made sense.

'Yes.'

'Why's she here? For end of life care?' Ward kept his
voice to a mutter, not wanting the sound of their conversation to filter through the door.

The woman crossed her arms, looking thoroughly
miserable. 'Well, I mean… I don't know the ins and outs
of her medical details, sir, but yes. That's why people
come here.'

Ward exhaled and shared a look with Nowak. Now it
did make sense, he reckoned. What had happened. Why.
They only had to hear it out of the horse's mouth.

Ward knocked on the door. 'Rebecca Callahan?
Police. Open the door.'

CHAPTER FORTY-THREE

'Rebecca? Open up.' Ward called through the door, not wanting to raise his voice in the peaceful setting. It was already late and he had no desire to wake other residents or cause a fuss.

'It's unlocked,' came a resigned reply from within.

Ward eyed the receptionist who nodded, still looking thoroughly unhappy, before he opened the door with a quiet *click*.

The warm, dim room behind the door took a moment for his eyes to adjust to. Ward's eyes fell first to the chair at the side of the bed, where a wig lay discarded with a pile of clothes and then to the wraith of a woman in the bed. She stared at him with measured calm, no hint of fear on her face. Ward could understand why now.

Beside her, a nurse was halfway to sorting out a drip, the liquid bag hanging and a needle ready to be inserted in the back of Rebecca's hand, which lay on the rail, waiting for her to administer. The nurse paused, her eyes wide as she glanced between Rebecca and the visitors.

'I can wait a little, Sarah, it's alright.' Rebecca drew her hand to her chest.

The nurse swallowed, and nodded. 'I'll uh... I'll come back soon.' She slipped past Ward and Nowak and grabbed the receptionist, hissing something at her.

Ward turned back to Rebecca.

She looked pale and drawn, with deep shadows pooling under her eyes and her face slack with exhaustion. The tiniest stubble of fresh hair was starting to grow on her otherwise bare head and her wrinkled hands lay atop the bedcover, clutching an old raggedy doll. The drip beeped softly on the far side of the bed.

'How long have you got?' he asked quietly, drawing in.

Nowak closed the door behind them.

'A couple months at best. A few weeks at worst. I feel it now,' she said, the strain of fatigue evident in her voice. No doubt the events of the past couple of weeks had taken it out of her, and if her mission was complete, then that too would be a release of the purpose keeping her alive.

Nowak sighed behind him.

Ward introduced them both quietly. 'Rebecca Callahan, I'm here to arrest you on suspicion of the murders of Paul Moore, Tony Brown, and Lee Brown and the attempted murder of Andrew Collins.'

She let out a dry rasp and lifted a hand as if to say, 'Go for it.'

Ward saw the daftness of it. What was he about to do, bundle her into the back of a police car and haul her to the station? It seemed she was terminally ill. He had no desire to do that to a dying woman, no matter what she'd done to earn that arrest warrant. Besides which, he could almost empathise with her cause—though he kept that to himself. She had sought revenge when the justice system had failed her sister and their family.

'I think we all know what's going to happen here. I'm still going to have to go through the motions and arrest you, but don't worry, I won't haul you down to the station in your present condition. It'll still go to court and trial. These things are long, convoluted. They take more time than you have. There won't be a conviction whilst you're alive if what you say is true,' he said bluntly, but there was no point mincing his words. 'I think that's why you did it, right? You didn't have any time left and you took matters into your own hands.'

She nodded.

'You didn't want them to get away with it, not whilst you could still do something about it.'

'I have nothing left to lose now, and I have nothing else to gain, either.' There was a satisfaction and finality in those words that resonated deeply with Ward.

The woman in the bed before him was so very nearly gone. Her doctors would be able to confirm that with Ward whilst he made the arrangements for her custody—no doubt right there under police guard for now.

He still needed the full story to put the whole, decades-long affair to bed. Even if she would never stand trial for what she had done. Ward had mixed feelings about that. Justice would be escaped... and yet, hadn't it already? It wasn't her place, but she'd delivered her own version of justice when the verdict of the courts had not done so. A justice that had been born of deep pain caused by her victims for what they had done to her sister and indirectly to all of her sister's loved ones. Years, decades, of emotional torment.

Rebecca had suffered so much already, and still continued to do so, it seemed. Ward eyed the machine next to her. Her end would likely be long and painful. Had already *been* long and painful.

'Will you at least go on the record now and tell me what happened?'

CHAPTER FORTY-FOUR

TWO DAYS LATER

C *lick click click.* The rhythmic sound of Ward's keyboard joined the others. The office was quiet for a rare and blessed moment, aside from the Christmas songs on Norris' radio. Across the desk divider, Nowak hummed along to *Jingle Bell Rock.*

DI Ward was typing up Rebecca Callahan's statement, recorded on his phone for the record on the evening of their visit. She'd remained under police watch at the hospice whilst they figured out how on earth they could accommodate her without disrupting her medical care. Ward suspected with the extenuating circumstances that they found themselves dealing with, she'd be allowed to remain there and pass away with dignity and peace.

Her condition had already deteriorated significantly since they had visited. Ward suspected that the only thing keeping her going had been the sheer damn grit of hcr willpower to see her vendetta completed. And perhaps the knowledge that she didn't have enough left in her to try to kill Andrew Collins again.

They'd processed Andrew Collins the morning after his arrest. They'd charged him with perjury and perverting the course of justice. He had been released on bail pending a court date. Ward expected him to be found guilty at trial if he didn't plead it in the first place.

The whole thing was a bittersweet mess. The actions of Tony Brown, Lee Brown, and Paul Moore all those years ago had left such a devastating and lasting impact on so many lives. They'd paid the ultimate price for their actions in the end, by Rebecca's hands.

The idea had been born of her diagnosis. Not the first time, but this time untreatable, for the cancer had spread too viciously to be contained or cured. Rebecca had realised that she was living on borrowed time and unless she did something, she would go to her grave with regret, knowing her sister had never found even the smallest shred of justice for what had happened to her.

Rebecca's pride and joy, her life's work, Forage had become a vehicle to deliver her justice in the end, and her intimate knowledge of British flora and fauna—poisonous and nutritious—had become an unlikely tool.

She had found Tony Brown's address online and sent him a free voucher—the wonders of the internet—though it had been pure and joyous chance that he had brought his brother Lee along with him. It had also been good fortune that Paul Moore had rang, though by that point, she had already researched his address too. She had been all too happy for him to pay for the privilege of his own demise and deliver far outside her usual area.

The fast-tracked forensics results had dropped that morning, along with Mark Baker's completed reports on the Brown brothers. It all confirmed what Andrew Collins, and then in greater detail, Rebecca Callahan had told them.

The toxins had been confirmed precisely as described in detail by Rebecca and from the evidence Ward and Nowak had uncovered in the greenhouse at her cottage. The four men—Paul Moore, Tony Brown, Lee Brown, and Andrew Collins—had been on her hit list. No one else had been involved with the rape case closely enough for Rebecca to blame for it.

Belladonna berries had poisoned Paul Moore. Both meals had been poisoned and his wife had had a lucky escape by not consuming any of the other meal that had found its way into her home that evening. The concentration of belladonna berries alongside an unknown medical issue that Baker had managed to uncover in his autopsy had ensured an even more swift death than Paul might have otherwise encountered. Perhaps that was a small mercy given the violent horror of his end.

Poison hemlock had taken out Tony Brown. It was an incurable toxin. From the moment he had ingested the quantity as a bitter garnish with his rich steak and sauce, he had been doomed.

Deadly webcap mushrooms had ended Lee Brown. Hidden in an innocuous mushroom risotto, he hadn't known until it was far too late to save him, even with an emergency trip to hospital.

The brothers had attended her restaurant without the slightest recognition of Rebecca after so many years—after all, they had last seen her as a young teenager at their trial, if they'd even noticed her at all. She had been able to watch, smiling politely at the other customers, whilst the brothers greedily devoured her delicacies laced with their hidden gifts.

A 'culinary Trojan Horse', she had called it, smiling darkly as she had stroked that old doll's hair while lying in her bed. Her sister's doll, she'd explained. One she'd kept close for all those years and the last reminder she had of Lizzie.

It had been the perfect crime on Rebecca's account, manufactured through skill and luck combined for a speedy conclusion. The only thing she regretted was the tarnishing of the Forage brand—her life's work.

'Make sure they don't mention the business in court, or in the papers,' she had begged them, not wanting it to come into disrepute. 'The mission has nothing to do with what I've done.' She had insisted that it was a good brand with a powerful and necessary message and she didn't want to ruin whatever legacy she had left with it.

Ward suspected that ship had sailed. He wondered why it mattered to her. She had weeks to live, at best. They'd never get her to trial. She'd never pay for what she'd done. Her legacy would be what it would be.

She had seemed content once she had finished giving

her statement. As though she had the finality of closure for her and Lizzie. They had left her exhausted, dozing off in bed – with the nurse glaring at them as she returned to administer pain medication and a cocktail of drugs – and Ward wondered if he would see her alive again.

'I can pass now,' she'd said. 'There's nothing else to stay for. It's done.'

CHAPTER FORTY-FIVE

THREE WEEKS LATER

Ward gratefully breathed the cold, fresh air even though it seared his lungs. It was a freezing, fresh day, with blue skies stretching over the Wharfe Valley as far as the eye could see. One of the crisp days that heralded winter's true arrival, for frost braced the landscape that morning, glittering and pale everywhere he looked.

Behind him, the ruins of Bolton Abbey soared, a silent sentinel to the rush of the River Wharfe under his feet. He stood on the bridge at the Cavendish Pavilion, his forearms resting on the wooden barrier, watching the iron-tinged water rush beneath the bridge.

Up the valley, the trees of the Strid Wood were mostly bare, their upturned arms spearing into the sky. Ahead on his right, the foothills soared, and out of sight, the summit of Simon's Seat stood beyond them. He had no desire to climb that day, though Oliver, shuffling impatiently at his feet, would have made a good crack at it.

Why had he come? Ward sighed, a plume of misty breath erupting before him. He'd needed to clear his head—sometimes he did after a case.

He'd booked a few days off, today was the first. Nowak had still rung him first thing to give him an update. Rebecca Callahan had passed away overnight, peacefully in her sleep at the hospice.

Daniel Ward didn't know quite what to think about that. The river's white noise soothed his tumultuous thoughts of life and death, right and wrong, actions and consequences. He stood, rubbed his gloved fingers together to try and get some movement back into the frozen digits, and clicked his tongue at Olly. 'Come on, lad.'

Olly sprang to his feet and strained at the lead, tail wagging so fast it blurred. Ward stepped off the bridge and walked past the Cavendish Pavillion, heading up into the woods on the well-marked trail to follow the river for a while. He'd walk to Barden Bridge, he reckoned, then head back down the other side of the river on the more strenuous path to give them both a leg stretch and keep himself out of puff enough to distract from all the unwelcome thoughts.

It had been an age since he had visited the place. He ambled slowly, pulled along by Oliver more than anything else, as he drank it all in. It was the same as he remembered and yet, not at all. Had the Cavendish Pavillion been there when he was a kid? He couldn't recall…

Mum had brought him and Sam once—at least, that was the time he remembered most. It had been the height of summer then. Baking hot. They'd entertained themselves for hours on the stepping stones across the river. They'd pushed each other in. A lot. Shrieking and splashing, laughter and hollering... That day had been a happy day, with their mother watching on from the riverbanks with the half-smile on her face that he so missed.

Every time he passed her painting of Bolton Abbey in his apartment, he thought of that day. Was it nice to be back? He wasn't sure. It wasn't like that day—he'd changed so much, it was the opposite season, and like Rebecca Callahan, his mother had gone where he could not yet follow.

That painting had inspired his visit though. He'd avoided a lot of places his mother had taken them, after all, but he was done with that. Why deny himself a life for the sake of avoiding grief? He found that grief quieter today. Still there, always painful, that little nub deep inside him, but today, he could sit with it, walk with it, acknowledge it, and not be consumed by it.

A little grief for Rebecca Callahan sat there too, and her sister and parents. For those who had suffered so much at the hands of others. He could understand her quest for revenge. How greatly the law had failed them when they'd needed it most.

Ward stepped to one side to let a couple of laughing toddlers race past, a tangle of smiles and hair and flying scarves, their mothers' warnings hollering after them, puncturing the constant rush of the river close by.

'Be careful, Teddy!'

'Slow down, Ella!'

Olly's tail wagged as his nose followed them and then he bounded back onto the path with Ward, trotting around another couple who walked the trails too. It was busier than Ward would have thought for a weekday in early December.

Up ahead, a flash of red caught his eye. A beret— another couple of women approaching him on the trail. Oliver yapped and strained on the lead, tugging toward the familiar face that sat under that red beret.

With Oliver's fuss, there was no way he wouldn't be noticed, even though already, he kind of wanted the ground to swallow him up, because he didn't know what on earth to do or say.

Oliver's yap drew her attention. She glanced at the dog, frowned, then up at Ward, and stopped. 'Oh!'

'Eve.'

Her surprise gave way to a smile. 'Detective Ward.' She bent to fuss Oliver. 'And who's this little chappy? Hello, Olly. Hello, mister. Yes, I know, it's very exciting isn't it? How lovely to see you again.'

Ward couldn't help but smile too. 'Careful,' he warned. 'You'll stoke his ego...'

Eve laughed and scratched Oliver under the chin, turning her head to look up at her friend. 'Soph, this is the detective I was telling you about, the one who helped me when the shop was burgled.'

'Nice to meet you,' her friend said noncommittally, scanning him up and down in that evaluating way women did that made Ward feel uncomfortably seen, and then giving Eve a pointed glance. 'I'll uh... go ahead.

Look at the river.' She shoved her hands in her coat pockets and wandered off.

'How's everything?' he asked, keeping his tone light.

Eve rose. Oliver whined. 'Alright, thanks,' she said, wrinkling her nose. 'The shop's all fixed up now. Luckily the insurance covered it. They still haven't found who's responsible or recovered any of the money. Though, I'm sure that's long spent by now.'

'And you? Are you alright?' He stepped closer.

'I'm alright—honestly,' she tacked on the end with a chuckle as he raised an eyebrow. 'With the CCTV I feel a lot safer. And knowing you're over the hill if I need anything.' She glanced up at him under lowered lashes.

That made something flip-flop in Ward's stomach. Was he entirely misreading the situation or was she giving him *The Look*?

He'd been thinking about life's choices in connection to the Callahan case. How choices both actively made or passively avoided shaped lives for worse and for better. In that moment, he knew he had a choice.

He could keep being a cowardly prick.

Or he could *carpe* the bloody *diem* out of that moment.

He'd decided he didn't want to wonder 'what if' anymore.

He spoke before he could chicken out. 'Look. Do you want to grab that dinner we never got around to?'

She froze for a second before blinking, a shy smile spreading.

Excuses bubbled on his tongue. They wanted to

erupt. To take it back. Tell her he was sorry he'd asked. He was stupid. An idiot. A moron. Delusional. What the bloody hell was he thinking!? He clamped his jaw shut as her mouth opened.

'Um…sure. Yes.'

For some reason, it still came as a shock. He'd expected that he'd entirely misread the situation and had already set himself up to be disappointed. Why was his stupid bloody heart hammering so fast? Gods, he felt like a daft young lad all over again.

'Great. I'd better give you my number. My *non*-work number, I mean.'

'Of course.' She looked satisfied, he thought, as he glanced sidelong at her again when she dipped her gaze to her pocket to grab her phone.

As they swapped contact details, it elicited something within him that he'd not had for a long time—hope. That maybe there was the spark of something there. The start of a better future that he'd be able to build for himself out of the ashes of his former personal life.

'Great!' he said, wincing as he came off with the enthusiasm of a puppy. 'I guess… Enjoy your walk and we'll sort something out?'

'Definitely,' she said warmly.

As he stood aside to let her pass it still felt awkward. They were still relative strangers. Too unfamiliar to hug. Too formal to shake hands.

'See you soon, Eve.'

'Bye, Daniel,' she said, sending a thrill through him.

As he walked away with Oliver whining in her direction, a massive grin spread over his face, making his cheeks ache. *She said yes!* He couldn't quite believe it.

A tendril of something good was taking root amidst all the heartache of his almost-complete divorce and the darkness of his job, and in the midst of a grim winter, he was going to seize it as hard as he could and not let go.

CHAPTER FORTY-SIX

Vigour fueled Ward's steps all the way to Barden Bridge and back, and he found himself humming along to some of the Christmas songs on the radio on his way home later that afternoon as the sun set on one of those fiery red kinds of evenings that set everything alight. It was more Christmas cheer than he'd managed to scrape together in years, but he was glad for it. It was nice to have something to lift the spirits—to look forward to—at last.

He stopped for a pub meal and a pint on the way home—why not, after all—at the Dog and Gun in Oxenhope, warming himself by the open fire, with a steak and ale pie. Meanwhile, Olly snoozed happily at his feet and the pub's other patrons created a pleasant buzz of chatter around him. Even though he was alone, he didn't feel as isolated as usual. Maybe he'd suggest it as a location for his and Eve's date.

Then, it was only a short hop over the last hill to

home, his apartment in Thornton just off Thornton Road itself. It was dark as he stepped outside, the winter night unpleasantly bloody freezing in contrast to that cosy pub. He hurried them both to his car and set off, the car's heating blasting on high to try and make up the deficit.

When he parked up, it was another quick dash into the apartment building, grabbing his post from the box on the way up, and then his flat. He gratefully shut the door behind him and kicked off his boots. His feet ached after all that walking and his legs burned in a pleasant, well-earned sort of way—a preferable alternative to the 'you're old, lazy, and fat' achy tune they usually sang.

Olly stretched generously and slowly beside him, letting out a wide yawn.

'Aye, lad, let's get you some dinner.' Ward sauntered to the kitchenette with Olly trotting behind him, his tail going ten to the dozen as Ward chucked the post on the counter and opened the cupboard with Olly's food. The dog wasn't daft.

He fed the dog then schlepped over to the kettle to pick through his post and make a decaffeinated coffee. A bill from Yorkshire Water came first. It was going up by another couple quid a month. Then the gas & electric company—they wanted another tenner a month. Why did the bills never come *down*? he asked himself. Ward tutted and shook his head.

Then came a pile of leaflets. He half-heartedly shuffled through a couple of takeaway menus and the local community booklet when something fell to the floor from between them.

Ward bent to pick it up.

A Polaroid.

The kettle bubbled above him, almost at the boil, but Ward had stilled and cold flooded him. He straightened slowly, holding that grubby photo between his forefinger and thumb. His skin *crawled*.

The edges were dirt-stained, as though it had been dropped outside in the mud. But the picture was still all too recognisable.

It was Katherine.

She was out somewhere he didn't recognise. The photo had been taken from a short distance, but close enough to capture her from the waist up. She was smiling, as though in mid-conversation with someone off-camera and unaware that she was being photographed.

He'd not recognised her for a second. She'd changed her hair to a pixie cut. She'd never had hair like that—he guessed that the photo was recent and that Katherine had chopped her hair off since he'd last seen her. It suited her, he thought fleetingly. She looked happier. Freer. But he felt no relief at that, only incandescent panic that obscured any rational thought.

Because someone had used a red permanent marker to slash a giant 'X' across her photo.

Ward turned the Polaroid over.

The back was blank, save for more mud spatters.

The kettle clicked off, making him jump, but Ward ignored it. Instead, he rushed back to his jacket hanging in the hallway, rifling through the pockets for his phone.

It was getting later but Ward didn't care. Katherine was in danger. And it was his fault.

There was only one person who would dare send a message like this. Only one person who Ward could have provoked into such a response.

Bogdan Varga.

Those choices that he'd been so self-satisfied with earlier, the very ones that had led him to pluck up the courage to ask Eve out to dinner—successfully—had now backfired in his face. Spectacularly.

His choices had stacked up and led to this. Whatever *this* was. He'd pushed Varga too far, hadn't he? What other damn choice had he had? Like he could leave the crime lord alone to wreak havoc on Bradford and the surrounding area like he did with every place he blighted?

Ward would hunt Varga as doggedly as Varga taunted him and damn it, Ward detested the man even more in that moment. That the lowlife was willing to drag yet more innocents into it to try and... what? Escape the law? That clearly wasn't going to happen.

No. Ward knew *exactly* why Varga taunted him with threats to Katherine. To prove a point. To prove that the bastard could and that he was untouchable. Now, no matter that it was Ward hunting Varga, someone else was going to pay the price.

Daniel Ward's fingers stumbled, sausage-like and clumsy, as he fought to stop them from shaking and find Katherine's contact details. He scrolled to 'W' before remembering that he'd finally stopped being bitter enough to call her 'Wicked Witch'. She was back to regular old 'Katherine' now.

He punched the *dial* button.

Every vacant ring of that unanswered call was a punch to the gut. He couldn't breathe, damn it. Where was she? Why wasn't she picking up? Gods, Katherine. They might be almost divorced, but he'd never forgive hims—

'Hello?'

It was her voice.

Katherine.

She sounded... fine. A little annoyed, actually. Perfectly typical, then, for when she spoke to him.

'Katherine?' Ward said raggedly, sucking in a great breath to replenish his crumpled lungs.

'Daniel? What do you want?' Her voice held a bite of impatience.

'Are... are you alright?' Damn it, she sounded completely fine. That panic still lashed in him, as embarrassment rose. Had he been foolish?

'I'm fine, why? What on earth are you calling me for at this time?'

Ward took a deep breath, exhaling shakily to try and still his nerves. She was fine. *Fine.*

'I—I just...' he stuttered, closing his eyes. Trying to make sense of whatever the hell any of this was. 'I just wanted to check you were alright,' he said, perfectly aware of how lame he sounded. Warmth flooded his cheeks, even as he braced himself on the counter, that stupid disgusting photo clutched in his hand.

'I'm going out on a date, *actually*. Look, I don't have time to speak. If it's not important, it'll have to wait. Bye.'

She didn't wait for him to reply before she hung up.

Ward stared at his silent phone for a second. Then he stared at the photo. It was her. Definitely, one hundred percent her—and recently. He could barely even think that she'd admitted to him she was on a date—a fact that would have crucified him months ago amid the bitterness between them back then.

He was still trying to work out what had happened.

I don't understand.

Or did he?

Varga played complicated games.

Taunts.

Lies.

Threats.

Ward knew then what this was.

This was a warning.

Perhaps his last one.

Mess again with me, Ward, and I'll hurt you.

And somehow, Varga understood that to hurt Ward, he would best hurt those closest to him to serve the most painful blows. Ward could even see Varga's disembodied, crooked smile as he imagined the man smirking with satisfaction at playing this game.

Varga was coming for Ward and, worst of all, the price might be paid by those dearest to him.

Have I gone too far?

Ward couldn't give up. If this was what it came to... That fear still swirled within him, as chaotic and overwhelming as a storm. He couldn't back down. Not after how far they had come.

Of course, Varga was going to threaten him. Ward had just helped to orchestrate the takedown of one of his biggest assets.

Ward couldn't be a coward.

Not now.

He had to stop Varga before the monster harmed those he cared for.

Ward crushed that Polaroid in his hand.

I haven't gone far enough. And I won't stop until Varga can't threaten anyone else again.

A NOTE FROM THE AUTHOR

Thank you all for following DI Ward and the team through another book! If you enjoyed it, I would gratefully appreciate a positive review on Amazon, and also recommendations for the book/series to your crime fiction loving friends and family! Word of mouth recommendations in person and on social media are hugely important to helping the series find new readers. Please could you do that for me? Thank you.

I really hope you enjoyed this latest case and the locations it visited. Close to my heart is the real farm shop above Thornton village, Robertshaw's Farm Shop. It's a wonderful local business with the best of local Yorkshire produce and I adore supporting them as a customer. If you're ever in the area, I really do highly recommend their food and drink.

Forage, however, is an entirely fictional brand, and of course, I know none of our wonderful local producers would have a poisonous quest for revenge in mind!

It was great to *finally* get Detective Ward a date with Eve, and you can expect some more of that side-story in the next book. I love that I receive so many messages from you all cheering Ward on in his (sort of tragic to date!) love life, asking after Olly the dog, loving Patterson's growth throughout the series, and enjoying the team banter. It is so touching that you care about these characters I write too. Thank you!

Hmm...where to next, dear readers? See you soon, in the next instalment, *The Power We Exploit*. Please do sign up for my newsletter at www.megjolly.com to be the first to hear of new books in the series, and join my Reader's Club for lots of extra goodies.

Warmly yours,
Meg Jolly

ABOUT THE AUTHOR

Meg is a **USA** Today Bestselling Author and illustrator living amongst the wild and windswept moors of Yorkshire, England with her husband and two cats. Now, she spends most of her days writing with a view of the moors, being serenaded by snoring cats.

Want to stay in touch?

If you want to reach out, Meg loves hearing from readers. You can follow her on Amazon, Bookbub, or sign up to her newsletter. You can also say hi via Facebook or Instagram.

You can find links to all the above on Meg's website at:
www.megjolly.com

Printed in Great Britain
by Amazon